ROCK YOUR HEART OUT

CRYSTAL KASWELL

ROCK YOUR HEART OUT

First edition. March 10, 2016.

Copyright © 2016 Crystal Kaswell.

Written by Crystal Kaswell.

Cover by Melody Jeffries.

Also by Crystal Kaswell

Inked Love

Dirty Rich

Pierce Family

Standalones

Come Undone Trilogy

Sign up for the Crystal Kaswell mailing list

Chapter One

The room is dark except for the yellow light streaming from under the closed bathroom door. Quiet except for the *tap-tap-tap* of the shower.

Then there's no more *tap-tap-tap*. The shower is off.

I grope the wall for the light switch. Nothing. Still dark.

Okay. No big deal. My brother knows I'm coming. I knock just in case my ETA text messages didn't get through. "Drew. It's me. Take your time."

No response. Maybe he didn't hear me. I go to knock again but the handle turns.

The bathroom door pulls open. Light pours into the main room. It surrounds a muscular man in a soft, yellow glow.

That's not Drew.

Thank God, because he's naked.

Completely and totally naked.

There's a strange naked man in Drew's hotel room, and he's between me and the exit.

I take a step backwards. There's nowhere to go. I'm

against the wall. My heart beat speeds up. This guy doesn't look menacing but that's not enough to convince the nerves in my stomach to settle.

"Hey. Didn't think you were coming," he says.

His voice is calm. Not threatening.

I take a deep breath. This must be an innocent mistake. The guy at the front desk gave me the wrong key.

Please let it be an innocent mistake.

"Alice?" he asks.

I shake my head. I'm not Alice. Given the way he's standing, tall and proud and utterly naked, she must be a sexual partner.

He reaches for something and the room illuminates. He's no longer highlights on hard muscles. Actually, he's really familiar. Green eyes. Dark blond hair hanging wet around his face. Soft lips curled into a welcoming smile.

I know him. Know who he is.

Relief floods my limbs as I exhale. That's him. Tom Steele, the drummer in my guitarist brother's alternative rock band, Sinful Serenade.

He's not dangerous. He's my brother's best friend.

Give or take. Drew isn't really the friendly type.

"Did you change your hair?" he asks. "Your nose maybe? Don't get me wrong. You look good. Just different."

I shake my head. My mouth is too sticky to form words.

He's naked.

My eyes won't co-operate with me. They trace a line down his body. Strong jaw, soft lips, broad shoulders, sculpted torso.

I've seen plenty of men naked in photography classes, but none of them made me feel sweaty and flushed.

My gaze goes lower.

To his happy trail.

Lower.

Holy shit.

He's pierced. There's a barbell stud going through the top to the bottom of his tip.

My jaw drops. "Is that a..."

"Prince Albert?"

It's impossible to speak. I nod.

"It's an apadravya. Like a Prince Albert but on both sides."

"Oh."

"It's new," he says. "Real new, actually. I'm out of commission for another three weeks. But I still have a mouth and two hands, so hop on the bed."

Me... on the bed... with Tom.

He steps closer. "You're not Alice, are you?"

Finally, I collect some hint of my senses. "No, I'm sorry." I press my back against the wall. Nerves collect in my stomach. Not fear but embarrassment. "Isn't this Drew's room?"

"We switched." His eyes fix on mine. "How did you get a key?"

It is an honest mistake. That's a relief. How did I get this key? At the desk. Asking for Bruce Wayne. It's hard to think given the circumstances. I say the first thing that makes it to my lips. "You're naked."

He laughs. "You're observant."

I can't drag my gaze away from his piercing. "Didn't that hurt?"

"Not as much as you'd think."

"What's the point?"

He studies my expression. "If you don't like it stop staring."

I press my eyelids together. "Sorry."

"You want to tell me what you're doing in my hotel room?"

"I thought this was Drew's room."

Somehow, I manage to look him in the eyes. That's definitely Tom. We've never met—I was in boarding school when the band was forming—but I've seen him in music videos and on the cover of *Rolling Stone*.

Tom pulls a towel around his waist. That makes it easier to think.

"I'm Drew's sister. Willow." I dig into my purse and pull out my driver's license. "Here. See."

Tom glances at the ID then returns it. "You shoulda told me before I let you gawk." He goes to the bed, digs through an open suitcase, and pulls on a pair of boxers. "I don't mind. I'm not shy. But your brother will kill me if he finds out you saw me naked."

There's a tattoo of a lion on his chest. Thick black lines. The pattern continues down his arm, all the way to his wrist.

"I know I'm sexy as hell, but you should probably stop staring."

God, he's right. I'm being all kinds of rude. There's no excuse. "I'm sorry. It's just—"

"Been a while?"

"Something like that." My cheeks flush. It's been six years since I've had sex. Six years since I've felt a hint of desire.

"I feel you, kid. I'm under strict orders from my piercer: no sex for six weeks." He looks back to me with a playful smile. "Can't even fuck myself."

He's casual with that information. *Hi, I'm Tom, my cock is pierced, I can't fuck anyone for three more weeks. Not even myself.*

Tom gets dressed like it doesn't bother him that I'm

4

gawking. Skinny jeans. Converse. V-neck. Tight cotton hoodie.

Picture perfect, effortlessly cool rock star.

I press my hands against my sides and force myself to stare at the wall. Okay. We've got this mix up settled. Now I have to figure out what the hell I'm going to say to Drew about why I'm here. The truth isn't an option.

Tom's voice pulls me out of my thoughts.

"Hope I didn't scare you." He smirks and motions to his now clothed crotch. "I know it's a monster."

I clear my throat. "I wasn't expecting a naked man in my hotel room."

"You look rattled."

"Surprised."

"Intrigued?" He raises a brow.

My cheeks flush. "I've never seen a, uh, piercing like that before." I press my lips together before I shove my foot into my mouth. "I have a lot on my mind. That's all."

His eyes pass over me. "If you need something— money a place to stay—I can arrange that."

I study his expression for a clue to his intentions. He seems earnest but I don't trust my instincts when it comes to men. "No thanks. It's a family thing."

Tom raises an eyebrow. "As you wish." He taps a few numbers into the hotel phone's keypad and brings it to his ear. "Hey. You two finished? I ran into your sister at the front desk. You want me to bring her over?" Tom laughs at whatever Drew says. "I know. I wouldn't. I'm too beautiful to die." He sets the phone back in the receiver. His eyes meet mine. "He's ready. Room 417."

I nod. "Thank you. And sorry."

"I don't mind." Tom shrugs. "Just keep this between us."

"Sure." It's too mortifying to tell anyone. "Good night."

I grab my bag, sling it over my shoulder, and reach for the door.

"Willow—"

"Yeah?"

"There are leaked pics of me online. If you need to take another look."

Chapter Two

Drew's arms are folded over his chest. His dark brows are furrowed. His dark eyes are filled with frustration.

"What were you doing in Tom's hotel room?" Drew asks.

"Talking." I play with my bag's shoulder strap. "It's good to see you too."

"Yeah." He pulls me into a stilted hug. His eyes fix on mine. "Well, if he tries to cross the line, let me know and I'll kick his ass."

I keep my voice calm. It must be possible to reason with Drew. In theory. "Isn't Tom your friend?"

"Yeah, but you come first. He's a player. He'll hurt you."

Even I can see that. "Consider me warned."

Drew stares at me, tearing apart my intentions. He softens. "What's wrong, Wil? You look terrified."

I swallow hard. "I need a place to stay for a few days."

"Why?"

The door behind us opens. Kara Kendrick, Drew's girlfriend, pops out. She's wearing her sweater dress backwards and her usually straight brown hair is a messy tangle.

"Hey Willow! It's good to see you. It's been forever." She pulls me into a close hug. "You look good. Your hair looks pretty long."

"Thanks." I run a hand through my thick brown hair. "It's getting a little much."

"You would look cute with a long bob. Or black. Something dramatic to celebrate being a college grad." She slides her arm around Drew with a wistful sigh. "One more month and I'll be free too."

"Then two years to get your teaching credential," Drew says.

She nudges him. "Technicalities."

Drew clears his throat and motions to the door. "Kendrick. A little privacy."

She squeezes him tighter. "No."

"What do you mean no?" Drew asks.

She smiles, happy as a clam, and kisses Drew on the cheek. His frown fades away. Until he's... smiling? That's weird. Drew doesn't really smile.

But he's freaking beaming.

"You look like you're gonna pop a vein, baby. Nobody wants to talk to you when you're pissed." She runs her hands through his hair. "Your poor sister is probably worried you're gonna hit someone if she tells you what's up."

Drew pouts.

"Bet you already threatened to hit somebody," she says.

"Not exactly."

Kara looks to me. "Did he?"

I nod.

She throws him a stern look and pulls her hands to her

sides. "You get into a fight and that's going to be the last time you touch anyone for a while."

Damn, I don't remember Kara being such a badass. I make a mental note to ask her for tips on dealing with difficult men.

Drew stares into her eyes. "You're bluffing."

"Try me." Kara pulls him into the hotel room and motions for me to follow. "Couch is clean. I swear."

The room is a suite, with a bedroom and a separate coffee nook. I move into the latter and plant on the couch.

Drew sits next to me. "What happened?"

I take a deep breath. I can't explain that Bradley moved in next door. There's no telling what Drew will do. "I have an issue with one of my neighbors. He's really... difficult. I can figure it out. I just need a few days to think."

Drew stares back at me. "If someone is giving you trouble, I'll talk to them. Take care of it."

No. Drew takes care of things with his fists. "It's nothing. Just that I can't deal with it right now. I'm applying for this job at a studio in the city. It's mostly boudoir, people who want sexy photos of themselves to boost their confidence or as gifts for their partners."

Drew raises a brow. "Not a bad gig."

It's an awesome gig, at the best studio in Northern California. But I still need ten photos, ten sensual photos of a model in various states of undress, if I want to apply. I need a new model ASAP but there's no way I'm asking my brother or his girlfriend to pose in lingerie.

I look back to Drew. "It's a great opportunity. And the application is due at noon. So..."

"So?" He stares back at me. "Is that supposed to convince me to drop it?"

"Until noon. Please." I cross my fingers. There's almost no chance this will work.

Kara steps into the room with two glasses of water. She hands one to me and the other to Drew.

He gets up and plants a kiss on her lips. "Give us a minute, baby. This is kinda personal."

She stares back at him. I know that look. It's the *do I trust Drew not to threaten violence* look. Answer must be yes, because she nods and takes her turn kissing him.

Kara looks to me. "I'll wait in the other room. I have to catch up on my Russian literature."

They're happy. Functional. I never thought either of us would have anything like that.

Drew runs his hand through his hair. "Wil, tell me the truth. I know you didn't hop on a bus for five hours because your neighbor plays metal until three a.m." He leans closer. "I'm not seventeen anymore. I'm not going to jump straight to violence."

"Is there an intermediary step now?"

He leans back, not at all amused. "You still don't trust me."

"The last time I needed your help, you..." I pull my arms over my chest, unable to do anything but remember how thoroughly panic swallowed me whole that night. "What if he'd had a knife or a gun? You'd be dead right now."

Drew scoffs like he believes he could take a knife and/or gun-wielding guy with fifty pounds on him. Drew is no slouch, physically. But Bradley is a football player. He's taller, bigger, meaner.

"Do you have any idea how scared I was that something was going to happen to you?" I hug myself tighter. "It would have been all my fault."

"No, it would have been my fault. I knew what I was risking. And I knew I could take him." He looks me in the eyes. "What's wrong with protecting the people you love?

10

The world would be a better place if Bradley was dead." The name is poison on his lips. "Shoulda killed him when I had the chance."

"You're not convincing me that you're capable of settling things without resorting to violence," I say.

Drew nods. He must see my point. "I'm sorry I scared you back then. You had enough to deal with. Whatever it is that's wrong, I'll help. The answer doesn't have to be murder. Doesn't even have to be aggravated assault."

Maybe. I want to tell him. I really do. But there's something about the intensity of his expression. I can't trust him not to get himself hurt.

Drew's voice drops. "Is it Bradley?"

I say nothing.

"Don't you have a restraining order?"

"It expired." I bite my lip. "It's nothing. I just... I need some time to figure out everything. If you don't want me here, that's fine."

"Of course I want you here." Drew looks me in the eyes. "Promise me you'll be safe on tour with us and I'll let it go."

"I'm only staying a few days."

"Wil, promise or I'm hiring a body guard to watch you twenty four seven."

I can't promise that. But I can't let Drew know Bradley is trying to insert himself back into my life. I look my brother in the eyes. "I'll be fine. But I should really get to showering. I have to get up early if I want to finish the application in time."

I go to push myself up but Drew grabs my arm.

"You need money?" he asks.

"I can't take your money. Not after all the shit Mom pulled."

"I'm not like Mom. I'm not going to attach strings to it."

"Still. I don't want to fight. I need a place to stay for a few days. If that's not okay with you, I'll figure something else out." I take a deep breath. "You can pay for my hotel room if it makes you feel better."

He smiles as he pulls out his credit card and hands it to me. "It does."

"Thank you."

His expression gets overprotective. "Wait. Does your application need sexy pictures?"

Okay. Time for a white lie. "Any portraits will do."

Oh no. He's about to volunteer.

At least this part is true. "No offense, Drew, but you always look pissed off in pictures. I'll find a model. It's no big deal."

"Okay. But you have to promise you'll think about staying the rest of the tour if you don't get that job. It's only another two months. It will be fun. We can catch up."

My stomach twists. Reality sinks in. If I don't get that job, I don't have a better option than staying with Drew. Even so... "Two months is too long to let my photography lapse."

"Consider it," he says. "Kara's flying out of Portland. I can take you to the airport with her or you can leave out of any other city. Hell, Wil, you can come back home with us and crash in the spare room as long as you need. There are lots of photographers who need assistants in Los Angeles."

"I'll think about it." It might be my only option. I push myself out of my seat. "Thanks, Drew. I'll see you in the morning."

"Tom wasn't bugging you, was he?"

"No. He was a gentleman."

Drew cocks a brow. "Sounds suspect."

"He was fine."

"I'll talk to him." Drew's expression gets serious.

I know that look too. It means *if talking doesn't work, I'll hit him until he understands.*

"Think about staying." Drew walks me to the door. "I'll feel a lot better not knowing what's going on if I can keep an eye on you."

"I will. Thanks."

He gives me a half-hug and looks back to Kara, waiting on the king bed.

She smiles and joins our awkward goodbye. "Hey, Willow. We're going to a theme park tomorrow. Go-karts, mini-golf, laser tag. You should come. It will be fun."

"I have this application due at noon," I say.

"We can wait," she offers.

I try to imagine some version of reality where go-karts and mini-golf don't involve me sitting on a bench in the hot sun, waiting out another activity, but the vision won't come. It's not that I'm against fun. Just that I prefer to stick to the sidelines. It's safer. Less risk of getting hurt or embarrassing yourself or falling in love with a guy who hits you.

"Thanks, but I'm really tired. I need some time to think tomorrow." At least that's true.

She nods. "Then how about we meet for lunch? After your application is due." She nudges Drew.

He looks at her then back to me. "Yeah. Meet you in the lobby at noon."

I nod. "Okay."

He opens the door for me. "Everything is going to be okay, Wil. I promise."

Chapter Three

I slump on the concrete bench outside the hotel. Cold, evening air sinks through my thin sweater. Goose-bumps spread over my arms.

It's not okay. There's a convention in town—apparently, a valid excuse for the front-desk guy to be an ass—and every room is booked.

My phone is still dead. There are half a dozen hotels in walking distance. But first, I need to clear my head. I take out my camera and adjust the shutter speed to one more appropriate for the dark sky. My hands are shaky. This is going to come out blurry. I snap a few shots anyway. The aqua hotel pool hiding behind a black fence. The yellow glow of the streetlight falling over the sidewalk. The couple walking towards me—too far away for any details besides the way the woman is holding onto the man like he's a balloon string and she's afraid he'll fly away.

Wait a second.

That's Tom. And a woman who looks a lot like me. Must be Alice. She's a little shorter and a lot curvier.

Lighter hair. More makeup. Much sexier outfit—tight dress and stilettos.

There's something about Tom's posture. Almost like he's not interested.

I zoom in to his face and snap a few shots. The evidence is clear. He has his arm around her but there's no enthusiasm in his expression.

The insight disappears when I set my camera down. The world makes more sense captured in a photograph. I see all the things I normally miss.

Tom's eyes connect with mine. He nods hello. I nod back and attempt to avert my gaze to anything else. My camera. Maybe there are some decent sexy pictures that will get me out of this desperate situation.

Nothing.

It took me a month to work up the courage to arrange a shoot with an exceptionally friendly model. How am I going to ask a stranger?

A high-pitched squeal interrupts my train of thought.

"What the fuck, Tom? You're going to make me share with some girl who looks just like me?" The girl on Tom's arm glares at me with irritation.

"No. I'm over threesomes." Tom keeps his eyes on me as he addresses the woman. "Wait inside. Now."

She scoffs but obliges, pushing through the glass doors and throwing herself on the lobby couch. Her legs spread in a pose more desperate than enticing.

He looks at her with a hint of regret. "This is why I don't do repeats anymore. Too many feelings."

"Repeats?"

He laughs. "Don't think you're as innocent as your outfit suggests."

Is a sweater and jeans really innocent? This is how most people dress.

I stare back at still effortlessly cool Tom. It sinks in. Repeats. "You mean sleeping with the same woman more than once?"

He nods. "Not worth the trouble."

Wow. That's... slutty. I clear my throat and force myself to look Tom in the eyes.

Dammit, that same buzz of electricity passes through me. From one fingertip to another then right between my legs. It's not the gorgeous green color that gets me. It's the spark of mischief in them.

The lines of his tattoo peeking out from his v-neck.

God, he would look yummy in a photograph, pulling that v-neck halfway down his chest that *I know you want me* expression on his face.

"Eyes up here." He smirks. "Where you going with all your shit?"

"The hotel's booked."

"You can take my room. I'll sleep in the bus."

"No. You're..." I motion to the woman sitting in the lobby. "Busy."

His eyes drift to Alice then back to me. "I'm gonna let her down easy. I'm not in the mood anymore."

He's not? He seemed pretty ready to pounce when he thought I was Alice.

It's not as if she's lacking in any way. If anything, she's prettier than I am. She's certainly more endowed in the T&A regions.

"You eat dinner?" he asks.

My stomach growls. The last thing I ate was oatmeal and raisins and that was this morning. I shake my head, no.

"There's a strip mall down the block. A couple places are open all night."

"What about Alice?"

"She'll feel even more deprived if we get going and she doesn't get her lips around my cock."

There isn't a single hint of irony in his voice. He's so confident, so sure that women will be upset over not getting the chance to blow him.

It must be amazing to be that sure of yourself.

"Here." He slides my bag off my shoulders and around his.

"Okay."

He's already halfway to the door, too far away to hear me. I try not to gawk as Tom talks to the girl. Apparently, he hasn't mastered this whole letting her down easy thing, because she pouts and stomps, throwing one hell of a fit.

She glares at me on her way to the street. Tom follows a moment later. He stops next to me and shrugs, not at all aware of the effect he has on her.

———

Tom pulls the Thai restaurant's door open. "Best chicken and eggplant anywhere."

"I'm a vegetarian," I say.

He points to one half of the paper menu pasted to the door. "They have a vegetarian version."

He presses his hand against my lower back and leads me to a corner booth. There are all these clothes in the way, but, still my body hums with desire.

We're the youngest people here by twenty years. That doesn't spare Tom from female attention. A woman in a sharp suit, some Casino executive type, makes eyes at him.

"Give me a sec." Tom pushes out of his seat and approaches the woman.

One second she's all business, the next she's gushing, pawing at his hoodie. He leans in close, smiling and running his fingers over her wrist. Is the gesture sincere or a put on? I can't tell. Not without my camera.

He slides his arm around her so she can take a selfie then pulls a marker from his jeans and signs the back of her cell phone case.

He blows her a kiss goodbye as he makes his way back to me.

I cover my judgmental expression with the menu. "If you want to take her back to your room, I won't stop you."

"She was wearing a wedding ring." Tom presses my menu down and looks into my eyes. "I don't fuck taken women."

"It's none of my business."

"You were watching."

I bury my attention in the menu. The eggplant dish sounds good. Basil, soy sauce, red peppers, garlic. But I know I like pad thai. "I was just curious."

"About?" He shifts back in his seat, gives the menu a once over, and looks back to me. "I don't offend easily. You can lay all the judgment you want on me."

"I'm not in a position to judge anyone's love life."

"Love doesn't have shit to do with it."

"Or anyone's sex life."

The waitress interrupts to drop off waters and take our order. I stick with the pad thai. It's safe. Tom orders the spicy basil eggplant dish he recommended. The vegetarian version.

"You didn't have to do that," I say.

"I know. I don't do anything unless I want to do it."

His eyes bore into me, but I'm not sure what he's trying to find. Without the menu, there's nowhere to hide. I have to say something.

"Why did you reject that Alice girl?" I ask. "She was hot."

"You like girls?" He perks up. "Can I watch?"

"You want to?"

"Never seen two girls who were *really* into each other go at it before. Only women putting on some show for my amusement. If I wanted to see fake orgasms, I'd watch shitty porn."

"As opposed to?"

"Amateur stuff."

I clear my throat. Not going there. "I like guys."

"You embarrassed about that?"

"No. But... I can tell when a woman is attractive."

"Yeah. Alice is cute. We hooked up a long time ago. Supposed to be a one-time thing, but she knew I'd be in Reno and she called. Thought she wanted tickets or wanted to fuck me again."

"What about the piercing?"

"I don't mind giving without receiving." He laughs. "But the way she was talking... she was getting feelings. Expectations. Maybe they were real. Maybe she's full of shit and wants to nab a rock star boyfriend." Sadness flares in his eyes. "Doesn't matter. I don't do relationships."

"Why not?"

"Never felt that way." He studies my expression. "Come on. Lay the judgment on me. I know you're not screwing a different guy every night."

A chuckle escapes my lips.

He raises a brow. "Only once a week?"

I laugh harder. A big belly laugh.

"Okay, okay," he says. "I don't want to insult your game. Twice a week?"

My whole body goes light. All the tension of the day melts as I burst into giggles. No one teases me like this. I shake my head. "I don't have any game."

"Guys don't go crazy for that sweet and innocent thing?"

"I don't really date."

"Just pickup guys in bars and fuck them without learning their names." He shakes his head with mock outrage. "Willow, Willow, Willow. I expected better from you. They at least deserve breakfast in the morning."

"I'm not a monster. I make them coffee."

His interest perks. "Really?"

I hold a poker face for as long as I can (about fifteen seconds). Another laugh escapes my lips as I shake my head.

"Don't even make coffee. So greedy."

"Hey! I live around the corner from a Philz Coffee. I always offer them a few bucks to pick something up."

"So you make them feel cheap too?" He shakes his head. "What do you scream when you come if you don't know their names? 'Baby' or 'Oh God' or 'Fuck yeah'?"

"What do you scream out when you come?"

"Only one way to find out."

He can't be serious.

Tom laughs. "Kidding. You seem like a nice kid, and I know better than to get between Drew and someone he wants to protect. You and I... we're just friends."

Tom and I are going to be friends. I can do that. I nod. Just friends. No problem.

I'll only be around him a few days if I get the gig.

There's a buzz on the other side of the bench. That's a loud vibrate alert. Tom attends to something on his phone. I check the rest of the pictures on my camera for anything remotely appropriate for this assignment. There's nothing.

The waitress interrupts our silence with a promise our food is almost ready. Once she's gone, Tom slides his phone into his pocket and turns all his attention to me.

CRYSTAL KASWELL

"How often *do* you get laid?" he asks.

"That is incredibly classified."

"Suit yourself."

Okay. Two can play this game. I tease back. "If you're such a proud manwhore, why did you get a piercing right before going on tour?"

"There's no time like the present. If you want something, why wait?"

"But you're permanently changing your body."

"I did my research. Read about the risks, found a piercer with experience. After that, there's no reason to waste time deciding. Do it or don't." He leans closer. "What did you think?"

Think? It's not possible to think in this state. That piercing, god that piercing. What would it feel like in my hands, my mouth, my—

"You do like it." He laughs. "My eyes are up here, kid."

"I know." I finish my water. How can I be this attracted to Tom? I haven't wanted anyone in years. He's hot, yes, but there have been other hot guys. I go on dates. Kiss even.

I never feel anything this intense. Hell, I never feel anything. Period.

The waitress drops off our food and refills our waters. She fawns over Tom, fetching him several kinds of hot sauce and brushing her hand against his wrist without asking permission.

When she's done flirting, he scoops his dish and a fair helping of rice onto a side plate and passes it to me. "Try it."

"You don't have to do that."

"I thought we covered this. I don't do things unless I want to do them."

22

"Okay. Thank you." I try a bite of eggplant. It's good. Tender. Spicy. After I swallow, I lick the oil off my lips.

He watches me with a cocky smile. He knows I like it but he doesn't brag about it.

I scoop a quarter of my noodles onto a side plate and offer them to him. "Fair is fair."

He nods. "I like a generous woman."

Oh, god, he's talking about sex again. I take a long sip of water in the hopes of cooling off.

It doesn't help.

We eat in silence. The food is good. Especially the eggplant dish. When I'm stuffed, I thank him for dinner and attempt to relax.

Tom finishes a few minutes later. He pushes the plates aside and leans closer. "You want to tell me why you're here?"

"At this restaurant—"

"In Reno. Drew didn't mention you coming, so I know it was last minute. And the way you've been acting. You're running from something."

I swallow hard. I can't tell Tom. He might relay the information to Drew. I shake my head. No. I'm not telling him.

"I can reword to make it a demand," he says.

"It's not any of your business."

He looks upset. But why? Tom barely knows me. He doesn't have any right to expect me to share my secrets.

An idea hits me. Perfect. It gets me out of answering without telling him to go fuck himself.

I look back at Tom. "I'll tell you. If you do something for me."

He sits up, intrigued. "I'm listening."

"I have an application for a photography job due at noon tomorrow and I don't have any pictures for it."

He shifts back to teasing, shaking his head in mock outrage. "Procrastinating on your homework. I expected better from you, Willow."

"Hey! You have any idea how hard it is to ask someone to get half naked so you can take sexy pictures of them?"

"It can be *hard*."

Oh. I clear my throat. "Are you familiar with boudoir?"

He nods.

"I need a model. I have ten photos due tomorrow. You wouldn't have to get naked. Just underwear."

"Sure. I'll do it."

What?

"Try not to look so surprised." He smiles, the picture of confidence. "You want to use my hotel room or you need some place sexier?"

My head is swimming. Tom is going to pose for me. I take a deep breath. "No. The hotel room is perfect."

For Tom.

Half-naked.

In front of my camera.

Chapter Four

I scan the room to assess the lighting situation. There are reading lamps on each side of the king bed. There's a bright fluorescent bulb above the couch. Then there's the bathroom.

My options are limited. But I can work with that. I take a few pictures of the room to see how it looks on screen. Too dark, no contrast. I turn my camera to Tom. He looks right into the lens.

"We starting already?" he asks.

"Not yet."

Click. It's hard to make out his expression. But one thing is certain.

He's trouble.

He plays with the zipper of his hoodie, raising a brow. "You need me to start stripping, Mistress Photographer?"

Oh yeah. Trouble.

It takes great restraint to stay calm and professional. "Not yet. We'll start with you fully dressed."

I set my camera down and mess with the lights. With

no way to angle them, my options are limited. I arrange the lamps *sans* shades until the room is filled with an angelic glow. The soft lighting will be a perfect contrast to the mischievous look in Tom's eyes.

When I'm finished, I turn my attention back to him.

Deep breath. I'm a photographer. If I want any chance of working with clients, I need to get over my shyness. Doesn't matter that my current model is smoking hot and about to strip. It's part of the job.

I look at Tom like he's a prop. Okay. That's it. I point to a spot in front of the bed. "Can you stand there?"

"Naked?" He teases.

My cheeks flush. He's a prop. "No. As you are."

He moves. His hands go to the zipper of his hoodie. He raises a brow. "Do I need to model?"

"If you want."

Something in his expression shifts, more posed and more relaxed at once. He *is* modeling. And he's good at it too. His expression is playful and sexy. It's perfect.

Click, click, click.

"Tease the camera." I motion to his zipper. "Like you're teasing me."

"You sure? Don't want to get you all worked up and send you home wanting."

My cheeks flush again. It's damn hot in here. I have to tease him back, make him think I'm as comfortable with this as he is. "It's an occupational hazard."

"Shit. Never thought I'd want to be anything other than a drummer." A cocky smile spreads over his face as he unzips his hoodie. He raises a brow as if to say *do you want me? I know you do.*

My, does he look good on film. Digital, technically. It takes great effort to stay professional. Somehow, I manage. I can't do many things, really. I can swim for hours. I can cook a decent meal. And I can take a fantastic set of photographs.

Hopefully.

"Take off your shirt." It comes out more demanding than I mean it to. "Please."

"You're so polite, Mistress Photographer. Are you trying to butter me up to get me naked?" He winks.

"Would I have to butter you up?"

"No. But my ego always enjoys a good stroking."

"You're trying to make me blush, aren't you?"

Tom smiles. "I'd never."

"Right. You're a nice guy."

He nods. "The nicest."

He spends ages pulling his shirt up his stomach, revealing inch after inch of defined abs. He has those v-lines. They make it nearly impossible to concentrate.

Tom doesn't wait for my order. He sits back on the bed and spreads his legs in a position that invites someone between them. Me. Well, the camera.

Prop. I need to think of him as a prop. Even if my palms are sweating and my mouth is dry.

Okay. It's way too hot in here. I set the camera down and do away with my sweater.

"Didn't realize it was *that* kind of photo shoot." Tom winks and pats the bed next to him. "I won't bite. Unless you want me to."

"No. It's just—"

"Where have I seen that before?" His eyes go to my chest. Well, the tattoo just above my chest.

"Drew has one." It's quite dramatic. A shattered glass heart, broken and bloody. "His is on his shoulder."

Tom's eyes fix on my chest. "Can't say I find his nearly appealing as yours."

"Thanks." I try to come up with some way to change

the subject. There are way too many memories attached to this thing. Awful memories that will get in the way of getting this done.

"Does it mean anything special?"

I swallow hard. "I got it after I broke up with my ex. To remind myself... of something. That I could survive a broken heart, I guess." I can't handle this conversation. It's too revealing. I point to the tattoo on Tom's chest. "What about your lion?"

"Loved *The Lion King* when I was a kid."

"You did not."

"You're right." He spreads his legs wider. "My mom, adopted mom, is an anthropologist. She always had tribal art on the walls." He points to her chest. "This is one of her favorite paintings."

"Did you get it for her?" I ask.

"Not exactly."

"What about your arm?"

"Liked the design."

"That's it?"

He nods. "Tell you what. I'll think a little harder about my next tat."

"It's your body. You should do whatever pleases you."

"Oh, *that's* what you're after." He reaches for the button of his jeans.

Oh God. He's about to take them off.

"No." I bite my lip to keep from blushing. Okay. I need to get back behind my camera. Out of the fray. No chance of getting hurt. I line up another shot of Tom. That's better. "Lie on your back. Please."

His body stretches long as he leans back. That's yummy. I snap more photos than I could ever use. This angle isn't quite right. I try getting closer but that's not it. The left side. Yes.

Without instructions, Tom slides his hand down his torso. Like he's going to start touching himself.

Deep breath. This is normal boudoir stuff. If I can't handle it, then I won't hack it with actual clients.

God, he's sexy. A natural. *Click, click, click*. His hand skims the waistband of his jeans. *Click, click, click*.

His hand is on the waistband of his jeans. The button.

I can't take it anymore.

I clear my throat as I set my camera down. "Maybe try a few sitting up."

He smirks, his eyes catching mine as he sits up straight. He knows how badly I want him. It's written all over his face.

Still, he is an accommodating model. He messes around on the bed. Copies half a dozen men's magazine glamour model poses. Kneeling. On all fours. Sticking his ass in the air.

"That better?" he asks.

I laugh. "You're better at being sexy."

"Am I?" He cocks a brow.

"You know you're sexy. Don't pretend otherwise." Thank goodness for my camera. I could never, in a million years, say anything this potentially embarrassing without the photography equipment shielding me. "Give me a few more. Be yourself."

He does. He shifts back on the bed. Oh lord. He unzips his jeans. Slides them off his hips. To his knees. His feet. He leans back, over the edge of the bed.

Oh, shit. "Tom, you're going to fall."

He does fall. With quite the thud. I bite my lip, bracing myself for a bad reaction.

But he jumps to his feet and laughs it off. He's a little scraped, but it's no big deal.

I set my camera down. "Are you okay?"

He nods to his scraped knee. "Occupational hazard."

He's effortless about everything. It must be nice to take life in stride. To be fearless.

I look back at Tom. "Those are great. I should have plenty."

"Let me see."

"After I edit them." And after a cold shower. "You're a good model."

"I know." He gets back into his clothes and walks to the door. His voice gets serious. "You can tell me tomorrow. About what it is you're running from."

Oh. That. I nod despite the dread forming in my gut. "Goodnight."

"Sweet dreams, kid."

The heavy door slams into the frame.

I plug my computer into the wall and get to uploading the images. The slow progress bar gives my thoughts time to sink in. They're heavy enough to weigh me down.

My first priority is getting far away from Bradley. Done. For now. My second is getting this application in. If I get the job, I'll move into a nice building with security and front gates that lock. If I don't get the job, well, I'll figure out something less depressing than crashing in my brother's spare room until the end of time.

One day, when I'm good enough, I'll open my own studio. I'll get magazine assignments. Editorials. Portraits. Beautiful photos that are packed with personality. I can fill in the gaps with headshots and boudoir.

Finally, the photos finish uploading. I go over them one by one. In every single shot, Tom is relaxed, confident, hot as the molten center of the Earth. It must be nice being that comfortable with yourself, your sexuality. Knowing how badly everyone wants you.

He lives with gusto. I try to imagine myself in one of his poses, confident and sexy and seizing the fucking day, but the mental image won't come together. The Willow in my imagination is awkward and stiff, afraid of what might happen if she so much as takes off her tank top, desperate to get out of the spotlight and behind the camera.

I narrow it down to ten photographs. There's no time to give each image the editing it deserves. Better be as efficient as possible. Exposure. Color. Contrast.

My eyelids get heavy. Okay. It's nearly three a.m. I can finish this in the morning. I get ready for bed, set the alarm clock to give me enough time to finish editing, and surrender to the embrace of the comforter.

It's been such a long day.

———

THE WEIGHT SHIFTS AS A MAN SITS ON THE BED. "I'VE BEEN thinking about you all night," he says. "Can't sleep."

The voice is familiar. I need it in my ears. Need him in my bed.

I shift closer, until the heat of his body warms mine. That electricity again. This time it's not a hint. I'm buzzing like a power line.

His mouth goes to my neck. Then down my chest. He pulls my tank top aside. His tongue flicks over my nipples. It's aggressive and precise at once. Nothing like with Bradley. Leagues better.

His lips trail down my stomach. Below my belly button. His hands go to my hips. He pulls my shorts down an inch. His lips press into the now revealed skin. He does it again. Again.

Until he's almost there.

Who is he? I should know, I should care.

Then his mouth is on me, and my whole body is abuzz. I thrash and tug at his hair.

My lips part and a sound escapes. A moan.

And then I'm saying something.

"Tom."

His name.

What, Tom?

There's no telling with his face planted between my thighs. His hair is about the right length. The right color.

Pleasure overwhelms me. Hard to focus on figuring out who he is. It's just a dream. What does it matter? I arch my back as my sex clenches. How long has it been since I've came?

Too long.

I tug at his hair. Almost.

His lips press against my thigh. "Not so hard, kid." He looks up at me. "Save it for round two."

Those mischievous green eyes.

Tom.

His tongue slides over my clit.

Oh, God, Tom.

Nothing else matters. Nothing but the pleasure spreading all the way to my limbs. My body shakes as an orgasm overtakes me.

I reach for him and he comes closer. His body is on top of mine, warm and heavy in just the right way. Hard. He's hard—his shoulders, his chest, his abs.

His cock.

I slide my hand below his belly button, over a soft tuft of pubic hair. My fingers brush his shaft. His tip. The hard metal of his piercing.

"I thought you had another three weeks." I groan as I wrap my hand around him.

"Not for you."

He takes my hand and presses it against his hard chest. I spread my legs as he shifts into position.

Almost.

Almost...

Chapter Five

That dream. God, that dream. I need a swimsuit and a pool and about a million laps. Something to clear my head. Something to think about besides the angles of Tom's body.

Almost there. The cursor hovers over the *Send* button. I double-check the email. Cover letter attached. Resume attached. Ten edited photos of sexy, boudoir perfection attached.

Here goes nothing. I click *Send*. A second later, the message is sent. And just in time too. It's fifteen till noon. It takes forever to edit with a track pad.

My still-damp hair sticks to my skin. The air conditioning in the lobby is cranked up high, but I'm sweaty and flushed. Even twenty minutes after a shower.

Coffee. I need coffee if I'm going to even fathom getting through today. I find a Thermos of complimentary java and fill a paper cup to the brim. It's bitter. Stale. So much for rescue. A little cream and a lot of sugar help take it up to semi-decent.

I sink into one of the cushy chairs and hug my bag into

my lap. The room comes into focus. It's bright outside. The big glass windows mean the entire lobby is backlit. There are about a dozen people here. Most are waiting, sipping drinks, staring at cell phones. Normal hotel stuff.

Crap. Tom is walking towards me. I cross my fingers that he hasn't seen me. How am I supposed to look him in the eyes after that dream?

No luck. He nods hello. A moment later, he plops next to me.

He takes a long sip of a black iced coffee and holds up two pastry bags. "You eat breakfast?" He offers me one of the bags.

"Supposed to have it with Drew."

"It's almost noon. Count that as lunch."

I take the bag. There's an egg, cheese, and avocado bagel inside. Doughy comfort food. Perfect. I take a greedy bite, chewing and swallowing too fast to actually taste it. "Thank you."

His eyes go to my complimentary coffee cup. "There's a Peet's down the street if you want something decent." He holds out his iced coffee, offering it to me.

I take a sip. Damn that's good. It's black but there's no bitterness. It's rich and chocolaty.

When I try to hand it back, Tom waves me away.

"Keep it." He opens the other bag and bites into his bagel sandwich. "You look like you're about to come."

"I do not."

"I like it." He steals my complimentary cup and takes a sip. "No wonder. That's total shit. What do you normally drink in the mornings?"

"I can get my own beverages."

"You want to fight over it, or you want to tell me?" He takes another sip, sticking out his tongue with distaste. "I've got things to do, but I'll wait."

He seems earnest about it. Demanding actually. Okay, if he wants to get me coffee, I'm not going to turn it down.

"Dark roast," I say. "Or cold brew iced coffee if it's a hot day. I like it sweet and creamy. Almond milk if it's available. Half and half if it's not."

"Picky all of a sudden."

"Sorry."

"Don't be. I like a girl who knows what she wants." He smiles. "Even if she's bossy about it."

Oh. He's talking about sex. My cheeks flush. "Are you... bossy?"

"I know what I like."

"Oh." My head fills with delicious mental images of Tom back on that bed, unzipping his jeans, issuing all sorts of illicit demands.

"You look fucking adorable when you blush." He pushes out of his seat. "Good thing I made that rule about us being platonic or I might get ideas."

"What kinds of ideas?"

He cocks a brow. "Don't go thinking about me like that, kid. I'm not the kind of guy you want to be involved with."

I nod to Tom. "Yeah. Sure. We're just friends."

"Good." He smiles. "You have a phone?"

I dig my now charged phone out of my purse and hand it to him. He taps a few things into it. Adding his number, no doubt. His cell buzzes in the front pocket of his jeans. Ah, he texted himself.

He hands back my phone. "My eyes are up here."

"Oh yeah. Sorry." It's still too embarrassing to make eye contact. I pretend as if the beige wall opposite us is fascinating so I won't turn every shade of red.

"I'll text you what time we're leaving when I know."

"Thanks."

"Better get out of here. Got a lot of shit to do."

I try not to gawk at his ass as he walks away.

I fail.

––––––

DREW AND KARA TAKE ME TO A COFFEE SHOP DOWN THE street. We spend an hour catching up. Despite their insistence that I join their fun group outing, I decline.

When they finally accept my *no* as the end of it, I stream one of my favorite movies, *Bringing Up Baby*, in the hopes of laughing away the sexual tension plaguing my body.

My phone buzzes with a text message. From Tom. He added himself to my phone as *Tom Steele, Irresistible.*

Tom: Has your computer melted from the heat of my photos yet?

Willow: Almost. Send me your email and I'll send them to you.

He does. So I do. A moment later, my phone buzzes with another text.

Tom: Damn, kid. It doesn't take a lot of work to make me look sexy as fuck, but these are good.

Willow: Is that a compliment?

Tom: Yeah. These are awesome.

Willow: Thank you.

Tom: Guessing you're not at the theme park.

Willow: No. It didn't sound like my thing. Why didn't you go?

Tom: Had shit to do. I have a proposition for you. What are you doing?

I'm not doing much of anything besides soaking in the air conditioning, but a proposition from Tom sounds like more than I can handle.

Really, I need to start putting my life in order, one thing at a time. Okay. That isn't the most exciting activity but it's necessary.

I check Yelp for my options. Online appointments, short walk from here. Done.

Willow: You think a salon called A Cut Above is any good?

Tom: Doubtful.

Willow: I hope you're wrong. I have an appointment in half an hour. I'll see you later.

———

TOM IS SITTING ON THE SALON COUCH, LEGS SPREAD IN that relaxed position confident guys always take. The one that says *you're lucky to have the chance to drop to your knees and blow me.*

Not that I'm wondering what that metal stud would feel like against my tongue.

Dammit. Since when do I fantasize about giving head?

"Hey, kid. What's up?" Tom smiles and pats the spot next to him.

The girl at the counter looks at him with lust. She's pretty. Short black hair and plenty of boob to fill out her low-cut blouse.

Tom shoots her a friendly nod. She bites her lip, grips the counter like she's gonna pee her tight black pants.

"Did Drew ask you to keep an eye on me?" I ask.

Tom nods. "Want to tell me why? Since you owe me an explanation for what you're running from."

"Just Drew being Drew."

"Uh-huh." He shifts up, bringing his knees a bit closer together. "You're full of shit."

"I don't need an eye kept on me."

"Course." He takes a long sip of his iced coffee. "But Miles and Drew are with their girls and Pete's not interested in company. So, as my new, platonic friend, you have to keep me entertained."

"That doesn't sound like the give and take of a healthy friendship."

Tom points to his mostly full drink. "I'll let you share my iced coffee."

The way he's laughing, I must be drooling.

"You want me to leave, say the word. I'll find some*one* to do." His gaze goes to the eager receptionist. He looks at her like he's considering the possibility of fucking her, fingering her, eating her out, something.

"No. You can stay." I take a seat next to him. "You look like you spend a lot of time on your hair."

"You calling me vain?" He runs a hand through his wavy, dark blond hair. Shakes his head in mock offense. "So rude, Willow. Gonna kick me out of bed without breakfast too?"

"Not exactly vain. But you know you're handsome."

Like a young Brad Pitt, really.

Fuck, I'm gawking.

"You keep staring, you're gonna give me a complex." He smiles wide. "Willow, Willow, sitting there, who is the fairest of them all?"

"Shut up. You know you're beautiful. I've seen you in magazines. You soak it in."

"Have you?" He raises a brow. "Which ones? Was I naked?"

"Some of the time. But there was never anything showing." My cheeks flush. "I buy anything about Sinful Serenade. To support Drew, you know? If I'm ever Annie Leibovitz famous, he can buy all my stuff."

His knee presses against mine. Thankfully or tragically, we're both wearing jeans. That makes the heat spreading through my body tolerable.

Yes. Platonic friends. I can do that.

I grab a stack of hairstyle books to keep myself occupied.

Tom leans closer, watching everything I'm doing. His chest presses against my back. His chin rests on my shoulder. "You going for anything in particular?"

"Something less... well, less." My long hair is heavy against my neck and back. I flip through a dozen pages of similar long haircuts, the kind of safe thing I normally do.

"Going shorter?" he asks.

"Yeah."

Tom drags his fingertips over my shoulders. "Here?" His fingers graze my neck. "Or here?" They move up to my chin, tracing the line of my jawbone, all the way to my ear. "Or maybe here."

A shiver runs down my spine. God damn, those fingers on my body... There's no doubt about it. My sex drive is not only awake. It's raring and ready to go.

I swallow the gasp that rises in my throat. "I'm not sure."

I need to concentrate on something before I melt. I devote all my energy to the style book. Maybe I can work up the courage to do something shorter. It's just hair. It shouldn't be a big deal.

Tom taps me on the shoulder. "That one's a lot less innocent."

It is. Chin length, choppy, and streaked with bright blue.

"I'm not innocent," I say.

"Of course not. How many guys have you slept with?"

"How is that your business? How many girls have you slept with?"

"I lost track after two hundred."

That's so...

I can't even.

"Ooo, the judgmental look again." He shifts to the left, grabs his coffee, and returns his knees to a *blow me, please* position. "You're cute judgmental."

"I'm not judgmental. Just surprised."

He stares back at me, challenging me.

"If you were going to ballpark it..."

"Four hundred. Maybe five."

My jaw refuses to stay in place.

"I'm always safe. Even with oral."

"I'm not judging."

"Get tested every three months."

I nod. "That's very responsible of you."

"Always been clean."

"That's great."

"You're blushing."

"No, I'm not."

"Yeah, you are." He laughs. "It's cute."

I stare back at the hairstyle. "It's too much. I'll look silly."

"You'll look hot." His fingertips brush my shoulder. "But do whatever makes you happy."

He thinks I'll look hot. I press my eyelids together, attempting to imagine myself as the kind of woman who could pull off such a bold style.

Tom runs his hand through my hair, pulling it back to approximate the length of the cut. "You should do pink. To match your cheeks." He shifts, looking me in the eyes. "Do you want to do it?"

I do. I want to do something different.

Tom brushes a stray hair behind my ear. His fingers linger on my cheek. "Then what are you waiting for? Do it."

He makes it sound easy. I'm sure, for Tom, it is that

easy. He wants something, he takes it. No hesitation. No second guessing. No doubt.

"Willow!" A hairdresser with a messy pixie cut and a sleek black dress calls my name.

Salvation. I stand and nod goodbye to Tom.

"I'll be here," Tom says.

"What a nice boyfriend, waiting for you. Wish my husband would do the same." She smiles. "I'm Gina."

We shake hands. I don't correct her.

"You know what you want?" she asks.

My gaze goes to Tom. He's half looking at his phone, half looking at me. Those green eyes, that smile on his face, the lines of the tattoo peeking out from his v-neck...

Yeah. I know what I want.

And it's different.

It's really fucking different.

Chapter Six

My hair is short, just past my chin, and the tips are pink.

It's perfect.

I'm not that naive girl who didn't know better. I'm dangerous, sexy. The kind of girl who demands what she wants. An edgy photographer who doesn't take shit from anyone.

I thank the stylist as she pulls back the cape. It takes me a full minute to regain my senses.

Tom is at the counter, not quite flirting with the receptionist, but certainly soaking up her admiration.

"Oh my Gosh. That song... what's it called? *No Way in Hell.* That one's my favorite. The beat is amazing. Even my friends who only listen to dubstep like it."

"Thanks, honey." He leans closer, smiling at her.

"And the lyrics... Oh my Gosh. Sweet. Is it really true that... what's his name? Your singer. Did he really write that about his girlfriend?"

"Yeah. He's crazy about her."

"What about you? Crazy about anyone?"

"Nah, I don't do that kind of thing."

She giggles. "What's the lyric in the song?" She starts humming. "No way, not me, I don't do this kind of thing?"

"That's it.

Tom smiles but there's a hint of irritation in his expression. He must be tired of hearing this over and over again.

She hands back his credit card.

What the hell is his credit card doing out?

He signs the receipt and hands it back to her. "Thanks a lot, honey. I'll pass the compliment on."

"Sure." The smiles falls off her face as she looks at me. She leans in closer, to whisper. "Is that your girlfriend?"

"No. Just a real good friend. Thanks for taking such good care of her."

"It was all Gina." She giggles. "But Gina only listens to country. I doubt she recognizes you."

"What are you doing paying for me?" I ask.

"It's no big deal."

"It's a big deal to me." I look at the flirty receptionist. "How much was it?"

Tom grabs my wrist as he makes puppy dog eyes at her. "Don't tell her. She's real demanding."

She nods, attentive, ready to follow any order he has. "Of course not. Bye, Tom!"

He shoots her a flirty wave as he pulls me out of the store.

His hands go to my waist. He holds me in place, my body pressed against his.

Dammit. I'm not going to let lust distract me from my point. I swallow the sigh rising in my throat. "Tom Steele, how much was that?"

"About two hundred dollars."

"What?"

"I tipped well." He runs his hand through my now chin-length hair. "You look great. Badass and sexy."

I look badass and sexy.

Deep breath. "Okay. I will pay you back as soon as I get a job."

"About that."

"Yeah?"

"Let's talk over lunch. There's a Thai place around the corner. Or would you prefer something different?"

"I don't want to talk over lunch. I want to pay you back."

"You will. Later. I trust you for it."

"Fine. Thai is good." My stomach growls at the thought of that spicy eggplant dish. "But I'm paying."

"Whatever you want."

"It's super cheap, isn't it?"

He nods.

———

AFTER WE ORDER—THE EGGPLANT DISH FOR ME, SHRIMP curry for Tom—I check my email on my phone.

Oh, God. It's here. A reply to my application. I take a deep breath. That was too fast. It's either great news or terrible news.

Here goes nothing.

Dear Willow,

Thank you for applying. You show great promise. Unfortunately, we've selected another candidate with more experience.

Best of luck

No.

No, no, no.

I drop my phone on the table and look towards the floor. What the hell am I going to do now?

"Hey. You okay?" Tom says.

No. "I didn't get the photography job."

"Sorry, kid."

I need to clear my head before I think about this. There must be something I can do, something better than playing Drew's shadow indefinitely.

I grab my camera and line up a few shots. The neatly arranged hot sauce. The steam coming off a bowl of noodles.

And Tom, staring at me with an expectant expression.

"You sure we can't do nudes this time?" he asks.

My cheeks flush. I'm nervous enough that the rejection only barely stings. Tom is quite the subject. I mess with the blinds until the lighting is just right and snap half a dozen shots.

"What's the point of these?" He sets his elbow on the table, leans against his palm, bored.

Impatient, demanding Tom. He looks great on the screen. The pictures are bursting with personality and he's barely doing anything.

"Practice for me." I line up the condiments and take another few shots. "You owe me for that paying for me bullshit."

"How can I owe you for paying for you? That doesn't make sense."

"You know it does."

He smirks. There. Photographic evidence that he knows he's wrong! Ha. My triumph is over quickly. Tom grabs the camera from my hands and taps a few buttons on it.

I try to grab it back but he stands and holds it up.

"Don't look at those," I say.

"You take naked self-portraits?"

"No."

"Then why not?"

I struggle to come up with an explanation. My pictures are personal, but I need to get over that if I'm ever going to be a professional. "Never mind. It's fine."

"These are good too." He hands back the camera. "I have a proposition for you. We have a photographer for our shows. Hazel. She's been talking about taking on an assistant for the tour. Would you be interested?"

"Hazel as in Hazel Alexander?" She's a legend of portrait photography.

"Yeah, that's it."

God, yes. I almost bite my tongue. I almost forget how to breathe. "Yes. Of course."

"Cool. I'll call her after we eat."

"Call her now."

He cocks a brow. "Demanding again."

"Call her now, please."

"Maybe… not sure what I get out of it." He smiles. "Maybe if you make it worth my while."

"Anything."

"Thought you'd say that."

God, his look is smug. I want to slap him and kiss him at the same time.

Tom shifts back, slides his knees open to that *blow me* position. "I need to do a little work rehabbing my image. Since my—" He motions to his crotch. "Haven't been going home with lingerie models on my arm. Tabloids are forgetting how much they love me."

"So, what, you need to go to the clubs and dance with other celebrities?" I ask.

"And I need someone to capture it." He points to me. "Someone who will look natural on my arm." His eyes scan my body. "No offense. Cause you look good in that tight sweater. But the women I have on my arms tend to dress a bit more—"

"Slutty?"

"Tsk. Tsk." He shakes his head in mock outrage. "So judgmental of women who show off their tits and ass."

"I'm not judging. If I had any, I'd show off."

Tom's eyes go straight to my chest. He doesn't even pretend he's not staring.

"You have some." Desire spreads over his face. "Bet you look damn good naked. Was hoping to get you that way when I saw you in my room."

My cheeks flush. I look for a sign he's joking, but there's none. "You do realize that platonic friends don't have these kinds of conversations?"

"Who cares what people usually do? Our friendship, our rules."

That makes sense. Kind of.

"If it bugs you, I'll stop." He makes eye contact. "You want me to stop?"

My cheeks flush.

Tom smiles. "Didn't think so."

"I would like you to get to the point. Please."

His gaze goes to my chest for a long moment then it's back to my eyes. "I need help maintaining the rock and roll image. Should only be once every couple weeks."

"Okay."

"You're judging again."

I shake my head. "Just curious."

"Things go better if the press is talking about me taking home a lingerie model than if they're asking why we canceled our second tour or looking for my biological mom or realizing Miles was MIA for three months."

"Oh."

"Yeah. The other guys, they don't want attention unless

it's about their musical talents. Miles, when he was single, he didn't mind so much—the playboy thing. But it's better if people don't look too close. They see the cracks."

"You're keeping the attention on your slutty ways so no one bothers your bandmates?"

He nods.

It's sweet in a strange way.

Tom may be a bad boy, but he's a hell of a great guy.

"I want the pictures you sent me. For my Instagram." He smiles. "There are gonna be a lot of vibrators running out of battery tonight."

He's effortless with that claim. *Hey, I'm Tom. Women are going to masturbate to my photographs tonight. No big deal.*

Wait. He thinks women are going to masturbate to photographs I took? I'm not sure if I should be flattered or offended.

"How do you want me to credit you?" he asks. "Do you use your real name or a stage name?"

I can't use my real name. Bradley might look me up. Okay. Might as well do like Drew and channel the dark knight. "How about Willow Wayne?"

He laughs. "Like Batman?"

"Is that a problem?"

"No. Just didn't think you were into rich guys who beat people up." He pulls out his phone.

"Are you going to pay me?"

"Sure. Let's say, I get you for five sessions. A thousand bucks each session."

I can't have heard that right. A thousand dollars per session. That's insane. I can afford a new camera, new lenses, new lights. I'll be halfway to startup costs for my own studio. And that's before whatever salary I get from Hazel.

I nod. "Yes. God, yes."

"You're gonna need some different clothes. For when we go out."

"Sure. Anything."

"You shouldn't let me know how bad you want it." He leans closer. "If I was less scrupulous, I'd take advantage of that."

My breath catches in my throat. "You're not scrupulous."

"True." His gaze goes to my chest. "And I don't have to blackmail my way into getting laid."

"Of course."

"But still. You've got a lot to learn about negotiating."

I nod. Sure. I'll learn about negotiating. Anything as long as I can have this job. "Can we call Hazel now?"

"It's kinda fun making you wait."

"Please."

"I bet you look good begging on your knees."

Lord help me, I'm more than willing to beg on my knees for the chance to work with Hazel Alexander. "Don't tempt me. I'll do it."

"Don't. If you get on your knees, I'll get ideas."

Yes.

So.

Many.

Ideas.

Tom dials his phone and holds it to his ear.

Damn. Voicemail.

I'm still waiting to figure out what the hell my future holds.

Chapter Seven

T he mall is bright, clean, totally void of personality. Dark tile floor, high ceilings, big windows letting in the desert sun.

My eyes stay glued to Tom's jeans, to the pocket where he keeps his phone. Hard to remember what we're doing here. Hazel still hasn't returned his call.

She needs to say yes.

I have no clue what I'll do if she doesn't say yes.

The air conditioning sends goose bumps over my flesh. I rub my biceps with my palms to fight a shiver. It doesn't help. A *brrr* escapes my lips.

Tom slides his arm around my waist, pulls my body into his.

It's not cold anymore.

It's scorching.

This is not at all appropriate for platonic friends, but God knows I'm not about to point that out. His body feels good.

Too good. My mind goes blank except for this loud voice screaming *more*.

I step aside. It's the only way to keep my wits about me. We're ten feet from a chain department store. I guess we're here for clothes. So I can look like the proper kind of hit-the-clubs woman who belongs on Tom's arm.

My gaze goes back to the front pocket of his jeans.

"Willow. Hello." He waves his hand in front of my face. "What's interesting in my pants? Besides the obvious."

I say nothing.

"If you want me to whip it out, you should ask. Staring won't get you anywhere."

Whip it out? Seriously? The man is deranged if he thinks I'd actually ask that.

"You okay?"

I shake my head. "What if Hazel says no?"

"She won't."

"How do you know that?"

"You want me to call her again?"

"Of course."

"Hmm... I don't know. What's in it for me?"

"Please."

He lets out a soft groan but says nothing about it.

"Please." I press my palms together. Self-respect is much less important than working with Hazel Alexander. "I'll beg."

"Don't beg. I'll get ideas." He slides his arm around my lower back and holds me in place. His other hand goes to his phone. He dials and brings the thing to his ear. "Hey, Hazel. It's Tom."

Success! I can just barely hear her on the other line.

She's no-nonsense. "Yes... if you know she's dependable... Lot of grunt work... Look forward to meeting Willow tomorrow."

"Later." Tom hangs up his phone and slides it into his

pocket. He releases his grip around my waist then looks at his arm like he's not sure how it got there.

"She said yes?" I ask.

He stares back at me with a wide smile, clearly enjoying tormenting me. "Did she?"

"You're killing me."

"Yes, she said yes. She's looking forward to meeting you."

I throw my arms around him and squeeze tight. Tom steps back, surprised, then he moves forward. Hugs me back.

He feels good. Hard. Safe.

"You that excited?" His voice is apprehensive.

"Yeah." I pull my arms to my sides. "Sorry. I shouldn't have jumped at you like that."

"It's all right. Just surprising."

It is? But he's experienced. "You've slept with 500 different women."

"Don't really stop to cuddle." He runs a hand through his hair. "I just... uh." He shoves his hands into his pockets. "You're going to stay through the tour?"

Fuck yes. I'll stay anywhere to work with Hazel Alexander. I nod.

"Then you'll need clothes. You only have that." He nods to my messenger bag. "You need help picking out stuff for clubs or you have that covered?"

"I can manage." Probably.

"Just, uh, make sure you pick out some lingerie."

Say what? I stare back into Tom's eyes but it doesn't help me figure out what he's getting at. "Why?"

He pulls out his wallet and counts out a thousand dollars in hundreds. "It's a surprise."

He is incredibly obvious about handing me the money.

I shove it in my purse before anyone can get ideas about mugging me. "What is this?"

"An advance on your salary. We're going to take our first set of pictures today. Get everything you need for the rest of the tour. Plus at least one set of matching lingerie."

I raise an eyebrow. He just smiles and nods to a bench outside the department store. "I'll be here."

―――――

It takes two long, exhausting hours of shopping to get everything I need. After I finish, Tom leads me to the parking garage, back to his flashy red convertible. It's a bright contrast against the beige concrete walls and the dusty asphalt.

Tom unlocks the trunk, stuffs my bags inside. Something in his expression changes. The softness in his eyes is disarming.

He leans against the car next to me. "Listen, kid. I hate to risk ruining the mood but I need to know what it is you're running from."

"Why?"

"A deal is a deal."

It's true. A deal is a deal. I take a deep breath. The air smells of gasoline. It's quiet. I can hear my heart beat.

"You're not okay," he says.

"Yes, I am."

"You're running from something bad, huh?"

"No. Just..." I pull my hands into my lap. "Just the normal stuff."

"Normal. Is that why you're cringing?"

"I'm not."

"Yeah, you are. Whatever it is, it's not normal."

I turn to face him. "It's very normal."

"Bullshit. You want me to call Hazel and tell her you're a liar?"

"Would you really do that?"

"I might." He stares into my eyes. "Been known to do whatever it takes to get what I want."

"You swear you won't tell Drew?"

"Why should it matter if—"

"Swear or I'm not telling you."

He nods.

Panic fills my stomach. I stare back at Tom. There's something earnest about him, something trustworthy. But that's not enough. I need to be sure.

"Seriously," I say. "If you tell Drew, everything is going to be fucked. You have to promise."

"I won't tell him. We're friends. Any secret of yours is just between us. Same goes for any secret of mine."

"Okay."

His shoulder presses against mine. He's warm.

"I live in an apartment in Berkley. A little studio in a six unit building. Mom didn't take me changing my major to photography too well. I moved out before she had the chance to kick me out. The place is a great deal and about all I can afford. I don't really have a choice about moving. Not without some serious cash."

He stares back at me. "I get that."

"My ex-boyfriend showed up as my new next door neighbor. Convinced my landlord that he's a nice, dependable guy I guess."

"He hurt you?"

"Someone always gets hurt when a relationship ends."

"He hit you?"

I can't answer that. "I don't want to be around him. That's all."

"Yeah, sure."

His fingertips brush my wrist. The touch is soft and delicate. How can someone who comes in like a God damn wrecking ball have such a delicate touch?

I say nothing. He responds with silence. We lean against the car, him looking at me, me trying hard not to notice how he's staring.

Minutes pass. My heartbeat, my breath—both slow to something normal. Until the only thing mixing me up is how badly I want the comfort of Tom's arm around me again.

I step sideways, adjust my clothes, anything to keep my hands busy and my mind occupied.

"You have a picture or something?" Tom asks. "For our head of security. I'll make sure he keeps it from Drew."

I nod. There are lots of pictures of him online, from his college football days. I pick the most recent one.

"Thanks." Tom borrows my phone for a minute then hands it back. "It's okay. I'll make sure he's not around."

"It's nothing."

"Yeah. Of course."

I nod. Of course it's nothing. But I'm not selling that story. Not even a little bit.

Tom studies me. He must decide I'm okay, because the serious look drops off his face.

He slides his arm around my waist. "You're probably caffeine deprived. Let's get a coffee or something."

———

AFTER AN ALMOND MILK LATTE AND A ONE-SIDED conversation about horror movies, I am over-caffeinated and sufficiently distracted. It's clear why Tom runs around like a monkey on cocaine. The man drinks an ungodly amount of iced coffee.

His fingertips skim my palm. He's back to his usual bouncy self. No cracks, no softness, no signs he's ever been hurt.

He looks me in the eyes. "You feeling properly energized?"

"Yeah."

"Good. I have an idea. Want to indulge me?"

"Depends on what your idea is."

"The tabloids need to know about my new fuck buddy," he says.

I'm not following. "You don't have a fuck buddy."

"Sure I do." He nods to me. "She's a mystery girl with an edgy hairstyle and great taste in men."

He means me. Okay. This might work.

"You're game?" He asks.

Maybe. I nod anyway.

"Then let's take a picture of us fucking."

Chapter Eight

et's take a picture of us fucking.

Has breathing always been this difficult?

"The hair really does match your cheeks," Tom says.

"Are you out of your damn mind?"

"And you think I would be fuck buddies with someone so shy." Tom shakes his head. He points to the department store across from us. "We're going to take a picture in that dressing room and you're going to leak it to a celeb news site."

"We're going to take a picture of us fucking in that dressing room?" I blink way more than any person should. "You don't mean..."

"Of course I don't *mean*... We'll cheat it. Don't tell me you don't know how to cheat a shot."

My body responds with gusto. Heart racing, heat building between my legs. It takes my head a few moments to catch up. The assignment is unorthodox, but I can do it. "What if Drew sees it?"

"He won't."

"You sure about that?"

"If you even say the words TMZ around Drew, he glares at you and threatens to hit someone." Tom nods. "If he does see it, I'll explain what we're doing. He won't like it, but fuck him. You want to spend your life making decisions because you're worried your brother is going to hit someone?"

"That's not it, exactly."

"Willow, it's your life. If you don't want to do it, tell me. But if you do want to do it, then fucking go for it. Don't let anything stop you from taking what you want."

"I'd be more receptive to your message if I didn't think you were trying to manipulate me."

"I don't need to manipulate women into pressing themselves against me. If you aren't game, I'll find another model." He scans the coffee shop, his gaze fixing on a tall woman with light hair. "But I'd rather not lead her on."

No. I don't want him pressed against that other woman.

He looks at me. "Are you in or out?"

I take a deep breath, cultivating the *go for it* confidence spread over Tom's face. I can do that too. I can be the kind of person who says *yes* to life instead of hiding behind my camera.

In theory.

Enough hesitation. I'll figure out what kind of person I want to be later. Right now, I need to please my client. I make eye contact. "I'm in."

"Then let's go."

———

TOM TEARS THE TAGS OFF THE BLACK LACE BRA AND PANTY set I bought at the department store. "I like your taste. Classy."

My cheeks flush. I try my best to shift into professional mode. We're in the handicapped stall of a dressing room, not a studio, but I can do this.

"Is the goal something we're taking for our depraved pleasure or something that belongs on Instagram?" I ask.

"Either way."

"They're different. The former will be messy, more about the physical and less about the props or anything. But you've seen pictures on social media. People pose them, get their latte arranged next to their book, next to their plate of grapes. No one really sits that neatly. You know?"

He nods. "Pretty and smart. Picked a good fake fuck buddy."

He's thinks I'm pretty and smart. I'm not sure which is more flattering. I clear my throat to keep desire from swallowing me whole.

"I want it to look like you leaked this picture. It's up to you."

"Then I don't need this." I point to my camera, return it to my purse, and fish out my cell. "It should look heat of the moment. Like we were so desperate to fuck that we nearly ripped off our clothes."

"This is why I need you, kid." He pulls his t-shirt over his head and drops it on the floor. "Good?"

My gaze goes to his chest, his stomach, the soft tuft of hairs below his belly button. Very good. Great. Amazing.

I unlock my phone, open the camera app. "Maybe a few like this. Sorta... you stripping for me."

He cocks a brow. "You're enjoying this, aren't you?"

"A woman should enjoy her work."

Tom laughs. He motions to the waistband of his jeans. "These too."

"Not yet." I snap a few shots of him, waist up. God, he's yummy. Unbearably yummy. It's practically objective.

I grab the bra and panties and toss them aside. Time to think like a photographer. If we were going to fuck in here, we'd have a few good options. There's the seat. Big enough for me to climb on top of him. Or he could lift me and push me against the wall. Or turn me around and take me from behind.

A flush spreads over my cheeks and down my chest.

I pull my sweater over my head and toss it on the ground.

Tom's eyes go to my exposed skin. My shoulders, my neck, my chest. His cheeks flush. He's checking me out.

He wants me.

But he made it clear we're only friends. I'm keeping this professional. Well, as professional as pretending to fuck in a dressing room can get.

I press my cell to my chest. "Come on. Let's get posing. Grab me and press me against the wall."

"Bossy all of a sudden."

"Just do it."

"As you wish, Mistress Photographer." Tom slides his arms under my ass and lifts me. "Wrap your legs around me."

I do. It puts us in quite the compromising position. He shifts, holding me against the wall. His crotch presses into mine.

"Not sure if this will come out well." I hold my phone over my head, press my cheek against Tom's to shield my face from the camera, and take half a dozen photos.

"Can't complain about the working conditions." He

shifts his body into mine, pressing me harder against the wall.

God, that feels good. I take a deep breath so I won't be totally red. "Can you set me down?"

He does. I focus all my attention on the pictures. Most of them are garbage—a whiff of hair or a strange angle on the floor—but a few are in the right direction. They focus on the tattoo spanning his shoulder blades, his arms around the mystery girl with short pink-tipped hair.

I show Tom the winners.

He points to something on the image. "Your straps are showing."

I stare back at him, unblinking.

"Keep your top on, kid. But push the straps to your shoulders or something."

"You better hope you're right about Drew not seeing these."

"I'm not worried about Drew. Push comes to shove, I can take him." He motions for me to adjust my top.

I pull my tank and bra straps off my arms. They hang under my armpits. It's unflattering from straight on, but it should work from overhead.

"Okay. Press me against the wall." I brace myself for the slight impact.

"Mmm, so bossy." He slides his arms around me and pulls us into position.

Somehow, we're closer this time. I can feel his heart beating against my chest, his breath against my neck.

His lips brush my skin. His fingers dig into the fabric of my jeans.

I shift, trying to get comfortable, trying to focus on taking pictures. *Click, click, click.* Then another angle and a few more for good measure.

"Wlllllw." Tom's voice is muffled. "Yrrr ttts rrr prsssd tooo myyy faaaa."

"Huh."

He brings his hand to my shoulders and adjusts my position. "Your tits are pressed into my face."

"Oh."

"Not complaining. Just means... shit." His grip around me tightens. He blushes.

Why is Tom blushing?

I squeeze his shoulders, trying and failing not to slip.

Oh.

He's hard.

His erection is pressed against my crotch. Lots of denim in between us but there's no denying it.

Tom is hard.

My brain refuses to focus on anything else.

"Guess this is how actors feel when they shoot sex scenes." Tom blushes. He lifts me higher, so we aren't pressed quite as closely together. "You want down?"

"No." I take a deep breath. "Two more."

He motions to my chest. "Be careful with those things. I can't exactly get my rocks off with the salesgirl who was checking me out."

"No? Why is that?"

"It's not nice to tease a man who isn't allowed to masturbate." He smiles, confident, but still blushing.

"You look really cute with your cheeks pink," I say.

"You're blushing too." He grabs my hips and holds me against the wall. "You know, the mall will close eventually."

I bring my phone over my head and snap another set of pictures. Then I try a few from the side. "Okay. Let me down."

Tom keeps me pressed against the wall as he shifts

back, breaking the contact of our bodies. I slide down the wall, setting my feet down one at a time.

He's still hard. I only barely manage to avoid gawking. It's really a marvel of denim technology that his jeans contain him.

Tom is not at all shy about resting his chin against my shoulder to check out the pictures. It's not as if he's intentionally rubbing against me. Just that he's not avoiding me. Not at all awkward. It's remarkable how comfortable he is with his body.

I go through the pictures, pointing out the winners and deleting the others. When we're finished, he helps me get my straps back into position and sends the photos to himself.

"I'll take care of leaking these." He shifts into his clothes. "You okay, kid?"

"Yeah. Great."

"Gotta say, that was the first time I ever paid to get hard."

That only makes the blushing situation worse. "I... uh... well, that's not really... exactly what you were paying for."

Tom smiles. "You're cute."

"Uh... thanks."

"Come on." He slides his arm around my waist. "Let's get out of here before I get any ideas that will get me into trouble."

Chapter Nine

We grab Mexican food on the way back to the hotel. There's a sleek black bus parked behind the building. It's unmarked.

"It's not bad once you get used to it." Tom nods hello to a tall, burly man in a black polo shirt and black slacks. "Our head of security, Xander."

He introduces me, and Xander opens the doors for us.

"After you." Tom helps me onto the steps.

"Thanks." I climb into the mysterious vehicle. It's not quite as dark on the inside. It's nice, actually. Clean, well lit, huge.

There are two people sitting on a couch in the front. A leggy woman with dramatic features sits in the lap of a tall blue-eyed man. She's about my age. He's a few years older.

"Hey," he says. "You must be Willow. I'm Miles Webb." He points to himself. "Vocals, lyrics, sex appeal."

"I'm Meg Smart," she chimes in. "Do I get a snappy introduction?"

He squeezes her. "Meg Smart. Wit. Beauty. Medical

services." Miles laughs. "Okay, I can admit that needs some work. How about—Wit. Beauty. *Jurassic Park* references?"

She attempts one. "Meg Smart. Future Doctor. If she can ever escape her boyfriend's immense sex appeal and actually crack open a book."

He grabs her and pulls her into an especially deep kiss. When they're done necking (it takes several minutes), we go through a round of handshakes, and they turn their attention back to the TV. They're playing a *Star Wars* video game. She's winning.

Tom gives me the grand tour of the bus. From front to back, it goes: TV area, kitchenette/table, bunk beds, and private bedroom. When the band isn't spending the night in separate hotel rooms, they take turns in the bedroom. Mostly it's for sex.

"Yes! I knew I'd get you." The woman squeals. "Miles... I still won, even if you're..."

"Mhmm." He presses his lips against her neck. His hands slide around her waist.

A moment later, they're making out like no one is watching. She pulls herself away with great effort.

"You're Drew's sister, right?" She waves to me.

"Yeah."

She looks up at Tom. "You angling for another black eye? You mess with my new friend, Willow, and I'll be the one to give it to you."

"Why you complain so much? Shit worked for you. Shit worked out for Kara," Tom says.

Meg nods reluctantly.

"You should accept that I'm a fucking genius," Tom says.

"Next time you meddle, can you skip the part where my heart is broken and I barely manage to find the energy to study for finals?" Meg asks.

"Where's the fun in that?" Tom teases.

Miles chuckles. He's the Sinful Serenade singer. His voice is just as sexy in person. I replay one of their more popular tracks in my head. It's breathy, tortured. He's taller than Tom. A little less built but certainly no slouch.

Gorgeous blue eyes.

Chiseled features.

He's anyone's definition of handsome.

I will my body to react, to want him and not Tom. Yes, he has a girlfriend, but it's only a test.

I stare at his strong, tattooed chest. He's sexy but my body is apathetic.

Meg looks at Tom curiously. "Hey. How come I haven't seen you with any girls lately?"

Tom's hand plops on my shoulder, and my God damn body floods with electricity. I swallow the sigh rising in my throat.

"This is a girl," Tom says.

Miles whispers something in Meg's ear. Her jaw drops. Her cheeks go red.

She looks at Tom. "You did not." She turns back to Miles. "Why would Tom get his cock pierced?"

"Babe, you should ask him that." He runs his hand through her hair. "Unless you're requesting—"

"Not if I have to go six weeks without hearing you come." Her cheeks turn red. "Oh, God. Sorry. I forgot you guys were there."

"Please," Tom says. "You two are louder than Pete. Where the fuck is he?"

Miles nods to the bedroom. "Sleeping off his hangover."

"How do you know?" Tom's voice is sharp.

"Talked to him. Something people do instead of trying to run each other's lives. You should try it sometime," Miles says. "The man is going batshit over that girl. He needs to get the break up over with and get to work on getting over her the fun way."

"That's his brother." Meg swats Miles playfully. "Is that what you'll do if I dump you?"

"Why? You have plans to dump me?" He repositions her, so she's straddling to him. "Better convince you to reconsider."

"Miles..."

"Mhmm." He's back at her neck, sucking on her skin with great concentration.

I clear my throat. It does nothing. Okay. They're way too into each other to care.

He pulls down his shirt and points to a tattoo on his chest.

She sighs with pleasure and drags her hands over his exposed skin. It's hard to tell from this angle, but it's entirely plausible that his hand is under her skirt.

Tom rolls his eyes. "Yes, you're in love and you can't keep your hands off each other. We've got the point."

Miles laughs. "God, I can't imagine the blue balls. How long has it been, Tom?"

"Three weeks."

Miles looks at his girlfriend. "He can't even masturbate for three more weeks."

"The free porn shows you two put on really help," Tom says.

"Aw, poor Tom likes watching us make out too much." She feigns pity.

"Yeah, you stop at making out..."

She blushes. "I thought you were asleep."

"Then why were you screaming?" Tom asks.

Meg blushes. "Sorry. I was trying to keep it down." She pushes herself off her boyfriend and makes eye contact with me. "Come on. If we wait until they're done with the pissing contest to eat we'll die of starvation."

———

I MUST BE THE BAND PET. EVERYONE TAKES THEIR TURN sitting with me, making conversation about work, school, or music. Drew stares intently at my new hairstyle but he keeps any commentary to himself.

"Tom give you a hard time or anything?" he asks.

Technically, yes. But that's not the question. "No, he's been great. He talked to Hazel about hiring me as her assistant."

Drew beams. "You're gonna stay?"

I nod. "Yeah."

Drew's still posture softens. "I'm glad you're here, Wil. If you need anything, let me know. Anything."

Okay. He's calm enough I can tease. "What if I need condoms?"

Drew throws me a *come on* look. He must be in a good mood. It's usually pretty easy to get a rise out of him.

"I hope that joke means you trust me," he says.

"Enough."

"Good. I've missed you. I'm not gonna fuck this up." He nods goodnight then joins Kara in one of the bunk beds.

Those things are tiny. The two of them barely fit.

I finish *Bringing up Baby* by myself. When I look up and turn my computer off, Meg and Miles are on their way to bed. They share a bunk for a while but eventually retire to separate spaces.

The giggles and mumbles of late night conversation turn to the soft breathing of sleep. The bus is quiet. Tom is on the couch, watching a movie with headphones. I guess the band's bassist, Pete, is still in the private room, sleeping or brooding or surreptitiously engaging in sexual activities.

That leaves me and Tom as good as alone. I try to stay busy color correcting portraits of my friend Cassandra. They're the kind of thing Hazel shoots but not nearly as good. I only manage to stay busy for half an hour before the couch beckons me.

I turn off my computer, put it with my things, and join Tom.

He's close. Really close. His shoulder presses against mine. The outside of his knee presses against mine. I can feel all the warmth of his body. I can hear his inhale and exhale.

"Here." He pulls an ear bud from one ear and hands it to me.

It's been ages since I've shared headphones with someone. It's sweet. Intimate.

The sounds of the film fills my ear. Soft rustling of the wind. A voice in a foreign language. The images on screen are bleak blue scenery. Snow and the empty sky.

The cable tugs. It's not meant for two people.

"This is *Let The Right One In*. Have you seen it?" He scoots closer, to give the headphones slack.

"No. What happened so far?"

"I'll restart it." He reaches over me. His hand brushes my stomach on its way to the remote.

"You don't have to do that." It's a waste, really. I won't be able to pay attention with Tom in such close proximity.

"It's no big deal." He restarts the film and settles into a spot on the couch next to me.

He moves closer, closer, until I'm practically in his lap.

I try to focus on the stark images of the opening credits. The movie is beautifully shot.

He pats his chest. "You can lay down. You must be tired."

"I'm not tired. Someone kept giving me caffeine."

"Blaming me for your lack of self-control? So tacky. I'm disappointed in you, Willow."

The screen flashes with a snow covered school. It looks cold. It looks cold but Tom's body is warm.

I clear my throat. "Where is your car?"

"Roadies take turns driving it. Gives them some time alone. You don't get many chances to hear yourself think on tour."

"Don't you get sick of that?"

"I'd put up with a lot worse for the chance to get on stage every other night."

"Plus all the money."

"Yeah." He laughs. "There's that."

"And the women."

"Don't need to be a rock star to get women."

"Doesn't seem to hurt you."

"It's too easy now. I miss the challenge." He turns me so I'm facing the TV. "You're gonna miss the good part."

I try to keep my eyes on the screen, but I fail. This—watching the light flicker on Tom's face—is the good part.

———

"What are you..." My eyes blink open. My surroundings come into focus slowly. Where's my bed? My *Roman Holiday* poster?

There's an arm under my ass.

"Now you wake up."

Tom. I'm in his arms, pressed against his chest. He's carrying me somewhere. To my bed. Only it's not my bed, it's a bunk on a tour bus, because in the last two days my life has turned upside down.

"You could have left me on the couch." I sling my arm around his neck for support.

"I could have done a lot of things." He leans, setting me on a bottom bunk. "This will be yours for a while. You can take my next turn with the private bedroom."

"Thanks, Tom." I slide onto the mattress. I'm tangled in a blanket but I feel cold.

"Take off your pants."

"What?" I must be hearing things.

"Your jeans. Shouldn't sleep in them."

I look back to Tom, but he's gone. I shift under the covers to strip to my tank top and panties.

The bunk has a small privacy curtain, like the bunk on a train. I go to pull mine closed, but Tom is back.

He sets a pair of boxers and a t-shirt on my bunk. They're his.

He kneels next to me. "There's an extra tooth brush in the bathroom."

I nod. "Thanks."

"Sweet dreams, kid."

"Yeah, you too."

Under the covers, I change into the temporary paja-mas. They smell like him. It should bother me, smelling like a strange man I barely know, but it's utterly intox-icating.

I climb out of bed, brush my teeth and wash my face. He's back on the couch, stripped down to his boxers, watching something.

He looks lonely all by himself.

Maybe I'm projecting. Manic, bossy, know it all Tom can nail any single woman in a twenty mile radius. He revels in his manwhore status, makes a point of avoiding relationships.

But he's human. He must get lonely.

His eyes meet mine. He motions to my bunk *go to sleep*.

I nod *of course*, climb into my bunk, and pull the curtain closed.

But sleep isn't happening. My mind is racing. And my body—it's way too keyed up to sleep.

What was it he said? *There are gonna be a lot of vibrators running out of battery tonight.* That's the only way I'm going to relax enough for decent sleep.

I can't masturbate on the bus. Maybe in the private room. But not here.

I press my lids together and take deep breaths. They don't help. I'm flushed, needy.

But I'm not bold enough to do anything to ease the situation.

Chapter Ten

L ight hits my face. It's bright enough that it's well past morning. I roll out of bed, expecting my feet to hit the hardwood floors of my bedroom. But that's not happening. I'm never going back there.

It's quiet on the bus. I must be alone. I brush my teeth, get dressed, find my phone.

I've got half a dozen texts from Drew—updates on where he is, the hotel's address, that kind of thing. Then a few from Tom.

Tom: Your fantasy is waiting for you.

There's a picture message attached. An iced coffee.

Tom: Bet you were expecting something else.

Tom: You gotta clean up that dirty mind, kid.

Tom: Get here soon or I'll have to find some other way to occupy my time.

There's an address. A coffee shop. I get dressed and get off the bus. Xander, the security guy, is the only person around.

He nods *hello*. "Good afternoon, Ms. Denton. Your

brother went to someplace called Voodoo Donuts. It's a few blocks away."

"Thanks, but I'm not looking for Drew."

He smiles. "Tom is at a coffee shop around the corner. You need help finding it?"

My cheeks flush. "Yes, please."

Xander gives me directions and mimes zipping his lips in an *our secret* motion. I thank him and make my way through downtown Portland.

The coffee shop is hipsterville. It's white and clean with uncomfortable looking silver chairs. Industrial metal blares through the speakers. It's on vinyl, of course.

A barista stares at me with judgment in his eyes. That *you know nothing about coffee, you fool* thing. Ah, the same as San Francisco proper. That's one thing I won't miss about home.

Tom is sitting in the back corner, gaze glued to his phone.

What the hell does he do on that thing all day?

I ignore the too-cool-for-school employees and make my way to Tom. He greets me with a nod.

"Hey, sleeping beauty." He points to an empty glass. "Drank your coffee."

"What happened to my fantasy?"

He looks up at me with mock outrage. "Are you trying to tell me that I'm not your fantasy?"

I nod.

"Ah, I see. Too many clothes for your fantasy." He pulls his zipper to mid-stomach. "This better?"

"It's a start."

Tom laughs. "It's all you're getting. Do you have any cash left over from shopping?"

"It's in my suitcase on the bus."

He fishes his wallet from his skinny jeans and pulls out a ten. "Treat yourself to a pastry." He winks.

Tom runs his hand through my hair, mussing it. And there it is. Coffee is no longer necessary. I'm awake. Wide awake.

Something about it tickles. I laugh. "Stop it."

"Looks better now."

I reach for his hair and mess what I can grab. "That looks better."

"Oh, you're after a war, huh?" He reaches for my hair.

I duck and reach back for him. He's at least five or six inches taller than I am, and he's fast. I jump at him, reaching high, laughing as my fingers dig through his bangs. He reaches back effortlessly sliding his hand through my hair and flipping it in every direction.

"That tickles," I gasp. Then laugh.

He doesn't stop. So I don't stop. Okay. Here goes nothing. I rise to my tiptoes and jump.

Shit. I throw my arms in front of me to catch my fall. But I don't hit the ground. Tom catches me, holding me against his chest.

His arms slide around my waist, holding me up, holding me against him.

God, he smells good.

The room is dead quiet. Everyone is staring at us. We're making a commotion in the cool, peaceful coffee shop. How uncouth. I press my face into Tom's chest in an attempt to hide.

Only my body doesn't get the hiding message. My body gets an entirely different message. Hard muscles under soft cotton. His hand presses into the small of my back. His mouth hovers over my ear.

"You're knocking this whole 'land on a gossip blog' thing outta the park." His voice is light, joking.

"Do what I can."

He shifts, sliding his hand into my back pocket in a *we're a couple* gesture. He nods to someone. A knowing, *yeah I am that guy* kind of nod.

I motion to the exit.

Tom stays put. "You need your coffee, kid."

"I'll get one somewhere else."

"Promise is a promise." He releases his grip around my waist and moves into the line.

It's even more awkward feeling the stares without him to deflect the attention. That's one good thing about a gorgeous rock star friend. Everyone looks at him.

I slide next to Tom, hanging as close as I can. To deflect the attention. Not because the warmth of his body is totally intoxicating.

He orders two more iced coffees, his black, mine with almond milk. I sweeten my drink with simple syrup and move to the grey street. It's drizzling but I prefer a little mist to a lot of stares.

Tom is a few paces behind. He takes in my expression with an amused smile. "Not big on attention, are you?"

"Not really. I'd rather be behind the camera than in front of it."

His voice drops to a whisper. "Let's go somewhere quiet. Just you and me."

———

WE PICK UP LUNCH AT A SANDWICH SHOP, FIND TOM'S CAR around the corner, and drive through clean, tree-lined downtown Portland. Tom navigates the one-way streets expertly. We cross a freeway, and all of a sudden we're done with big buildings and wide streets. We're in a neighborhood on the hill. Rows of perfectly imperfect houses pass by. I snap half a dozen photos, but they come out blurry. We're moving too fast.

It's beautiful here. Even better as we make our way into Washington Park. It's a massive thing, twice the size of Golden Gate Park, and surrounded in tall pine trees. Everywhere I look is a deep shade of green.

We park at the rose garden. Tom slides his arm around my waist. Totally inappropriate for platonic friends, but pointing that out will only lead to him not touching me.

I follow his lead as we make our way down a set of concrete steps. It's still raining but it's light, more of a mist, and the sun is peeking out from behind the grey clouds.

Wow. It's beautiful here. There must be a hundred different kinds of roses. The air is crisp and clean. It even smells of flowers.

I shift away from Tom's grasp so my eyes can lead me. There's a perfect red rose. Deep crimson and flush with petals. A white rose, as pure as snow. They're all beautiful and alive.

Tom presses his purple converse clad foot against the grass, testing for mud. "No fresh air on the damn bus."

"You must be used to that, living in Los Angeles." I follow Tom along a stone-lined path. "You seem like you'd fit in there."

"Fuck you very much, too."

That's an insult? "I didn't mean—"

"It's okay. I do seem like that. I'm vain, I go to clubs, I sleep with models and actresses. I'm your typical Los Angeles B-list celebrity douchebag." He presses his palms against a concrete railing. "It's what everybody thinks of me."

I'm sure it's not the most opportune time, but I have to capture his expression. I pull out my camera and take a few photos of Tom.

He looks away, at the ground.

The pictures are beautiful. The soft lighting, the tranquil scene, the hint of pain in his eyes—but they don't tell me why he's upset.

I put the camera down and move closer.

The concrete is cold against my skin. I stare out at the next level of the garden. It's flush with roses, but it's the deep green petals and thorns that dominate the picture.

"What's inaccurate about that image?" I ask.

"Nothing." He looks up at the sky. "I'm shallow. Don't know when to mind my own business. Only care about money. Only in it for the pussy."

"I've seen you turn down three or four women."

"Only cause I can't come."

"I don't believe you."

He shrugs. "Guess we'll see in—"

"Nineteen days?"

"Don't count. It will give me ideas."

"Oh."

"Fuck this serious shit." His fingers curl around the railing. "There's nothing I can do now."

"Are you okay?"

"Will be."

I move a little closer. "What happened?"

"Nothing." He's quiet for a while, his gaze on the flowers below us.

I break the silence. "You're not a typical B-list celebrity douche-bag."

He says nothing.

"More like C-list."

That elicits a smile. "Would you prefer someone more famous?"

"No." I move closer. Until we're touching. My heartbeat picks up. A flutter builds below my stomach. Moves lower. Lower. "And I don't think that the fame matters to you, whatever you want to claim."

"Of course it does. I'm an attention whore."

"If you insist."

He turns, leans against the concrete banister. His posture screams *leave me alone* but there's this sadness in his eyes. I can't go anywhere. It feels wrong.

I stare at the flowers from afar. They're beautiful but infinitely less interesting than Tom is.

I line up another picture. The composition is perfect. It's moody, raw, authentic.

Yet, I don't want to click. I don't want to be behind the camera. I want to be here, with him. Whatever that means.

I set my camera on the soft ground and turn back to Tom. After a few more minutes of staring out at the sky, he speaks.

"My mom, adopted mom, Ophelia. She loves roses."

"Yeah?"

"First day I got to her place, she had this big bouquet of roses on her dining table. But no ring. No sign of a boyfriend. Nothing. I lived to piss people off, so I looked at her and asked 'who the fuck bought you the roses, lady?' Pretty sure I added a few things about her being ugly."

I move closer. Until I can feel all the heat from his body.

"She looked me in the eyes, and she told me she bought them for herself. Of course, being a little asshole, I stared back at her and called her a loser."

"You didn't."

"I did." His gaze shifts to me. "She didn't blink. She stared at me with all this love and patience, and she said, 'you can't wait for people to give you things you want. You have to ask for them.'"

"Smart."

"Took me a while to figure out what she meant." He kicks the grass, muddying his shoe.

"Did something happen to her?"

Tom doesn't answer. He pushes himself away from the railing and makes his way down the next set of concrete steps.

He stops in front of a peach rose bush and stares intently at the flowers. "She always had roses. Every week or two, she got a new bouquet."

"That's really sweet."

He holds up our takeout bag and points to an amphitheater to our left. "Food's getting cold."

He shakes his head, shaking off his bad mood. I follow him to the empty stage and sit cross-legged on the still-damp grass. The butt of my jeans is going to be wet. At the moment, it's hard to care.

Tom plops next to me. He eats quickly, then lies on his back and stares up at the sky. It's not raining anymore. It's mostly blue and bright and beautiful.

But none of that really matters to me. The only thing I can see is the pain in Tom's gorgeous green eyes.

I have to get him out of his mood. I line up a picture of him lying on the grass.

He looks up at me, raises a brow. "You have to do that now?"

"You can have these for free. Something soulful and pensive to get all your fans thinking you're sensitive."

"Don't need them thinking I'm sensitive." He looks back at the sky.

Okay. Here goes nothing. I move closer. Until I'm kneeling next to him. But the angle isn't quite right. I sling my knee over his legs, straddling him.

"What the hell, kid?" He swats the camera away.

I snap another picture. He still looks sad.

Tom pushes the camera aside. He brings his hands to my shoulders, pushing my arms towards the ground. I let the camera fall into the soft grass.

He pulls my body onto his, but not to hold me. He wrestles me onto my back, keeps me pinned with his knees planted outside my thighs, his hands planted outside my shoulders.

We're lined up perfectly for some tighter version of missionary position. If only we weren't wearing all these clothes. And in a public place.

I sink into the damp grass. His body is hard, warm. Heavy in this delicious way.

"Not now." He shifts off me and plops back on his back. "If you pick up that camera again, I'm breaking it."

"You wouldn't do that."

"I'll buy you a better one. Guess I'm encouraging you to keep shooting pics by admitting that."

"Not if it's upsetting you." I stare at the sky. There are big, white clouds. One is rabbit-shaped. "If you ever want to talk or anything. I don't know a lot about relationships, don't have a lot of friends, but I can always listen."

"It's nothing."

"That's not true."

His voice drops. "Neither was what you said yesterday."

I swallow hard.

"I didn't call you on that bullshit about your ex. If you can't tell me the truth, why should I tell you shit?"

He's right. It's not personal. I don't tell anyone anything.

But that is personal, isn't it? I put Tom in that same *I can't trust you* category as everyone else.

It's exhausting, never trusting anyone. I wiggle my fingers reaching for Tom's hand. But I can't find it.

He lets out a heavy sigh but says nothing. For minutes.

When I can't take the silence or the wet grass on my back any longer, I get up and finish my grilled vegetable sandwich. I scrunch the wrapper into a tiny ball and toss it into our takeout bag.

There are a dozen other people in the garden, but there's no one within twenty feet of us.

A poster on stage announces a Shakespeare in the Park showing of *A Midsummer Night's Dream* in three weeks.

What was it Tom did yesterday, when I was obviously about to lose it? He changed the subject and filled me with caffeine. I haven't got any coffee, so I'll have to stick with the former.

I point at the poster. "You read any Shakespeare in school?"

"Didn't really do my assignments."

"Oh."

He shifts so we're eye to eye, a knowing look on his face. "You told me a secret yesterday. Part of one. I'll tell you a secret in exchange, but you have to promise not to tell a soul."

I make the *my lips are sealed* gesture.

"I would have failed out of school if I hadn't needed to maintain my GPA."

"Were you on the water polo team or something?"

"You enjoy thinking about me wet, huh?" He smiles, a hint of sadness falling off his face.

"Dripping wet preferably," I say.

He shifts back into his good mood. Mostly. He leans closer, raising an eyebrow suggestively.

I tease back. "I was on the swim team all through high school and college."

"If you talk about how wet you were, I'll get ideas."

I clear my throat. "You promised me a secret."

"I was in the marching band."

"You were not."

He nods. "On drumline."

I stare at Tom with disbelief. He nods, still the picture of confidence.

"But you're so cool now," I say.

"Drumline is the coolest part of band. Who do you think nailed all the girls in Color Guard?"

"You?"

He nods. "And half the cheerleaders."

"Charming."

He's quiet for a moment. His eyes find mine. He stares at me, picking me apart. Or maybe he's picking himself apart. I can't place his expression.

A cloud passes over us, turning the bright light to a soft glow.

Tom moves in closer, and brings his mouth to my ear. "Thanks," he whispers.

And then he gets up, moves away, and all the pain in his eyes is gone. He's the same bouncy guy, no cracks, no signs anything has ever hurt him.

Chapter Eleven

Wwe arrive at the sound check just in time. Hazel is here.

She looks just like the picture on her Wikipedia page. Round glasses straight out of the 70s, loose men's clothes, short grey hair. She's shorter than all the guys in the band by at least six inches, but she commands their attention.

Talking ceases as she makes her way into the room.

"If you don't get back to making trouble, I won't have anything to photograph." She smiles, friendly but no nonsense, and looks me dead in the eyes. "You must be Willow. What was it, Willow Wayne?"

I nod.

"Let's stick with Willow. I'm Hazel Alexander." She offers her hand to shake.

I take it. "But stick with Hazel?"

She nods, releasing my hand. She looks back to the band. They're mostly shooting the shit, waiting around as roadies set up instruments. Tom and Drew take turns glancing in our direction.

Her attention turns to me. The focus in her eyes is overwhelming.

"Let's see what you've got," she says.

Here goes nothing. I pull out my cell and show off my edited portraits. Hazel stares at them intently. She looks up to me, back to the portrait, swipes to the next picture, back to me, back to the portrait.

"These are very nice, sweetheart, but that's all they are. You can make a lot of money shooting nice headshots for actors. You can travel around the country taking simple corporate headshots and make a nice living. There's no shame in a nice living." She hands back my cell phone. "But you're too young to give up on work that interests you."

I nod, soaking in her advice the best I can. The pictures are nice. Only nice. Why would Hazel Alexander want nice? She's a photography goddess.

"Don't worry, sweetheart. I was high until I was twenty-five. You're ahead of the curve. But I'll be honest. I don't do nice. I don't do comfortable. I'm more than happy to pay you to fetch my coffee and change my lenses, but I'm not going to give you feedback on any more nice pictures."

I worked hard on these pictures, spent forever editing them.

Nice.

It's an ugly word. As good as *boring* or *bland*.

"They're good pictures, but they're empty. They don't say anything about this girl. They don't say anything about you." Her gaze shifts to the band. "You have a camera, sweetheart?"

I nod frantically, pull my camera from my bag, and hand it to Hazel.

She looks it over gently. "This will be fine for now." She

points to the power button. "Mind if I play around with it?"

"Of course not." I nearly bite my tongue getting the words out. This is a million times more nerve-wracking than Tom looking at my photos. Her feedback has the power to tear me in half.

She turns on the camera and looks intently at the screen. "I'll have you do some coverage once you get settled. First few shows, stick with me, get a feel for it. Live concerts get old, but the label made me an offer I couldn't refuse."

"Is it better than nice?"

"Better enough." She smiles. "Editorial work fills my soul, but my soul doesn't sign the alimony checks I send to my ex-husband. I'll need your help on any editorial assignments I can squeeze into the tour schedule." She looks back to the camera, holding up her hand as if to say *shush*. "Now this is something." She taps the screen. "This says something."

Hazel motions *come here*. I do. She's looking at a photograph of Tom, one I took earlier today.

"Willow, sweetheart, why were you holding out on me? This is a damn fine portrait." She shuffles through a dozen photos of Tom, stops on another. "Does he interest you?"

I stare back at her. She can't be asking if he *interests* me. I clear my throat. "He asked me to help him out with his bad boy rock star image."

"Yes, he would." She looks over at Tom, makes eye contact. "He's a handful."

"Yes."

"Charming."

"Is he?"

"Funny."

"I hadn't noticed."

"Yes, you had." She shuffles through the pictures until she finds one from the restaurant where Tom is mid joke and full of life. "The evidence speaks for itself."

She scans further back. Oh, God. All the way to the pictures I took in his hotel room.

"My." Hazel looks up at me. "Willow, sweetheart. You lied just a minute ago." She points to a picture of Tom leaning back on the bed, his body long and lean. "It's clear he interests you."

"He was helping me out with a job application. For a boudoir studio."

"Hmmm." Hazel pours over the pictures. "You have a knack for it, sweetheart. These are excellent. Granted, you have a perfect practice model here. Most of boudoir is helping your client get comfortable. Is that something you want to do?"

"Maybe. It was nerve-wracking but—"

Hazel holds up a particularly sexy image of Tom sliding his hand down his torso. "Yes, I imagine Tom didn't make it easy."

It's like Tom can tell we're talking about him. He nods to Hazel. When she turns back to me without responding, he makes his way towards us.

Hazel looks at me and raises an eyebrow in a *watch this* gesture. "Of course, once you're met one famous person, you've met them all. The size of the ego on some of them —worst part of the job." She turns to face Tom. "Thomas, sweetheart. We were just talking about you."

He slides his arm around her shoulder. "Yes, I know. Once you meet Tom Steele, everyone pales in comparison. I've heard that from a lot of different women. Oh wait, that's once you've fucked Tom Steele everyone else pales in comparison." He winks at me.

"Thomas, don't sexually harass my assistant. It's bad

enough you have her running around photographing you." She removes his arm from her shoulder. "Can't you take your own Instagram photos like a normal celebrity?"

"Why settle for normal when I could have the best?" Tom asks.

Hazel looks back to me. "You're lucky you're talented or your ego would be unbearable."

"Hazel, you wound me. Promise I'm your favorite."

"I prefer Pete."

"Ouch. Not even her favorite band member. Not even her favorite Steele brother." Tom smiles, reveling in their sparring. "What does Pete have that I don't?"

"An aura of mystery."

"What good is mystery?"

"He has a thigh tattoo."

"Thigh tattoo? That doesn't sound very mysterious, Ms. Alexander. Have you been sneaking into Pete's room to watch him shower?"

"I'm sorry darling, but I love a man with a steady hand and a quiet disposition," she says.

"She thinks you're too loud," I explain.

"Pete has a rhythm. Thomas, you forget how many times I've seen you pound on those poor drums of yours. A woman my age doesn't like it that fast and rough."

"Hazel, baby, you know I'll go any speed you want," Tom says.

"Sorry. My heart is set on Pete."

"Damn, this is the first time I ever lost a woman to Pete." Tom shifts his weight. "You know he has a girl, right?"

"Yes, and you've told me twenty times that he won't have a girl for long. You don't make it this long in my line of work without patience." Hazel smiles. "You'll always be my favorite Sinful Serenade drummer."

Tom mimes being stabbed in the gut.

Hazel chuckles. "Get back to work, sweetheart."

"Don't tell me you also ask Pete to model for your nudes," he says.

"Has he finally agreed?" Hazel teases.

"I'll put in a good word for you." He winks on his way back to the band.

Once Tom is out of earshot, Hazel turns to me. "He's very handsome."

There's no sense in denying that point. I nod.

"But you can't sleep with the talent. That kind of thing isn't done anymore."

"I'm not."

"You're thinking about it."

I must be blushing, because she nods, affirming her suspicions.

"Look all you want," she says. "But keep it in your pants."

———

THERE ARE ALMOST FOUR HOURS BETWEEN THE SOUND check and the opening band. I spend every minute of them learning from Hazel. She takes me through hundreds of concert tour photographs. The pictures she takes are great. Full of life and energy and passion. They're crisp, in focus, not at all staged.

I get lost in her directions. Once we get going, she'll take one side of the stage. Depending on the night, I'll take the press box, the venue's area for photographers, or the other side of the stage. Today, I'm going to act as her shadow. All I have to do is follow commands.

We make our way to the press area in the middle of the opening band's set. Our view is a little too angled, but otherwise it's perfect. I notice nothing about the band. I watch her work. The way she waits for the perfect moment then lines up a shot in the blink of an eye. Every few minutes, she asks for a different lens. A deflector. A coffee. A water. Something.

I'm so lost in her instructions, that I barely notice Sinful Serenade come on.

She chuckles and points to the stage. "Your muse."

Tom is standing behind his drum kit, teasing the audience by pulling his shirt up his stomach. One inch. Then two. Three. Four. Then it's over his chest, his head. A heap on the ground.

Women scream. At least five hundred. Maybe a thousand.

Hazel motions to my camera. "Take a few of him."

I watch Tom through my camera as the guys start the song. In an instant, he's lost in the music. His arms and wrists are strong and precise as bangs his sticks against the drums, the cymbals. His foot taps out a beat on the bass drum. He moves so fast he's a blur on my screen. Sweat drips down his neck and torso. His hair sticks to his skin.

God, he's fucking sexy.

As a subject.

I'm only doing my job here.

———

AFTER A THIRTY MINUTE POST-GAME WITH HAZEL, I FLASH my backstage pass to the security guard and go in search of the band. My text messages announce that Drew and Miles are already on their way to the airport to send off their girlfriends.

Leaving me as the lone woman in a group of depraved

men. If Mom knew, she'd be livid. I'm tempted to call her just to rub it in.

I bump into someone. One of the guys from the opening band. I forget his name. He's ridiculously tall and broad. He looks down at me with interest.

"Hey. You busy tonight..." He stares at me like he's trying to remember my name.

He's attractive. Okay, body, let's do this. Look at the attractive man and want him. He's tall. He's broad. He's buff. He has a full sleeve tattoo, colorful koi fish.

He's hot.

My body refuses to cooperate. Nothing. I copy Tom's player move and brush my fingers against his wrist. Strong hands. But nothing.

Absolutely nothing.

"It's Willow. I'm Drew's sister."

"Oh. Right." He steps back, no doubt aware of Drew's reputation for beating people up. "See you later."

It's a good thing my body doesn't care about him or I'd be offended. No matter. I step into the dressing room. It's the size of a hotel room, and it's packed.

Tom is sitting on a couch, two eager women on each side of him. He tells a story with an animated expression. His gestures are big and loud. But he's not really engaging with the women. He's in his own world, the same way he was when he was playing.

The women take turns trying to touch him. Mostly, they keep it above the waist, grabbing at his shoulder or reaching for his hair. He doesn't react to their affection. Not really. He just shifts to another girl and continues his performance.

He's still on stage, really.

"Hey. Willow, right?" A deep, patient voice asks.

It's not Drew or Miles. Must be Pete. I spin. Sure

enough, it's the fit, dark haired bassist. I know Hazel was teasing Tom, but there is something appealing about his reserved disposition. There's this hint of pain in his eyes, like there's an ocean of depth underneath his calm surface.

"Yeah, Drew's little sister." I shake his hand.

"You should introduce yourself as Hazel's assistant. Unless you're trying to scare off guys who aren't my brother." He nods at Tom.

He's really Tom's brother? Tom was effortless with that information with Hazel but the guys don't look alike beyond both of them being fit and handsome.

"We're foster brothers. Not blood relatives." He looks me in the eyes. "In case you were trying to figure out why I'm so much sexier than he is."

"That clears things up."

I give Pete a once over, willing my body to react to his the way it reacts to Tom's. He's dressed in all black, from the thick eyeliner to the dark converse. His clothes are tight.

He's sexy.

He's intense.

But... nothing.

I look back to Tom, surrounded by his gaggle of fangirls. Anger builds in my stomach. He just lets them touch him, flirt with him. Probably, he'll take one of them home, throw her on the bed, rip off the ridiculously short skirt she's wearing—

"He's awfully tacky, isn't he?" Pete nods to Tom.

"Isn't that the point of being a rock star?"

"It gets old pretty fast."

"Apparently not." Let's discuss anything besides Tom's flirting. "You're really good on the bass."

His lips curl into the world's tiniest smile. "That the

best you can do? Come on. At least ask my favorite movie or something."

"What's your favorite movie?"

"I mostly watch docs. You ever see *Devil's Playground*?"

I shake my head.

"Nevermind. Do me a favor."

"Okay."

"Follow my lead."

Pete makes eye contact with Tom and nods goodbye. Then he slides his arm around my waist and pulls me close.

He leads me towards the door.

"What are you doing?" I ask.

"You've got this look in your eyes, the same one your brother had whenever any guy talked to Kara. Like you're jealous enough to hit someone."

"I'm not jealous."

He offers his hand. "If you insist. But fifty bucks says this gets Tom to come running."

"Oh."

"Unless you'd rather watch him flirt."

"Okay. You're right. Let's... where are we going?"

"Doesn't matter."

He leads me through the now crowded backstage area. Mostly, it's the opening band and their entourage. Almost everyone stops Pete to say hello or ask for an autograph. It takes five minutes to go ten feet.

I'm about to slip through the crowd when an arm slides around my waist. It feels right, that arm. It's exactly where it belongs.

"Hey, kid. Where do you think you're going?" Tom asks.

Damn. That worked fast. So Pete isn't just handsome. He's smart too.

Unfortunately, my body insists on Tom. He's all that will do. God, does he feel good with his chest against my back, all that warmth of his torso sinking into my skin.

"It's almost midnight," I say. "I'm going to sleep."

"Don't think so. I've got an image to maintain."

Tom pulls me to a side door. He motions for his brother to follow.

We step outside. There's a perimeter set up around the club but there are a dozen fans waiting outside it. When they spot Tom, they scream with excitement.

Tom leans in close to whisper in my ear. "I can convince you."

"How?"

He slides his fingertips under my t-shirt and presses his palm against the small of my back. "Like this."

Chapter Twelve

The world goes silent. No rushing wind. No screaming fans. Nothing but my lungs emptying as I fail to fight my sigh.

Tom is pressed against me. His fingertips graze the exposed skin on my lower back. His heartbeat pounds against my chest. He looks me in the eyes, his expression pure mayhem.

The boy is trouble with a capital T.

"Get your mind out of the gutter, kid. We're going dancing. It's 90s night." He steps back releasing me.

The door swings open and slams shut. Pete. He surveys the scene and frowns.

"This isn't going to make you feel better." Pete pulls his hood over his head and looks at the women waiting outside the barricade. "I'll do the honors."

Tom stops him. "You should come out with us."

Pete shakes his head. He walks away without offering an explanation. But there's no confusion on Tom's face. Whatever is going on, it's something they share.

Tom was upset earlier, thinking about his mom. It must be about her.

"He'll change his mind." There isn't a hint of doubt in Tom's voice.

Cockiness or familial instincts? Hard to say with Tom.

He takes my hand and leads me around the corner, away from the action. From here it's only a few blocks to our hotel. It's dark enough that we're not immediately recognizable.

Tom wraps his arm around my waist. "You make a nice shield."

"You're lucky you're as hot, rich, and famous as you are, because you can be a real asshole."

He stops at a red light, checks the traffic, and pulls me into the crosswalk. "You think I'm hot?"

"You know you're hot." I follow him along the sidewalk.

"Maybe I don't. Maybe you and Hazel wounded my fragile ego."

"There's nothing fragile about your ego."

He feigns offense, tugging at his t-shirt like he can't stand how hot he is. It rises above his belly button, revealing inches of defined abs. He played most of the show shirtless but that was different. He was in his own world, lost in the music.

Right now, he's here.

It's not like when he was talking to those women backstage. He's not performing. He's really here, in this moment.

Tom drops his shirt. "You keep looking at me like that and you'll give me ideas."

Okay. I'm gawking. But he's teasing me. He's trying to cause this reaction. I keep my gaze focused on what's in front of me. There's the hotel. A mere two blocks away.

But there are people in front of it. Women. They're waiting for the band.

I nod at the crowd.

"Feeling shy?" he asks.

"You're free to soak in more adoration."

"Why does that sound like an insult?"

Because watching those women paw at him makes me want to throw up. I clear my throat. "It's not. You enjoy your fame. Good for you."

"Still sounding like an insult." He nods to the left and steps into a clear cross walk.

I follow him. "I'm tired and you're threatening to drag me to a 90s club to what—capture you grinding with a Victoria's Secret model? We're in Portland, not Hollywood. There are no celebrities here."

"I don't discriminate. Any beautiful woman will do."

"Well, there are half a dozen women right there." I point to the women waiting in front of the hotel. We're five blocks away now, too far to see if any of the women are up to Tom's standards. But, hey, he doesn't discriminate. It should be fine. "Bring one up to your room. I'll get the shot."

Tom stops dead in his tracks. "What the fuck is your problem?"

"I'm tired."

"Well, I'm going out, and I want you to go with me."

"Why?"

"Because you need to have some fun." His expression intensifies as he stares into my eyes.

No, I'm tired. I practice the words in my head, but they refuse to make it all the way to my mouth. It's what I always say to invitations. I'm tired. Physically, mentally, and emotionally tired. I always say no. I always want to say no.

But not this time. I want to say yes. I want to scream

yes and add *press your body against mine all night. Fuck the dancing, let's go back to your room.*

"Willow. Hello?"

The words are still stuck in my throat.

"You don't want to go, fine. I don't need an entourage to have a good time. I've never had a problem finding a *dance* partner before."

Acid churns in my stomach. Okay. I'm jealous. And worse, I'm jealous of a hypothetical person. I've got it bad.

I shake my head. "I'll go with you."

"Knew you'd change your mind."

———

DESPITE HIS ARROGANCE, TOM DOES THE GENTLEMANLY thing and walks me to my room.

"Thanks." I slide the key into the door and nod goodbye.

"You know what you're wearing?"

"A dress and heels?" There's no confidence in my voice. Security was supposed to move my stuff to the room. As long as I have my suitcase, I should be able to figure it out. I push the door open. "I'll wear clothes. It will be fine."

"All right. I'm gonna shower. Be back in ten. Unless." He nods to the closed bathroom door. "You want to try and take a peek again?"

"You're not going to let me live that down, are you?"

"Absolutely not."

"Are you wearing that?" I point to his jeans and t-shirt. He looks fine. Sexy, actually. A little sweaty, but that's only enhancing his appeal.

"No, I am not wearing this. But I'm glad to know your feelings on the matter." He shakes his head in mock outrage. "So judgmental."

Do not engage. Do not engage!

I nod back to Tom. "See you in ten minutes."

He kisses me on the cheek. "Until then."

Okay. Friends kiss on the cheek. In Europe. And maybe in Los Angeles too. Certainly none of my friends do it. But it's plausible that it's Tom's thing.

Of course, I haven't seen him kiss any of his other friends.

Hell, I haven't seen him hug anyone.

Only nine minutes to go. I take a cool shower in the hopes of convincing my body it doesn't want Tom. No good. I'm still flushed and wanting. It's all right. We're staying the night in Portland. I'm alone in this room.

I can take care of this need on my own. It's not as if I'll be thinking about him the entire time. Imagining those strong hands on my hips, that cocky mouth on my—

Fuck. Only three minutes to go. I dig through my suitcase. Organization isn't one of my strengths. I toss two pairs of jeans, three tops, and every God damn pair of underwear I own aside before I find a single dress. It's black and short. That's what people wear dancing. More or less.

Only two minutes to decide. I slide into the dress. Matching heels are nowhere to be found. But bright sneakers are very 90s. I slip into my hot pink Keds and line my eyes in purple.

A knock on the door disrupts my already unsteady hand. Shit. That's a mess. "Just a minute." I wipe my eyeliner clean with a wet tissue and answer the door.

Tom looks me over. He copies the tone I used earlier. "That's what you're wearing?"

"Is there something wrong with it?"

"It's 90s night. You need color. Come on." He steps into the room and crouches over the suitcase, pawing through my stuff. He tosses a navy mini skirt and a pink crop top on the bed. "That will be better."

That will certainly be less. The top is minuscule and the skirt is barely long enough to cover my ass. "I don't think so."

"Try it."

I shake my head.

He reaches for the bottom of my dress. "Don't force me to remove your clothes."

My heartbeat picks up.

"You have five seconds. Four." He looks me in the eyes, daring me. "Three."

I step backwards. "Okay. I'll try it. Wait in the bathroom."

"As you wish." He does as he's asked.

The room feels different without his presence. Colder. Less inviting. I change into the skimpy outfit as quickly as possible.

"Okay. You can come back." I press my hands over my stomach as I check my reflection. I can't wear this. It's nothing.

Tom looks me up and down. All that smugness falls off his face. His eyes go wide. His lips part. "That's no good." He pulls my hands to my sides, his fingers brushing my exposed skin.

"Why?"

Tom traces the exposed skin on my side, from the top of my skirt to the bottom of my crop top. "Just change back."

"Why."

His cheeks flush. "It's too sexy."

He's nervous.

"Change. Now." He shifts towards the bathroom, his body brushing against mine.

He's still close. Still warm. I reach for him, get the back pocket of his jeans. I need to say something. That I can be sexy if I want. That it doesn't matter what Tom thinks.

Only it does. I want him to think I'm sexy.

"Tom." My hand brushes against his hip. "I... I want to look sexy. You do. You always look desirable. Why can't I do the same?"

I go to step back into some bold, confident pose, but my foot catches on the bedspread. Shit. I slip and fall backwards. My ass hits the bed. Then slides down to the floor. Bam. I'm on my back, my legs spread. I press my hands into the ground to push myself up.

Tom's gaze passes over me. It stops between my legs.

"Uh..." His eyes cloud with desire.

He watches me with rapt attention as I rise to my feet. At my thighs, my hips, my stomach. By the time he works his way to my eyes, I'm buzzing like a power line.

Touch me, please.

Throw me on that bed.

Kiss me.

Something.

I try to speak but my mouth is sticky. My hands are clammy. I wipe them on the skirt. Damn polyester thing fails to absorb the sweat.

Tom moves past me again, reaching for my suitcase. I'm too nervous to balance. I cling to his shirt and tug at it to stay upright. He smells good. I can feel his hard muscles through the soft fabric. God damn, I really hate his stupid shirt at the moment.

I press my lips together. I want to respect his wishes. Just friends. I can do that.

In theory.

But I need to touch him. At least his arm. Something. I

try to pull him closer. He looks at me, this strange mix of lust and confusion in his eyes.

He shifts forward. It knocks me off balance, and I fall back on the bed.

He's on top of me a second later. An accident or on purpose?

His hands plant just outside my shoulders. His body lines up perfectly with mine. His chest, his crotch, his thighs—they're all pressed against mine.

His lips are three inches from mine.

He smells like mint.

The room is silent.

He stares into my eyes. I stare back.

His hand goes to the back of my thigh. He pushes me up, all the way onto the bed. But he doesn't move off me.

My lungs refuse to cooperate with me. Am I breathing? Is it even possible to breathe? There. I inhale. Exhale.

He's hard.

For me.

Electricity collects below my belly button. We're close to something perfect.

Then there's a knock on the door.

And everything is wrong.

Tom practically jumps off the bed. He moves to the other side of the room, his back pressed against the wall.

He wants me. He adjusts his clothes but that does nothing to hide the evidence.

Another knock.

"You convinced me." Pete's voice booms through the door.

"I'm glad." Tom yells back.

Damn. Cunt-blocked by Pete of all people. Given the expression on Tom's face, I'm guessing this is for the best. He's not enticed or excited or dripping with desire.

He looks uncomfortable, supremely uncomfortable.

But still hard.

"Why is he coming to my room?" I pull the blanket around my shoulders in the hopes of disappearing.

No good. I'm still here. The room is still warm with fluorescent yellow light. And Tom is still looking at me like I'm the last person in the world he wants to see.

"Told him I'd be here." Tom runs his hand through his hair. His expression shifts. All the way back to normal.

But he's still hard.

His eyes meet mine. "Get dressed. I'll wait outside."

"Tom... I..."

His expression screams *don't.*

No sense in embarrassing myself any further. I nod my best *everything is normal* nod. "I should be about five minutes."

"Sure."

"Great."

"Great." He steps outside the door.

Really, really great.

Chapter Thirteen

I t's difficult to concentrate with the sting of rejection spreading to my limbs. It's not as if we're anything, as if I have any right to expectations. Tom is sexy, rich, famous, adored. He has his pick of women, doesn't have any interest in a relationship. It's not going to happen.

I stay in my skimpy outfit. Hopefully, some male attention will nurse my wounded ego. Maybe my body will want one of the guys at the club. Maybe I'll finally break my dry streak and realize that sex is loads of fun.

Anything is possible.

The mood in the hallway is tense. Whatever Pete and Tom are discussing must be awful. They silence immediately. Pete nods a hello. Tom slides his arm around my waist then pulls it back to his side.

"Sorry," he mumbles then nods to the stairway. "Cab's waiting in back."

Pete looks from me to Tom for a second. His expression is doubtful but he remains silent. I'm liking this silence thing. Saves me from making a fool of myself again.

We follow Tom down the narrow staircase and out the

back door. The rain is no longer a mist. It's pouring. Within moments, my thin cotton top is soaked. The fabric clings to my skin. Picked the wrong day to skip a bra. At least this will be as painful for Tom as it is for me.

He takes one of the end seats.

Pete nods to the middle. "You want to take that or you want me to sit on Tom's lap?"

His attempt to defuse the tension fails miserably. My stomach tenses. Tom frowns, turning to face the window opposite us.

"I'll take it," I say. "I wouldn't want Hazel to get jealous."

"Any day now." Tom taps his fingers impatiently.

I slide into the middle seat. It's a tight fit. My thigh presses against his. There's no way to arrange my arms so they aren't touching Tom. I adjust my skirt and top so I'm as covered as possible. It makes little difference.

Pete takes his seat and slams the door shut. He gives the address to the friendly cab driver. Then we're off.

A bump sends me halfway out of my seat. The belt tugs against my lap. I grab onto the nearest thing to keep my balance. Turns out that's the thighs on either side of me. Now I'm groping two men at once. Maybe I can get two rejections at once. That will make this day even better.

Tom growls. He stares daggers at Pete's thigh. He's silent, of course. It's not like I'm trying to start a threesome back here.

I pull my hands back to my lap. But that does nothing to ease the tension in Tom's torso. He's still clenched, angry. I remind myself that his bad mood isn't my problem, that we are friends, and that friends communicate with each other instead of growling incoherently and pretending they didn't almost kiss.

"How long have you been a photographer, Willow?" Pete breaks the silence.

A distraction. Thank goodness. Tom shrugs his shoulders, shifting his gaze in my direction.

"I took it up in high school, but I didn't get serious until college." I play with my camera. "It was my major."

"Where did you go to school?"

"Berkley. I graduated in December. A semester early."

"Congrats. Can't do much better than working under Hazel Alexander."

"Thanks. She's amazing so far." I make eye contact with Pete. "I think she has a crush on you."

"Can't blame her. Everyone knows I'm the sexiest guy in Sinful Serenade."

"What are you basing that on?" I ask.

"Don't tell me you prefer someone else," Pete teases.

Tom jumps in. "Don't flirt with Willow."

Pete stares back at Tom. It's the kind of look that says volumes. It's not saying any of the volumes to me, but it must communicate something to them, because all talking ceases. Both men press their backs into their seats in silence.

The last two minutes of the ride pass at an agonizing rate. Mercifully, we arrive.

Tom reaches for the door, but Pete stops him.

"Tom, a word." Pete looks at me. "If you'll excuse us."

"Yeah, sure." I don't wait for Tom to move. I climb over him on my way out the door.

He lets out a soft groan as my ass makes contact with his crotch. The man has gone three weeks without coming. It's just physical. Not personal.

I stand under the club's awning to avoid the rain. The place looks nice. Ornate doors, clean walls, dim lighting that makes it hard to see inside.

I play with my camera to pass the time. The Whole Foods across the street isn't the most interesting subject, but the rain adds a lot to the shots. I barely notice Tom and Pete get out of the cab.

Tom grabs my wrist. "Come on. Let's dance."

"Uh." I follow him inside the club. "Okay."

We show our IDs to the bouncers then make our way up the stairs, to the main area.

The ceilings are high, the windows are wide, and the room is packed with people in bright colors. Britney Spears booms from the speakers.

Tom dances, mostly by himself. I attempt to copy his movements but there's no way my motions qualify as anything more than erratic swaying.

I slow. "I'm not a very good dancer."

"It's easy. Come here."

He grabs my hips and guides me until I'm moving in time with the rhythm. My posture softens.

His hands slide to my waist. My lower back. The skin on skin contact sends a buzz of electricity straight to my core. I want him and badly. Without all these damn clothes in the way.

He pulls my body towards his, leading with his hips.

Damn, he's a good dancer. Precise and rhythmic and seamless with his movements. My eyelids flutter together. I soak in the music, the feeling of his body against mine.

The song changes and he moves his body away. Not far, only six or seven inches, but it's enough that I go cold. My muscles tense. My gaze goes to the high ceilings.

Tom's fingertips graze my lower back. Up, up, up, all the way to the bottom of my t-shirt. He moves closer. Leans in to whisper in my ear.

But he says nothing.

He pulls back, releasing his touch. "You want a drink?"

"No thanks."

He's already gone. Halfway to the bar. I try to push out any feeling besides the music. This Shakira song used to be my favorite. I throw my arms over my head. I make circles with my hips.

A bearded guy in a t-shirt, thick arms dotted with tattoos, comes up to me. "Want to dance?"

Okay I can do that. "Sure."

He places his hands on my hips but keeps his distance. His gaze goes to my chest. First my breasts then the tattoo above them. "Nice ink."

"Thanks." I clamp my lips together, move closer so we won't have to talk any more. I'm sure this guy is nice, but I don't discuss my tattoo with strangers. It's too personal.

My body presses against his. Nothing. He's an attractive man. Friendly brown eyes. Short dark hair. His chest is sculpted. His shoulders are broad.

I bring my hands to said shoulders. Nothing. He slides his hands to my lower back. Nothing. Dancing with him is fine but I feel nothing.

"Excuse me." Tom bursts between us without another word. He raises his hands to show off the shots of amber liquid. "Whiskey." He pushes one of the glasses into my hand.

"I don't drink."

Tom looks to the bearded man. "Nice to meet you, but my friend and I have some shots to take."

"Doesn't sound like she's interested," he says.

"All right, up to you, kid. Stay and dance with this lumberjack if that's what you want." Tom slams his shot and steps aside.

"Excuse me." I nod goodbye to the bearded guy and follow Tom to an almost empty corner of the room.

He offers me the drink. "Still yours if you want it."

"No, thank you."

"Suit yourself." He slams the shot then sets the empty glasses aside. His hands go to my hips and he pulls me back to the dance floor. "You catch on pretty fast."

"Huh?"

"Your dancing. You've got the hang of it."

He keeps his distance this time. It's still close enough that my heart is thudding against my chest.

After a few songs, I relax into the rhythm. A long time ago, I loved dancing. It's not quite as freeing with my body keyed up over Tom's proximity, but it's still lots of fun.

Song after song, I lose track of everything but the music and his body against mine. We dance for the better part of an hour, our bodies swaying together, before we hit a slow jam.

I slide my arms around Tom's neck and look up at him. There's all this strain in his expression, like he's desperate to be thinking about something other than what's on his mind.

"You okay?" I ask.

"Yeah." He pulls back. "Just need another drink. You want something?"

"Water."

He nods and makes his way to the bar. I scan the room for Pete. He's on a couch in the corner, brooding. What is it these two guys are going through?

I try to keep my mind on the music, but it's hard to slow dance by yourself. Tom is back quickly. With a water and two double-shots of whiskey. He follows my gaze to Pete and nods *let's go*.

Tom takes my hand and leads me through the crowd. I guess it's dark enough that no one recognizes him. Or maybe it's the kind of place where no one cares. After all, we're trapped in the 90s. No sense in getting hung up on a modern day celebrity.

He plops on the couch next to Pete and hands his brother a drink. "Moping won't make you feel better."

"Neither will getting wasted."

Tom glares. He slams his drink and drops the empty glass on a side table.

I take careful sips of my water.

Tom holds up his drink to Pete. Nothing. To me. I shake my head.

Tom takes a swig. "Why the fuck is everyone glum all the time?"

"Don't start," Pete says.

"Don't do whatever the fuck this is." Tom finishes his drink and drops it on the table. "You think this is going to change things?"

"You think forgetting your name is gonna change things?"

"Everyone already knows my fucking name."

"God damn, you're an obnoxious drunk."

Tom looks at me with puppy dog eyes. "You think so too, kid? You think I'm obnoxious?"

"I'm not getting involved," I say.

"You won't hurt my feelings." He raises his eyebrows. "I have a massive *ego*."

"So I've seen," I say.

Pete's jaw drops. "Sticks, please tell me you didn't—"

"I didn't. Damn. You really think I'd be stupid enough to fuck Guitar Prince's baby sister? We're just friends. Real good friends." Tom looks me in the eyes. "Right, kid?"

I'm silent.

"You're making a fool of yourself," Pete says.

"Don't I always?" Tom turns to me, ignoring his

brother. "You looked miserable before. I hate to disappoint."

"Excuse me." I nod to the dance floor. "I uh... I really love this song."

Pete makes eye contact. "You want me to hit him?"

I shake my head. "It's fine. I've got it under control."

"If you don't—" Pete points to the couch. "I'll be here."

"We've got a chaperone. Fun." Tom motions for me to follow him. "Guess I'm not trustworthy."

I grab onto Tom's wrists and refuse to let go. "He's right. Whatever you're running from is going to catch you."

"I'm aware." He shakes off my hands then takes them and places them around his shoulders. "If you don't want to dance with me, don't. I'm not lacking for interested partners."

"That's charming."

"Just saying." He slides his hands to my hips. "If you're gonna do something do it right."

His hands make a compelling argument. I tighten my grip on his shoulders and sway in time with the music.

We stay close for a few songs. No words. Just the music and our breath.

Then the song shifts to something slow.

With his hands on my hips, Tom leads. He pulls me closer. Closer. His thigh shifts between my legs. Then his thigh is against my sex, the fabric of his jeans creating friction in my cotton panties.

My breath catches in my throat. No doubt my cheeks are as pink as my hair. God, that feels good. I grab at his shoulders. Stare up into his eyes. He's watching me, intently, studying my reaction. I nod the best yes I can muster. Whatever this is, yes.

He responds by pulling me closer. The friction is enough to send pleasure to every nerve in my body.

Tom brings his mouth to my ears. "Do you realize how much you light up when I touch you?"

I say nothing.

His fingers skim the waist of my skirt then settle on my lower back. It's completely appropriate for dancing. Normal. But my body doesn't feel normal. My body is buzzing, desperate to get those hands under my skirt.

One hand traces its way up my back, all the way to the bottom of my still crop top. Then under it. His fingertips grace my bare skin. I'm not wearing a bra. He's so close to touching me properly.

Why isn't he touching me properly?

My body throbs with need. I stare into Tom's eyes. There's no clue in them. No explanation. He's been clear about us being friends. This isn't what friends do. Friends don't dance like this.

Don't lead each other on.

"Excuse me." I step back. "I'm going to sit the rest of these out."

The song shifts to something faster.

"Willow, don't. I'll stop." His fingers graze my wrist. "Don't brood with Pete. It's no fun."

I will myself to push Tom away, but his body feels too fucking good. Okay. I need to focus on something else. On whatever it is that's upsetting him. "Yeah. But you can't run away from your feelings. You have to let the pain sink in sometimes."

"Not interested in pain. I prefer pleasure."

I stare back at him. It's hard to tell if he's serious, especially with the limited lighting. "What does that mean?"

"I'm not trying to be oblique, kid. But I'm more than happy to explain in detail if that's what gets you off."

Okay. He is mocking me. That's enough. "Stop it."

"Stop what?"

"Teasing me. I get that you're a slut. I get that you can nail any woman you want. I get that you can tell I'm attracted to you, that it amuses you that someone like me would want someone like you. Stop rubbing it in my God damn face."

"Doesn't amuse me."

"Yes it does."

"It doesn't. I... Forget it."

"Just stop teasing me. I don't care how long it's been or how many days you have left until you can finally nail the first girl who meets your stringent criteria." I take a step backwards. "I haven't had sex in six years, and you don't see me torturing my friends to pass the time."

Tom's jaw drops.

I continue before he says something to make me even more angry. "I've got the message. You can do better. We're friends. Platonic. That was your edict, not mine."

"Six years?"

"Yes."

"That's not possible."

I ignore his commentary. I need to stay focused on making it out of this alive. "Stop flirting with me. Please."

"Stop looking at me like you're thinking about me naked."

"Fine."

"Great."

I spin and head for the couch.

Pete has that same calm expression on his face. He leans in close enough to whisper. "You can go. I'll keep an eye on Tom."

"No, I'm great. Having a lot of fun."

It takes Tom the briefest of moments to find a dance

partner. He picks a blonde woman with long hair and a short skirt. His hands go to her hips, inches from her ass. She whispers something in his ear and clings to his shoulders like he's a buoy and she's lost at sea.

"He won't fuck her," Pete says.

"Cause he can't fuck anyone."

"True." Pete watches the action. "But he won't take her home."

"If I'm really lucky they'll start necking."

"They won't. He doesn't kiss on the lips."

I stare back at him as if to ask *really*.

"You learn way too much about a person's sexual habits on tour. Not that I can talk."

I look at him curiously.

"Phone sex. I get carried away. Or I did. Long story, not very interesting." Pete turns to me. "You like him?"

No sense in denying something this obvious. "Yeah."

"Tom's never thought about anyone that way. Not sure that he believes anyone will ever love him."

That's sad. The acid in my stomach settles down. It's hard to stay angry at someone who seems so lost. He's dancing with the girl, yeah, but he's not here. Not really.

Pete pushes off the couch and offers his hand. "Come on. Let's go. He won't keep making a fool of himself without an audience."

Tom is already on to a new dance partner. She paws at him. She's clearly not interested in Tom Steele, human being. She stares at him like he's a shiny celebrity trophy to show all her friends.

I nod a yes to Pete and follow him out of the club.

———

Back at the hotel, I brush my teeth and collapse in bed. Screw pajamas. I strip to my panties and hide under the covers.

My mind is racing. Almost three a.m. and I'm nowhere near sleep. I toss and turn for a solid hour, trying to think about anything but how good Tom's hands felt against my skin.

He was drunk.

Didn't mean anything.

I will myself to stop thinking about him, but that's a completely useless goal. Fine. I guess there's only one way to satisfy my desire.

I pull the covers over my head and slide my hand down my torso. It's been a while since I've done this. Haven't felt any inclination. My fingertips skim the waist of my panties. Already, I can tell it won't be enough. Won't help the situation any.

There's a light knock on the door.

No. Whoever that is, no. I slink under the covers.

They knock again.

"Willow, hey."

Tom.

Hasn't he tortured me enough?

Chapter Fourteen

"You up?" He asks. "I have to say something to you."

"Come back when you're sober."

"I'm sober enough." He taps on the door. "Please."

I want to know what it is that's so important it can't wait for a decent hour of the morning. But I'm not going to make this easy for him.

I pull a thin white tank top over my head and check my reflection in the mirror. It's practically transparent. Perfect.

I open the door. "Yeah?"

His eyes pass over me slowly. They linger on my thighs, my crotch, my breasts.

"Eyes up here, Tom." I copy his tone.

"Can I come in?"

Probably best not to make noise in the hallway at four a.m. I nod, yes, and plant on my bed. Tom closes the door behind him.

He sits next to me, his knee pressing against mine. "You were right. I shouldn't be teasing you."

It's a far cry from *I'm sorry, Willow. Let me make it up to you in orgasms. One for every asshole thing I said. Should be a solid eight, then I'll satisfy you with my solid eight* but it's something. "Okay."

"Yeah. Just. I never had a girl friend before. Don't exactly know the protocol."

"Pretty sure you know it doesn't involve grinding."

"I don't mean to flirt that hard. Can't help myself." He runs a hand through his hair. "No excuses. I'll cut it out."

"Great." I dig my toes into the carpet. It's rough, scratchy. "How was... that girl?"

"Subtle."

"I try."

"Didn't take her home."

"Why not?"

"Didn't feel like it..." He shifts, uncomfortable. "I'm gonna wait the whole two and a half weeks. Too frustrating otherwise."

"What happened to giving without receiving?"

"My cock isn't getting the message." He looks me in the eyes. "You've really gone six years without fucking anybody?"

"Yeah."

"You get fingered or eaten out or anything?"

"I don't think this is appropriate platonic friends conversation."

"Okay. Can I ask one thing?" His expression is earnest, concerned.

I nod. "One thing."

"How fucking horny are you all the time?"

"Honestly?"

"Yeah."

"I didn't really think about sex at all. Until recently."

"How recently."

"Until I walked in on you naked."

"That's not personal. Just that it's been years. It's not like you were practicing your photography taking nudes of hot male models, right?"

"True."

"You appreciate an attractive naked man. Nothing wrong with that. As soon as you see another guy, get laid, you'll realize I'm not special."

"I appreciate you writing off my desire. Maybe you should get a new platonic female friend, so you can realize I'm not special."

"Didn't mean that." He pulls the blanket aside, making room for me to get under it. "Go back to bed."

"I don't need to be tucked in."

"You want me to leave, say the word."

I say nothing. Instead, I make a point of stretching long as I lie on my back. My shirt pulls up my stomach, almost all the way to my chest.

Tom's gaze goes to my exposed skin. "You sleep in that?"

I nod.

His fingers graze the edge of my tank top. He starts to pull it down. Slowly. Too slowly. Heat races through my body. I bite my lip, squeeze my toes into the sheet.

Tom looks into my eyes. It's just like in the club. He's asking for permission. Half of me wants to tell him to go fuck himself with his mixed signals. The other half wants to beg him to get into this bed and to get me out of these clothes.

There. The shirt is back in place. His fingers graze the waist of my panties. They stay there.

I rock my hips forward, half an inch.

His fingers stay in place. Not moving closer. Not pulling away.

Just there. Teasing me. Filling me with anticipation.

I press my eyelids together. My lips part with a sigh. Yes. Please. Now.

He doesn't move.

I can't take this anymore. I have to know what this is supposed to mean.

"Tom, I..." A sigh breaks up my words.

He looks away. "You should get to bed."

What? He's leaving. He can't leave now. I'm on fire.

He shifts off the bed. "I... I'll see you tomorrow."

He opens the door and steps into the hallway. He's half lit, half in darkness. It would look gorgeous on film, but it's hard to appreciate anything at the moment. He spent the whole night working me up and now he's leaving.

"Goodnight, kid. Sweet dreams." He pulls the door closed.

———

I WAKE UP FLUSHED AND WANTING. NOTHING HELPS. NOT swimming laps. Not a cold shower. Not an egg sandwich and a massive cup of dark roast coffee. Even avoiding the band is a hollow victory.

When I can't come up with an excuse for why I, the lowly photographer's assistant, am the one holding up the drive to Seattle, I get my ass to the bus.

Only I'm not holding up anything. Tom is the only one here.

His eyes connect with mine. "Where the fuck have you been?"

"Out."

"I called you ten times." He folds his arms over his chest. "Next time try picking up your God damn phone."

"Why? It's not like you were worried."

"Who says I wasn't?"

"I found a pool and went swimming."

"Just tell me next time." He pulls his hoodie over his head and closes his eyes. "God damn, it's bright in here."

Someone steps onto the bus. Miles.

"Pretty sure that's called a hangover." He looks at Tom with a smug expression. "Thought you were above hangovers, Sticks."

"Fuck off," Tom growls.

"Thought that hangovers were a sign you couldn't handle your shit. That you were out of control," Miles says.

"You want to do this now?" Tom glares at Miles. "Cause I've got a fucking laundry list to back up my case. It's starts with Ativan and ends with Ecstasy."

"Ecstasy doesn't start with an X." Miles nods hello. "How are you doing, Willow?"

"Fine." I glance at Tom. "Xanax starts with an X. But those are both prescription anti-anxiety meds." I swallow hard. The therapist at my boarding school was particularly aggressive with medication. I'm sure the drugs help other people, but I hated feeling like I was living under a cloud.

"Sweet of you to help Tom make his argument." Miles looks me in the eyes. "Bring anybody back to your place last night or stuck hanging with Tom and Pete? Although... Wouldn't be a bad man sandwich if you're into that kinda thing. At least if you can get most of it from Pete and not Tom."

"A man sand—" Oh God, he means a threesome.

"Wouldn't that be a girl sandwich?" Tom asks. "The girl is in the middle. You don't call a pastrami on rye a rye sandwich."

Miles nods, accepting his point. "You and Pete ever tag team a girl?"

"Fuck off."

Light floods the bus as Miles flips open the blinds. Tom glares daggers at him.

"Didn't realize it was a sore subject." Miles laughs. "More sore for the lucky lady."

God help me, there's something appealing about the idea of the two of them at once. Maybe I fell on my head and woke up a sex maniac. That would explain the sudden influx of lust in my veins.

"Pete? Seriously. He's only ever been with Cindy," Tom says. "And don't talk about him like that."

"You ever listen to the man go at it on the phone? The shit that comes out of his mouth makes *me* blush. Bet he can get a girl off without even touching her."

"Isn't that the point of phone sex?"

"But without her touching herself."

"That's my brother, asshole."

"Not biologically." Miles shrugs.

"You ever have a threesome with another guy?" Tom asks.

"Once or twice. When I was using, fuck if I remember."

"Who?"

"Nobody you know."

"Drew?" Tom asks.

Miles laughs so hard he cries. "Fuck, Sticks, that's a good one."

"I could see it."

The laughter continues. "Okay. Sure. Who would Drew tap in? You?"

"No. Somebody he doesn't want to punch in the face."

"So, nobody." Miles shakes his head, apology in his eyes. "Sorry about the mental images." He looks back to Tom. "Who the fuck did you tap in?"

"It was in high school," Tom says.

"We went to the same high school."

"You were two grades above me."

"Who?"

"It was after you moved to Malibu."

"Mhmm."

Tom breaks. He feigns shyness. "Alan's girlfriend had a fantasy. It was her birthday wish."

Miles laughs. "You've always been giving." He looks back to me. "You ever have a threesome, Willow?"

"No. I don't really sleep around." I try to change the subject before my mind gives up on productivity and moves to the gutter. My birthday is coming up. If Tom just goes around granting women's birthday wishes—

"I'll be your wingman if you want to change that." Miles steps past Tom, pointing me to the kitchenette. "You have a hangover? Don't mind torturing Tom with the coffee grinder but you seem like a nice girl."

"It's an illusion. I'm actually a heinous bitch," I say.

Miles laughs. He pulls out a coffee grinder and fills it with fresh beans. It turns on with a loud whir.

Tom cringes. He lets out this loud groan that sounds equal parts anguished and turned on.

My cheeks flush.

Yes. Again.

Miles is watching me. Smiling. He taps the side of the grinder and turns it back. Whir.

Tom's groan is louder and even more anguished. "Fuck. You have to do that now?"

"Do what?" Miles grins away.

Whir. Whir. Whir.

"Fucking asshole." Tom grabs two pillows and covers his ears.

Miles laughs. He turns back to me. "What kind of guys do you like?"

Fuck it. I'm too frustrated to keep this to myself. "Guys who are clear about their intentions. Who don't blow hot and cold."

I can feel Tom's eyes on me. Sure enough, he's staring with this hurt look on his face.

Miles clears his throat. "Ah, dealing with a cunt-tease is no good. Kick that guy to the curb."

Tom looks at me. "Maybe he has an explanation. He was drunk and let his cock do the thinking for him. Maybe the guy realized he was crossing the line." His eyes go to the floor. "And it took every fucking ounce of will power he had to do the right thing."

Miles stares at Tom with a look that demands explanation.

Tom shoves his hands into his pockets. "You making coffee or you just giving me a headache?"

"Damn," Miles says. "Never seen you this pissy, Sticks. Those blue balls are getting to you."

"Fuck off," Tom growls.

"You're proving my point."

———

I thank Miles for the coffee and sip in silence, counting down the seconds until I will no longer be in the same space as Tom.

Ages pass while we wait for Pete and Drew to arrive. Once we're all settled in, the bus takes off.

I hide behind my laptop, pretending I'm busy editing photos. There's nothing worth editing on here besides the pictures of Tom half naked and God knows that's not going to help my situation any.

A groan breaks my concentration. From the way heat is building between my legs, it must be Tom's. Sure enough, he's on the couch next to Miles, losing at a shooter video game. They're teasing each other, caught up in the competition.

When Tom's eyes catch mine, his expression changes. Confused. Regretful even. There's so much tension between us. Even when I look away, I can feel it spreading through the air.

I try to think about my future. After this tour, I'll have enough savings to open a studio, but I need a focus. Don't get me wrong—I'll take whatever work I can get—but no one is going to hire a photographer who is okay at everything. I need to be amazing at one thing.

Headshots are fine. A little too nice. Editorial work would be amazing, but it's hard to come by, and it doesn't pay well. I need something steady enough to support myself. There's no way I'm taking money from my parents. Even from Drew.

Boudoir has potential. There's an appealing rawness to it. A sexuality. Too much, really. How am I ever going to convince shy clients to feel comfortable when I'm utterly lost in the sex and love department?

When we arrive in Seattle, I get set up in my hotel room and pour myself into collecting photographic inspiration. I don't stop until my stomach growls. Okay. It's about dinnertime. I need something to do after I eat, something that will keep me from thinking about Tom. I surf the net for inspiration.

There. Perfect. *Fight Club* is playing at a hip theater downtown. Shirtless, sexy, alpha male Brad Pitt is sure to replace Tom as my fantasy man. And the other great stuff about the movie. Cinematography, snappy dialogue...

Other sexy shirtless men.

I grab a sandwich at the coffee shop outside the hotel and take a cab to the movie theater. It's a beautiful night.

Crisp air. Dark sky. Everything is shades of blue and green. Even the theater. Its yellow marquee stands out against its soft blue exterior.

It's twenty minutes to show time. Perfect. I can grab a snack and a drink and relax before the movie.

Only there's no hope of relaxing.

Tom is here.

And there's a woman on his arm.

Chapter Fifteen

A pretty twenty-something woman paws at Tom's shoulder. She follows his gaze to me and scowls. Does he know any women who talk or does he only hang out with silent scowlers?

Tom nods a hello. He introduces us. "Anna, this is my friend Willow."

"Nice to meet you." She stares daggers at me, then flips her long, purple-red hair over her shoulders. She whispers something in Tom's ear.

He chuckles. "Not today, honey."

"Why not?" She draws a circle on his exposed forearm. "Don't you want to?"

The look on her face is desperate and hungry. So she wants to fuck him. Channel Alanis Morissette and go down on him... during the feature.

I shake my head. Hard to blame her, but I'm not going to watch them negotiate what they are and aren't doing.

Anger dances in my stomach. So much for Tom laying off any sexual activity until he's at full power. He might as well make her come during the film. The movie is packed with gasps and the pounding of flesh on flesh. It will be hard to notice any extra noise.

My cheeks are burning. "Enjoy *the show*." I push past Tom and his floozy of the night. It's not nice thinking such vile things about a perfectly innocent woman, but I don't have it in me to think anything else.

I buy my ticket and hide out in the bathroom. Light bounces off the white tile floors and the stark white walls. I wash my hands for the hell of it then practice scrunching paper towels into tiny little balls and tossing them into the trashcan.

Tom's on a date. Or with a particularly grabby friend. Maybe that's why he has no sense of boundaries—he's surrounded by women who don't bother to ask before they touch.

Not that he crossed a line.

Not that I wanted him to stop touching me.

I attempt to pep talk the girl in the mirror staring back at me. "Put up or shut up, Wil. Go for him or get over it. If you want the man, tell him this *friends* thing isn't working out."

She stares back at me, confused and lost. I'm Hazel Alexander's assistant photographer. This is a damn opportunity. Nothing is going to ruin that for me. Certainly not how badly I want Tom.

I buy a box of chocolate covered raisins at the concession stand and make my way inside the theater. The lights are still on. There's a guy in front doing trivia for swag. T-shirts and DVDs and all that.

Tom's date is easy to find. Her burgundy hair matches the seats. She's pretty. Really pretty. And curvy. I feel even more like a little girl next to her.

Any hint of confidence fades away. My stomach is a mess of acid. I pop a handful of candy in my mouth to chase away the bitter taste. Chewy, sweet, delicious.

The girl runs her hand through Tom's hair, and the bitter taste is back.

There's no way I'll enjoy *Fight Club* with this in front of me. I clear my throat as I walk past Tom and his date and take an aisle seat three rows up.

I try my hand at trivia but I haven't got a clue what any of the answers are. Oh, well. The die-hard fans will appreciate the prizes more than I would.

The emcee announces five minutes to show time and walks out of the theater.

I play a game on my phone to keep my mind occupied. Someone comes up to my aisle and points to the seat next to mine.

There are two-dozen empty seats here. Why pick this one? Not my issue. Maybe the guy is hot, and I'll be the one making Tom jealous. Anything is possible. I pull my knees into my chest so the jean-clad man can pass.

He takes the seat next to mine. I keep my eyes on my phone, doing my best to ignore him. There's something familiar about his presence. He smells good. He has strong hands. Exposed forearms. And a tattoo on his—

Fuck.

That's Tom. He's sitting next to me, *sans* date.

"We had different ideas about what we'd do during the flick." He raises his eyebrows suggestively.

"You really cock-blocked yourself with that piercing, didn't you?"

He chuckles. "Sometimes it's fun not getting everything you want."

Not for me at the moment. I slide my phone into my

purse and direct my attention to the movie screen. "Should I guess how your friend wanted to spend the feature?"

"If thoughts of me getting blown in a movie theater please you."

Only if it's by me. The flush in my cheeks spreads to my chest. "You really have girls that desperate to drop to their knees?"

He nods.

"Why not rip off her panties and finger fuck her when the lights go out?"

"Finger fuck?" He scrunches up his face. "You really haven't had sex in years."

"Thanks for the reminder."

"I like this movie. I'm not interested in a distraction."

"You'd take *Fight Club* over a blow job?"

"Not in the mood." He shrugs. "I can snap my fingers and a get a woman on her knees." He looks around the room, counting. "At least four here."

I do my own count. There are about ten women in attendance but half of them are cuddled up with male dates.

"I envy your confidence," I say.

"You can get at least five guys here to fuck you."

"Is that so?"

"Yeah, sure." He points to the twenty something glasses wearing guy sitting in the row across from us. "He was checking you out before I took this seat."

"I'm sure you're trying to help—"

"Yeah. You need to break your dry spell. Get out of your head. Have some fun. Not saying that Mr. Plaid Shirt over there is the right choice, but somebody. Trust me. Once you come a few times, you'll see... sex is no big deal. You'll be attracted to guys left and right."

"You're offering to get me laid?"

He nods. "As your wing man. Unless you prefer Miles."

No, the problem is that I don't prefer Miles. I don't prefer Pete. I don't prefer Mr. Plaid Shirt. Hell, I don't even prefer Brad Pitt playing Tyler Durden.

Tom's elbow bumps against mine. He motions to the armrest. "You can have it."

"I'm good at sharing."

"How about we go out after this? There's a local band I know playing a late show. Should be a lot of guys there. Drummers even."

"I don't have a thing for drummers."

"Sure you do. We play hard, we fuck hard. We're animals."

My head fills with the mental image of Tom pounding into the red head until she's screaming his name over and over and over again.

Damn photographer's mind is too imaginative.

"Shit. Sorry. That's not helping you cool down, huh?" His fingers brush against mine. "This whole movie is shirtless dudes grabbing at each other. You're gonna be begging for it by the time it's over."

"Tom, I know you're trying but—"

"Come with me to the show. I want your company."

"As...?"

"A good friend."

Great. I'm his good friend. I can live with that. As long as he's done blowing hot. "Okay."

He offers me his soda. "Anna didn't get to drinking it. She had her heart set on getting her lips around something else."

God damn, he's casual and confident with that information.

He takes a sip, testing the flavor. "Diet cherry coke."

I take a long sip. Nothing like artificial cherry flavoring. Tastes like cough syrup. Like the days I stayed home from school sick when I was a kid, before Mom and Dad split, before Mom wrote me off the way she wrote off Dad and Drew.

"Thank you." I take the soda and drink greedily. I can do sharing. I offer Tom my box of chocolate covered raisins.

He takes one and pops it in his mouth. Chews. Swallows. There's this hint of chocolate on his lips.

"You've got a little." I motion to the spot. "I can get it."

"Alright."

He blinks as I run my finger over the corner of his mouth. The pad brushes his lip. Soft. I'm close enough I can smell his breath. No hint of alcohol today.

I wipe the hint of chocolate off his lips and suck it off my fingers. Now, I'm the one getting ideas. Please, brain, think of something besides how Tom would feel in my mouth.

I clear my throat. "How's your hangover?"

"Greasy burger did the trick." He takes another chocolate covered raisin. "How long have you been a vegetarian?"

"Since I was a kid. We went to a petting zoo in third grade. A field trip, take the city kids to the country kind of thing. I was enamored with this adorable goat. She had a big pink bow, just like a stuffed animal. I couldn't eat meat after that."

"It's commendable, living by your principles."

"I guess so. It's pretty easy in Berkley. I don't really think about it."

"You go on dates?" He asks. "Normally?"

"Every once in a while."

"How often do guys ask if you eat—" He leans in close, lowering his voice as if he's scandalized. "*Other kinds of meat?*"

"Too often."

"What do you say?"

"This sounds like a way to ask without asking."

"I'm not." He leans back into his seat. "Already know the answer."

"How do you know the answer?"

Tom raises his brows. "You want to look me in the eyes and tell me you haven't been thinking about sucking me off?"

My God damn body buzzes like a power line.

"Don't lie. It's unbecoming." He takes a long sip of the soda. "I won't give you a hard time about it. Got a little carried away last night. Didn't mean to tease you. I..." He runs a hand through his hair. "Never mind."

"You were drunk."

"That's no excuse." He looks me in the eyes, confident and sure of himself. "I want to do this platonic friends thing. Pretty sure it doesn't involve you thinking about my cock as often as you do."

"Maybe you should stop talking about it then."

He nods. "Sure. You'll have to lead the way. Tell me if I'm crossing the line. Or being an asshole." He offers his hand to shake. "Deal?"

The lights turn off and a preview flashes on screen. Okay. Two and a half hours to divert my attraction to another hot man. Brad Pitt, I need you to step it up here. Take me back to my teenage fantasies.

I take Tom's hand and shake. "Deal."

Brad Pitt fails me.

He's sexy as hell, all sweaty and ripped. Even battered and bruised, the man is one hot piece of ass.

But he has nothing on Tom.

Nothing on the way my body, as Tom so aptly put it, lights up when his fingers brush my wrist as we wrestle over the armrest. On the way my stomach flutters when I go for the soda and grab Tom's thigh instead. On the tension that builds in my core when Tom goes for the chocolate covered raisins and gets the edge of my skirt.

It's innocent.

An accident.

Nothing.

But there's no convincing my body. By the time the credits roll, I'm antsy and flushed. What possessed me to wear a skirt? This would be much less painful in a pair of jeans. Very thick jeans with leggings underneath them. And a pair of long johns for extra padding between his fingers and my skin.

The lights turn on. "Excuse me. Ladies room." I practically jump out of my seat.

The bathroom is the same clean, white place. I stare at the girl in the mirror and try to think up another pep talk. Tom's intentions are clear. He's trying. Platonic friends? I'm there. I'm capable. I'm not melting under the weight of my desire.

A few splashes of cool water do little to dampen the heat building inside me. At least I have a convenient excuse. I'm desperately turned on by shirtless Brad Pitt and his macho need to beat people to a pulp. Yes, there's nothing I adore more than a man who turns to violence to soothe the pain in his soul.

In the lobby, Tom talks to another pretty twenty-something. This one has dark hair and an intense expression in her eyes. She's more polite than a lot of his admirers. She doesn't paw at him or run her hands over his gorgeous exposed forearms. She doesn't trace the lines of his tattoo or stare at the hint of taut stomach between the bottom of his t-shirt and the top of his low-rise skinny jeans.

He spots me and says goodbye to the fan. That cues the grabbing. He smiles politely but there's irritation in his eyes. He hides it well. Better than I did working at the camera shop. The girl pulls out her cell to take a selfie with Tom.

He mugs it up for the camera. But still, she grabs at him.

Okay. I'll cut in. I cross to Tom, slide my arm around his waist and look at him with *fuck me* eyes. "Baby, I've been waiting for you." I extend my hand to the girl. "Willow Wayne. Tom's girlfriend."

Her jaw drops. "But you always say that there's no sense in limiting yourself to one woman..."

"He always said a lot of things." I run my hand through Tom's hair the way the redhead did.

He leans into my touch, his lips curling into an expression of pleasure. Real or is he faking for the sake of the annoying fan girl? Hard to tell, but I like his expression. I drag my fingertips through his hair, down his neck, over his ears.

His eyes flutter closed. He practically purrs. So his ears are the spot. I make a mental note. There's a perfect space for it next to *his cock is pierced* under *things you shouldn't know about your platonic friends*.

"Yeah." He slides his arm around my waist, playing it up for the girls' sake. "Willow's great. We're madly in love. And it's about time we go back to the hotel and fuck until she comes so many times she begs me to stop."

She's some mix of star struck and dumbstruck. She nods for a moment, then her eyes fill with envy.

Tom presses his lips against my neck. For me or for the girl? Hard to say. Either way, my body is desperate for him to continue.

Chapter Sixteen

The bouncer guarding the door gapes.

"Holy shit. Tom Steele?" He asks. "What the fuck are you doing at this dump?"

Tom shrugs. "Matthew's a friend of mine."

"Shit. David's gonna flip. Aren't you playing tomorrow? Tickets sold out in ten minutes."

Tom smiles. "Nice to hear from a male fan for once."

"I'm sure most guys are intimidated by how often your vocalist sounds like he's about to come," the bouncer says.

Tom laughs. "Miles? Yeah. You should hear him going at it with his girlfriend. A man has never enjoyed fucking a woman as much as he does. And he used to get as much tail as I do." Tom shakes his head. "Hate to see a good man go down. Though his girlfriend seems to enjoy that part too."

The bouncer chuckles nervously. It's completely disarming seeing the six-foot-three, two-hundred-fifty-pound man star struck. He unlocks the door and motions for us to step inside.

"What's your name?" Tom asks.

"Jason Benes."

"You working tomorrow?"

"Night off."

"I'll leave you a ticket at will call." Tom leans in to stage whisper. "If you do me a favor."

"Keep the guys away from your girl? Don't think anybody is gonna mess with Tom Steele, even to talk to a girl that fine."

Tom makes eye contact with me and raises a brow. He turns back to Jason. "Willow here isn't my girl. She's a friend. And she needs to get laid. If you see any hot guys— and I'm talking grade A, six pack abs, buns of steel, piercing eyes—send them her way."

"Don't think I'm going to be able to pick out piercing eyes." The man chuckles. "But I'll do what I can."

"Any ringers for Brad Pitt—that's her type."

"Are his eyes piercing?" Jason asks.

"They're not," I jump in. "But I don't need any help finding hot guys. I've got it handled."

"Listen to the little minx. Already talking about fondling strangers." Tom *tsk tsks* in mock disgust. "Such a filthy mind." He shakes the bouncer's hand. "Jason Benes. I won't forget."

Jason laughs, still totally star struck.

The door swings closed behind us.

It's an intimate place. Room for a hundred people on a busy night. This is not a busy night. There are a few dozen people here, most of them talking instead of paying attention to the guys on stage. It's not that the band is bad. They're just not particularly remarkable.

The singer tries. He's not great, and his lyrics are inane, but he's trying. Not so much the guys on strings.

They look at the ground or at each other or, worse yet, at the drummer. Said drummer is committed to his playing, thrashing around with his long hair swaying left and right. He's loud. It's all very loud.

"Shit. Thought Matthew was better than this." Tom motions to the stage. "Look at that."

"Which one is Matthew?" I ask.

"Guitarist." Tom points to the man with purple hair. "He's got his fucking back to the audience."

"How do you know him?"

"Played in a band together way back when." Tom chuckles. "I was that kid in high school who started a new band every year. Only nobody ever took it as seriously as I did. Matthew was in the fourth or fifth band. Only he thought he could sing. As you can see from the man's stage presence, that was a nightmare."

As if on cue, Matthew turns back to the audience. Tom waves, and the man's jaw drops. He stops playing for a solid twenty seconds. The other guys in the band look around confused but they carry on.

"Fuck, that must have been eight, nine years ago." Tom runs a hand through his hair. "He's not trying very hard."

"Maybe he had other priorities."

"Yeah. Everyone does. Even back then. I lived in a nice part of Orange County."

"Really?" There's something about Tom that seems rawer than image conscious Southern California. Especially given the way he reacted when I said he seemed like he belonged in Los Angeles.

He nods. "Where do you think I learned the power of vanity?"

"You're not vain."

"Not as vain as some people." He brushes a pink-tipped

bang from my face. "We can't all spend hundreds on our haircuts."

I stick my tongue out at him.

He laughs. "Back then, everyone had an eye on college. First band, the guitarist dropped out because he was failing Spanish. The second, we practiced all summer, but everybody quit as soon as school rolled around. Must have gone through five or six bands before I met Miles."

"I've never heard the Sinful Serenade origin story."

"Always figured you weren't interested. Since you never came to shows. Even when we were playing all over San Francisco." Tom's gaze goes back to the band. "Drew talks about you a lot."

"He does not."

"You have to judge it by Drew standards. Anything that isn't an argument about how I'm a sellout for trying to get our music into some TV show is a lot."

"You're the one who does licensing deals?"

He nods. "Our manager is a fucking asshole. Had an issue with him a while back. Couldn't get him fired so I took over."

"One of your songs is on a soda commercial."

"Fuck, yes it is. You have any clue how much that endorsement paid?"

I shake my head.

"Let's just say I've never seen anyone that miserable to make a million dollars."

"Each of you or the band?"

"Geez, Willow. So greedy. Two hundred fifty thousand isn't enough for you? I'll have you know that I'm worth seven figures."

I actually gasp. Seven figures? That's *fuck you* money. Why isn't Drew rubbing that in Mom's face 24/7?

"Miles and Drew—they don't know what it's like to go

hungry, to wonder if you're gonna get evicted, to work six months saving every penny so you can buy a better drum kit. I don't have to tell you that Drew's family, your family is well off."

"Money doesn't buy happiness."

"Don't have to tell me that, kid. I'm the one worth seven figures."

"You like to brag, don't you?"

He nods. "I'm incorrigible."

"Very."

"Big word for a guy with a GED."

There's something about the way Tom says it. Like he wants me to ask about it. Like he's desperate for someone to ask about it, to show interest in Tom Steele, human being, and not Tom Steele, famous drummer.

I move closer. "You dropped out of high school?"

He nods. "Had to deal with some shit, missed some school. It was easier to study for the test than go back." His posture stiffens.

I consider asking what it was he had to deal with, but the mood is still light, and I want to keep it that way. I nudge Tom. "You still haven't told me how the band started."

"Started with Pete. He must have been twelve or thirteen when Mom fostered him. The kid had nothing but this beat up bass guitar. It was the only thing in the world he cared about. His dad, before he died, was a jazz musician. That's how he picked it up."

"How did you pick up drums?"

"One of my foster parents had a drum kit in the garage. Played on the weekends in some KISS cover band. I needed something to do. At first, I liked making enough noise to piss everybody off. But the drums are the soul of the song. They carry the rhythm. It's the one place where

I'm in control of shit, where the world makes sense." Tom gets a far off look in his eyes. "A lot of people think bass is a less cool guitar, but it's really part of the rhythm. Me and Pete create that together. It was the first way we ever connected. I know it sounds hokey—"

"That's how I feel about photography. The world makes sense when I'm behind the camera. I see things I don't normally see."

"The stuff you shoot with Hazel or something else?"

"I love doing portraits, any kind. Even the sexy ones we were shooting in your hotel room."

Tom looks me in the eyes. "You're good. You should go after that when you're finished working with Hazel."

"Maybe. I don't know. I want to, but—"

"But what?"

"I'm not really good with people. Being a photographer is all about dealing with clients. It's intimidating." I clear my throat. "It seems easy for you."

"It's a skill. You can learn how to work with people. Just takes practice."

He's really listening, but I don't want to talk about myself. I want to hear about him. I want to know everything there is to know about Tom. "You had the rhythm figured out. Then..."

"So impatient." He smiles, teasing.

Again, I stick my tongue out at him.

"You keep doing that, I'll get ideas about better uses for your tongue."

"Do you ever get ideas that aren't about sex?"

"My secret." He nudges me with his shoulder. His gaze goes back to the stage. "Guess someone has to entertain you." He shifts back into his story. "Miles and I were in the same school for a year or two. I was sleeping with a girl he was dating. I guess she was two-timing both of us. Don't think either of us cared much about her, but honor demanded we let our fists settle things."

"Could just let the girl decide."

"Wasn't about the girl," Tom says. "It was about being the man."

"But what does fighting prove?"

"Still don't know. Seemed like the only solution at the time."

"You get into a lot of fights?" I ask.

"Not anymore. But back then? Got into a fight every other day. Miles too. We beat each other pretty bloody before the principal broke it up. The next day, Miles comes by to say he dumped the girl, but I fight pretty good. He'd heard I was in a band. He'd written some songs. Acoustic stuff. Mostly about how his dad was a piece of shit. Wanted to put a band together. For a while it was just me, him, and Pete. Then Miles move up to Malibu, and we fell out of touch. I had a lot of shit to deal with." His eyes cloud.

I swallow hard. The same shit he referred to before, no doubt. I consider asking about it but there's something about his expression that tells me he's not in the mood to retrace those memories. "How did you guys get back together?"

"It's quite the anti-climactic story. Miles poured all the pain in his heart into his guitar and his singing, only he couldn't play guitar that well."

"You really throw down the insults."

"Truth hurts sometimes." Tom laughs. "He broke his hands too many times. Lost a lot of dexterity. Guess you'll have to ask Meg if he's back up to full strength. From the sound of things, I'm guessing he's pretty damn nimble."

"You really listen to them fucking?"

"Don't want to. Especially the last few weeks. Think

he's doing it to torture me. She acts all shy, but the second he starts touching her, she's DTF anytime, any place. You should have seen him when he was single. Girls go apeshit for those pretty blue eyes of his." Tom shakes his head. "The way he tells it, he was hanging out in some girl's dorm room and he heard this guy killing it on acoustic guitar a few doors down. Not playing fucking *Wonderwall* to get in a girl's pants, but playing this crazy Carlos Santana level shit."

"And that was Drew?"

"Bingo. Usually, when I tell the story, I throw in a threesome and a fight over the girl." Tom smiles. "Gotta keep people's interest up."

"Who is having the threesome?"

"Miles and Drew, of course."

I cringe. Not a mental image I need.

Tom laughs. "Don't worry. Pretty sure Drew is incapable of sharing."

"Please stop."

"But you're cute when your cheeks match your hair." He brushes a stray hair behind my ear.

And there it is. My heartbeat picks up. Heat spreads from my cheek to my chest to just below my belly. Tom is touching me. I need him touching me more. I need him touching me all the time.

I clear my throat. We're friends. I can do that. With the help of a distraction. "Miles found Drew. Then?"

"You sure you don't want to hear me speculate a bit more about Drew's sex life?"

"Positive."

Tom smiles, soaking in my discomfort. "I have a few more things to add. Really graphic details."

"Please don't."

He smiles but shifts back to his story. "Miles called me

from a show. Drew was in this band. Dangerous Noise. And he told me to get the fuck up to the bay. He knew we'd be a million times better than Dangerous Noise or than any of the half-assed bands I was in at the moment."

"Is Drew really that good?"

"Yeah. Gives him lots of latitude to make my life difficult."

My brother, the diva. I can see it. He's always been really insistent about doing things his way or not at all. "Is he even more trouble than he's worth?"

"Occasionally. In the pre-Kara days, all the time. Don't have to tell you that he's uptight."

I nod. Uptight is a Denton family tradition.

"Mostly, he just... he doesn't know what it's like to go without. Pete and I..." His expression hardens.

I'm not sure what he's going through, what he's thinking, but I have to do something to comfort him. I offer my hand.

He takes it without looking and squeezes. "Haven't gone hungry in a long time, and I'm not keen on remembering how much it fucking sucks. Fame isn't forever. Gotta capitalize on it now." He looks at me. "You want to call me a sellout too?"

"Depends on whether you were shilling for Coke or Pepsi."

He laughs. "I like you, kid."

I pull my hand away. "I like you too." Too much. But that isn't what we're doing. "It's been a while since I've had a guy friend. I've mostly avoided being alone with guys since my ex."

"That would make it hard to get laid."

"I haven't tried."

"Of course not." He looks me up and down. "If you applied yourself, you'd be taking home a different guy every night. With all due respect and platonic intention, you're smoking hot."

"I'm not smoking hot."

"Fishing for compliments is just as unbecoming as lying."

"I'm not fishing. I'm pretty. Cute even. But I'm not hot. My shoulders are too broad—"

"Your shoulders are hot."

"My boobs are too small."

His gaze goes straight to my chest. "In that getup, sure." He reaches for the zipper of my hoodie. "You mind?"

"No, it's fine."

He unzips slowly, slides the hoodie off my shoulders. His fingertips linger on the backs of my hands. Then they're gone and he's tying the hoodie around his chest like some preppy kid on his way to SAT classes.

"You look ridiculous," I say.

"Gotta tone down my sex appeal if I'm gonna be your wingman. Don't want guys to feel like they can't complete."

They can't. And judging by the confident smile on Tom's face, I'm pretty sure he knows it.

He brings his hands to the bottom of my tank top. He looks down at me as if to ask *okay?* I nod *sure* and he adjusts the top for maximum cleavage potential.

He stares at my chest. "Small, maybe, but very nice." His fingertips brush against my tattoo. "And this is fucking sexy."

My cheeks flush. Sense. I need to regain it. "I'm not saying I'm unattractive. Just not hot. I'm cute. Like your friend's little sister."

"You are my friend's little sister."

"You know what I mean."

Tom's eyes go to my chest. "Smaller breasts are more responsive."

I'm tempted to ask how he knows this, but the answer is probably experience with hundreds of pairs of breasts. That's hundreds of mental images I can do without.

"You're judging again."

"I'm not."

"It's science. All women have the same amount of nerves, give or take. The smaller the breast, the more concentrated the nerves."

"Educational."

"Plus you have nice tits."

My cheeks flush. "How do you know?"

"That see through tank top you were wearing to torture me. Worked you know. I was fucking—"

"Think you're crossing the line."

"See." He takes a step backwards. "Look how good we are at this platonic friendship thing."

The band finishes their set with a bow.

Tom points me to a brown haired man in a leather jacket. "What about him?"

"He's fine."

"Fine? He's better than fine. He's got a lip ring."

"And?"

"Try it. You'll like it." Tom nudges me towards the man.

"I don't think so."

He shakes his head. "Okay. We'll do this together."

Tom takes my hand and leads me to Mr. Lip Ring and his friend Polo Shirt.

"Hey." Tom presents me. "Have you met my friend, Willow?"

Mr. Lip Ring and Polo Shirt look at me for a hot

second. But I'm not what interests them. Tom is. They stare at him with disbelief.

"Holy shit, Tom Steele. You're a legend." Mr. Lip Ring grabs his cell phone and throws his arm around Tom. "You mind?"

Tom catches himself in an eye-roll. "Yeah. Sure." Despite the irritation in his voice, he entertains their picture fest for a solid sixty seconds. He turns back to me. "Willow, here. She's looking for a good time. Either of you want to take her home?"

Subtlety is not one of Tom's strengths. My cheeks are burning. I step backwards.

"You sound like a fucking pimp," I mutter.

"Too much?" He looks at the guys. "What do you guys think? Too much?"

They laugh nervously, utterly star struck.

"Not at all," one says.

"You're amazing." The other turns red.

At least he's as embarrassed as I am. I back away slowly and turn my attention to the stage. Much to my chagrin, there's a roadie breaking down the instruments. No sign another band is set to perform.

Tom takes my hand. "Let's go backstage."

The nervous guys offer a dozen different goodbyes.

"I think they would have preferred to take you home," I say.

"Can you blame them?"

Not in the least.

———

THE BACKSTAGE AREA IS THE SIZE OF A WALK IN CLOSET. There's a couch on one wall, a table of booze on the other.

A dozen people mill around, including the purple-haired Matthew. He waves Tom over to the couch.

"Where the fuck have you been the last few years?" Matthew asks.

"World domination." Tom leans over and whispers something.

I make eye contact with Matthew. "Please tell me he's not trying to sell you on fucking me."

He laughs. "Tom, I'm gay."

"Shit. Since when?" Tom asks.

"Since always. Where did you think me and Trent went off too after practice?"

"Trent too? Fuck. No wonder he wanted to go to the beach all summer. Probably getting his jollies checking me out in my speedo." Tom nudges his friend. "You had illicit thoughts about me, didn't you?"

Matthew blushes.

I lose interest in their banter. It's a lot more fun picturing Tom in a speedo. The weather is set to get hot as hell. He's the type of guy who's game for anything. I'm sure I can convince him to get in a pool at some hotel. Maybe even to skinny dip.

"Hey, kid." Tom nudges me. "If you're gonna think dirty thoughts, think them about some hottie. There's plenty of hotties here." He looks to Matthew for confirmation.

Matthew nods. He motions to a shorthaired guy in a sweater vest. "Heard he's on the rebound."

"There. Go." Tom nudges me towards Sweater Vest. "Now or I'll have to get involved."

Please, no. Tom is trying to be helpful but I do not want him involved. "Okay. Fine." It won't kill me to have a conversation with the guy. He's wearing a sweater vest. He's got to be harmless.

157

I bump into him as if by accident. "Oh, sorry."

"No problem," he murmurs.

His posture shifts as he turns to me. He takes his time checking me out then moves closer.

He's interested.

He's interested, and he's cute.

Why won't my body respond to that?

"I'm Willow," I say.

He looks down at me, checking me out. "You with the band?"

"Just a friend." I take a long look at Sweater Vest. My body refuses to find him attractive. Oh well. No sense in being rude to the guy. "You?"

"Friend of a friend." He looks down my tank top. "You need a ride home or anything? My roommate is out of town this weekend."

Okay. Sweater Vest doesn't waste any time. Better to get this over with before he gets the wrong idea. "No thank you. I came with someone."

I glance at Tom. He's watching intently, but the expression on his face is unreadable. When our gazes meet, he nods *go* but I can't bring myself to take the suggestion.

My body refuses to cooperate. It screams at me *I ask for Tom and you give me this? Are you even trying?*

Forget it. I nod to the couch. "Nice to meet you. Excuse me." I shift past Sweater Vest and take a seat. This flirting thing is overrated. I'll have to find some other way to get over Tom.

Sweater Vest plops next to me. His arm finds its way around my shoulder. Tom is still watching. Not proud. Not excited by my progress. But...

No.

He's jealous.

The devil on my shoulder urges me to use Sweater

Vest's interest to my advantage. *A girl has to take what she wants. Make Tom jealous. What's the harm? This guy is thinking of you as a piece of ass. He doesn't give a fuck about you.*

Sweater Vest shifts closer.

He leans in to whisper in my ear. "I'd like to kiss you."

My stomach clenches. No sign my body is interested in his. "Maybe later."

"How about now?"

Tom is staring, glaring even.

Make him jealous. Worst-case scenario, you have a bad kiss. It's possible Sweater Vest is a great kisser. That your body really will want his. You should give him a shot.

I look back at him. "Just a peck, okay?"

He nods. "Sure."

My eyes close. Bam. His lips press against mine. Nothing. Not even a whisper of electricity.

That's a peck. I pull back but Sweater Vest isn't relenting. He squeezes my shoulders. Then one hand shifts to my chest.

I go numb. This is how it starts. Sometimes it's just a kiss. Just a touch. But sometimes it's more. Worse. Sometimes it doesn't stop.

My hands. Where are they? I wiggle my fingers. There. That's something. It takes forever to find the movement in my arms but I get it. I push him gently.

Nothing.

I push hard.

He backs off, his expression irritated.

And then there are hands around his collar. The weight shifts as he's pulled off the couch. By someone.

By Tom.

Tom throws the guy against the wall so hard it shakes. "What the fuck was that, asshole?"

"Nothing."

"Get out of here before I make you regret that."

The guy stares back at Tom. "I wasn't doing anything wrong."

"You have three seconds left."

The guy doesn't move.

"Two."

Nothing.

"One."

Chapter Seventeen

Tom doesn't hit Sweater Vest. Not yet. He stares until Sweater Vest is cowering.

"She said she wanted to kiss me. How am I supposed to know she's a tease?" Sweater Vest looks at the floor.

Wrong thing to say.

Tom pulls the guy closer and slams him against the wall again. For good measure I guess. My mind races, urging me to jump in, to stop this, but my body refuses to move. I try to talk myself down. This isn't Drew and Bradley. Tom is stronger, bigger, infinitely more tenacious. Sweater Vest doesn't have a chance.

That doesn't stop fear from seizing my throat. I open my mouth to say *let's get out of here, now. Let someone else deal with this asshole.* Nothing comes. Air will barely make into or out of my lungs. Words are a lost cause.

"A tease? That's the best fucking excuse you can come up with?"

"She was into it."

"I'm gonna enjoy making you bleed." Tom pulls his arm back, ready to punch the guy.

"I didn't know she was your girl."

"You're not helping your case, asshole."

There's a thud as Tom's fist makes contact with the guy's face. The room goes silent. My thoughts go silent. The only thing I can hear is my heart pounding at the speed of light. Tom is going to kill that guy, and then he'll get arrested and go to jail. I can't live with that.

My mouth refuses to cooperate. Okay. Talk is cheap. Action is better. Let's do this, legs. Just stand up and walk out of here.

Nothing.

I'm frozen.

My stomach clenches with fear. My eyelids press together. I can't watch.

Thud. Another hit. Horrible mental images fill my brain. Blood and bruises and broken bones. I force myself to open my eyes.

Tom has the guy pinned to the wall with one hand. The other is curled into a fist. He's looking at me, studying me.

He makes eye contact. "You okay, kid?"

I open my mouth to respond. The sound that comes out is in no way comprehensible.

Tom looks back to Sweater Vest. "You're lucky I care more about her as much as I do." He grabs Sweater Vest by the collar and tosses him to the ground.

The asshole falls with a heavy thud.

Every single ounce of attention in the room is on us. The crowd parts as Tom steps towards me. He leans down and scoops me into his arms then nods to his purple-haired friend. They share one of those *no, you kick his ass* guy looks of understanding.

God, I'm being carried out of a room like a damsel in distress in a cheesy B-movie. I can't bring myself to feel embarrassed. I slide my arms around Tom's neck, clinging to him, pressing my eyelids together.

His heartbeat is steady. His muscles flex against my back, cradling me. He's strong. I'm going to be okay. As long as Tom is here, I'm going to be okay.

A door opens, and cool air rushes around us. The pitter-patter of the rain fills my ears. Something goes around my shoulders. My hoodie. My feet make contact with the ground as Tom sets me down. He leans me against the wall and presses his body into mine, holding me in place. There's something comforting about the weight of his body, like a heavy blanket warming me on a cold night.

He runs his fingers through my hair. Over my cheek. My guard is down. I'm defenseless.

He stares into my eyes with an intense expression. "Are you okay?"

I can't pretend I'm okay. That this is even close to okay. I shake my head.

"You want to go home or you want me to beat that guy bloody?"

"Home. Please don't hit anyone."

Surprise spreads over his face. "You sure? Guy needs to learn his fucking lesson, or he'll do it again."

I shake my head. "I don't want something to happen to you."

"I can knock that guy unconscious before he gets one punch in."

"But if someone calls the police..." I stare back into his eyes. "You could get arrested. Convicted. That will fuck up your life. Your tour. Your reputation."

"I don't care about that."

His voice is earnest. He really wants to kick the guy's ass. But for me or for some macho need to prove himself?

His breath is warm against my neck. His fingertips are soft against my chin.

My legs shake. I wrap my arms around him for balance but it isn't necessary. He keeps me pinned to the wall.

Anyone else, I'd be terrified. But with Tom, I know he'll take care of me. I know he'll protect me.

Tom's expression softens. He slides his hand to my waist. "Come on, kid. I'm a lot more concerned with getting you home than with teaching that little asshole a lesson."

"Matthew can do it for you," I offer.

"Yeah." He holds my body against his. "But only if you want him to."

"No violence on my account."

He nods. "You okay to walk?"

"Yeah." Still shaking but my legs are finally ready to cooperate.

Tom leads me to the street. He hails a cab, helps me into the backseat, and gives our address to the driver.

He pulls the safety belt over my waist. "You're doing a bang up job helping with my bad boy rep."

"Thank goodness."

"You really commit to your work."

"I try."

"Anyone can try. You accomplish shit."

My laugh eases some of the tension in my back.

Tom slides his hand under my chin. He nudges me gently.

I look up at him. His green eyes are filled with concern. The intensity of it takes my breath away.

Inhale. Exhale. There. I've got it, more or less.

Tom leans closer. "Your ex, he hit you?"

I don't have it in me to deny it. No. That's not it. I want to share this part of myself with Tom. "Not at first. At first, he was sweet with a bad temper. He'd blow up over the littlest things, but he wasn't violent." I swallow hard. "Then one day... he was. We'd been together about six months when he slapped me. We had been fighting. I'd said awful things. I thought it was my fault."

Tom wraps his arm around me.

"He apologized. I told myself he meant it. The next time it was worse. But his apology was sweeter. Flowers, chocolates, crying until I told him I forgave him. I really thought that he loved me, that he just got a little carried away sometimes. Even when it was so bad I was showing up to swim practice bruised enough the coach called my parents."

"What did they do?"

"Nothing. At first. Eventually they decided to let someone else deal with it, and they sent me to boarding school."

"Willow..." Tom's expression darkens. "Did he rape you?"

My heart thuds against my chest. "Only once. In the beginning, first eight or nine months, I said yes. I wasn't quite ready, but I wanted to make him happy. After a while, I couldn't take how empty it made me feel, and I told him I didn't want to have sex anymore."

"And after that?"

I take a deep breath. I've told people what happened but only in vague terms. Never in this much detail. Never the ugly parts that show off how weak I was to take him back again and again.

"I guess... back then I still thought that love could be that ugly. That it could include calling someone a cunt or a bastard until they were crying. My parents were vicious with each other. Our place was nice by San Francisco standards, but it was small enough that I could hear every insult, every sob. Bradley, my ex... at first he seemed safe. He was older, a college football player. Even after he started to lose his temper... he always tried so hard to apologize, to prove he loved me. I guess I wanted to believe in love. That someone loved me."

I lean into Tom. He still feels good, safe. There's no way I can be just friends with him. There's no way I can do anything but fall in love with him.

"We were together for such a long time. It got all mixed up. I really believed that he loved me, that he only hurt me because he lost control. Things were bad with my parents. I didn't have anyone to talk to. Drew thought they couldn't get divorced fast enough. But I couldn't stand the idea of our family being torn apart. It feels stupid now—"

Tom presses his cheek against my neck. "Everybody wants their family together."

"I'm sure you went through worse than I did."

"It's not a competition."

"You can talk about it if you want." I play with my skirt. "I'm a pretty good listener."

"Another time."

"I want to know you, Tom. All that pain that you pretend you don't feel."

"Not right now, kid. I want to hear this."

I nod. "The night that it happened... That he raped me... It was right after my parents announced the divorce. They got into this horrible fight and they kept going at it. I snuck out sometime after midnight. I had to be somewhere else."

"How old were you?"

"Fifteen."

"Jesus." His expression darkens but he says nothing.

"Bradley was in a bad mood. Drunk. Like normal, but he didn't stop at normal. He didn't stop when I said no." My fingers brush his palm. "I didn't fight back. He was bigger than I was. There was no point in struggling. In trying to leave before he was asleep or passed out."

Tom squeezes my hand.

"Drew showed up sometime that night. I don't remember exactly how it went, just that he took me home, made sure I was safe, and left to settle the score. I was sure Bradley was going to kill him. Or that he'd end up in jail. I cried so hard my throat closed." I take a deep breath. "He came home bruised and bloody. His hand was broken. The doctor told him he might never be able to play guitar the same way. If he lost that... I would never have forgiven myself."

"Do your parents know what happened?"

"Bits and pieces. I filed for a restraining order. A few months later, mom sent me to boarding school. I'm not sure if it was because she was sick of me lying or because she was worried about my safety. It didn't matter. It was better than seeing them fight all the time."

"That must have broke your heart."

I nod.

Tom runs his hand through my hair. "I'm sorry you went through that."

"Thanks."

He looks out the window. His expression hardens. "I doubt it's what you want to hear at the moment, but if anyone ever hurts you like that again, I'll kill him."

I shouldn't want to hear it. But I do. I want Tom protecting me. I want Tom in every way it's possible to want a person.

The ride passes in silence. Just our breath and the quiet hum of the car's hybrid motor. When we get to the hotel,

Tom pays the driver and helps me out of the cab. He slides his arm under my shoulders, holding me upright.

Tom takes over, leading me to the elevator, punching the button for the proper floor, fishing my key out of my purse and opening the door.

It's hard to navigate the room in the dark. It's already a mess—clothes and suitcases spread out over the floor, photo equipment all over the table.

Tom helps me to the bathroom then steps back. He stares at me, his expression filled with uncertainty.

I grab my toothbrush and squeeze a little paste on it. It's late. I'm ready to collapse in bed but not alone.

I turn back to him. "Will you stay with me tonight?"

He thinks it over for a minute. "You've got two queens. I can stay in the other."

"No." I bite my lip. "Will you sleep with me? Not sex. But in my bed. Holding me. I get nightmares sometimes. After tonight... I don't want to wake up alone."

He runs a hand through his hair. His eyes go to the ground. "I don't know if that's a good idea. I don't really do that."

"You don't hold people?"

He shakes his head.

"You never want that kind of comfort?"

"An orgasm is more than enough." His expression is confused.

Does he really mean that?

I can't tell. I want that comfort, but not if it's going to make him feel as shitty as I do. "It's okay if you don't want to hold me. I understand that it's not a normal request." I turn back to the mirror and get to brushing my teeth. It's strange, him standing behind me as I get ready for bed. Intimate.

Tom goes to the door. The deadbolt clicks. Locked. Then he's back, behind me.

"I want to," he says. "You have an extra toothbrush?"

I shake my head, spit, and offer him my toothbrush. "You can use mine."

"I usually sleep naked."

So my body can still feel desire. A hell of a lot of desire. Enough to push away everything else.

"Boxers okay with you?" he asks.

"Naked is okay with me."

"Nice try."

There's a heaviness to Tom's smile. This whole night is heavy. I miss our easy conversation, the way he makes me feel light and free. No one else has ever made me feel like that, like I could float.

I wash my face, change into my pajamas, and wait on the bed.

Tom takes his turn in the bathroom. He steps into the main room and strips. Once he's down to his boxers, he slides into bed and lays his body behind mine.

He's awkward, stiff. He really doesn't do this.

I press my back against his chest, my ass against his crotch. His cock stirs but I know better than to read into that.

He feels good. Hard. Safe. Strong.

After a few minutes, Tom relaxes enough to pull me closer.

"I shouldn't have pushed you that hard," he whispers. "This wouldn't have happened—"

"You want to know the truth?"

"Yeah."

"I only let him kiss me because I wanted to make you jealous." I press my eyelids together. "I really like you,

Tom. But if you only want to be friends, I understand. I'd rather be your friend than nothing at all."

"You're a sweet kid."

"I'm not."

"Yeah, you are. If our roles were reversed, I would have asked you to kill that guy."

"Would you really kill him if I asked?"

"Maybe not kill, but I'd get pretty close." He exhales slowly. "Why? You want me to?"

"No. Violence only begets violence."

"See what I mean?"

"You're a good guy, Tom."

"We'll have to agree to disagree on that point."

I shake my head.

He runs his hand through my hair. "Try to sleep. We can talk in the morning."

I still can't relax. My thoughts are racing. My shoulders and neck are tense. Hell, I'm tense everywhere.

Keeping this up is impossible. Giving him up is worse.

What the hell am I going to do?

I take deep breaths, willing the answer to float into my brain.

It doesn't.

I shift closer to him. "Are you up?"

He runs his fingertips over my shoulders. "Yeah."

I turn around, bringing us face to face. Even though it's dark, I can see all this affection in his eyes. How deep does it go?

Friends?

Or more than that?

Tom rubs my shoulder. "You're tense."

I nod.

He looks me in the eyes, studying me.

I reach for him, run my fingers over his cheek. Words

form and dissolve on my tongue. There's no easy way to explain my feelings, so I say nothing.

"Close your eyes," he whispers.

I do.

He drags his hand down my neck and shoulders. I gasp. A groan of pleasure escapes my lips. I need Tom's fingers on my skin, erasing the memories of anyone else touching me.

He lets out a deep sigh. The good kind of sigh. He wants to do this. Needs to do it.

He drags his fingers over my chest, over the neckline of my tank top. Then under it. Just barely. The lightness of his touch sends shockwaves to my core.

All the ugly parts of the day fade. My body takes over. It doesn't care about tomorrow. It doesn't care about defining our relationship. It only cares about one thing: Tom's hands on my skin.

I dig my fingers into his bare torso, soaking in the feeling of his hard muscles. "Please."

He presses his forehead against mine as if to say yes.

His fingers brush against my nipple. I gasp, arching my back and squeezing my toes to contain the desire that spreads through me.

Yes.

He moves slowly. Peeling my tank top off one shoulder then the other. Teasing one nipple then the other. His touch is soft, precise. He brushes his thumb over me. Again and again. My breath hitches. My heartbeat picks up.

He stays slow, patient. The tension in my neck and shoulders melts. Everything else melts until I'm pure need. By the time his hand slides down my stomach and into my pajama bottoms, I'm too desperate to think anything but *now*.

His forehead is warm against mine. He's looking at me

with hunger and need, yes, but there's much more to it. He's giving something of himself to me.

He brings his other hand to my shoulder, cupping my chin, my cheek, my neck. The intimacy of it leaves me breathless. I have no choice but to close my eyes.

His fingers brush against my clit. I'm so keyed up that the light touch is enough to send sparks to my core. My lips part with a sigh. My fingers dig into his skin.

His touch stays slow. All the need that has been plaguing me collects between my legs. Tom. God, Tom.

Little by little, he strokes me harder. Until I'm panting. Until there's so much pleasure inside me I'm not sure I'll ever be able to breathe properly again. I squeeze his hip as an orgasm rises up inside me. I press my cheek against his, soaking in all the warmth of his face, his body, his hands.

There. Pleasure spills through me as I come. I gasp and moan. Incomprehensible things that barely resemble words. It feels damn good. Much better than my hand. Much better than with Bradley.

Tom wraps his arms around me and pulls my body into his. No words. But I can feel his heart beat, hear every inhale, every exhale. All that tension is gone. I'm calm.

For once, I really believe everything is going to be okay.

Chapter Eighteen

Morning hits me like a ton of bricks. It's bright but it's damn cold. I don't need to feel the other side of the bed to know that Tom is gone.

My heart sinks.

If he's gone... Then what the hell did last night mean?

There's no way I'm going to clear my head here. After my usual morning routine, I find the hotel pool and swim laps for the better part of an hour. My thoughts settle bit by bit. I have to demand an explanation from Tom. It will gut me to walk away from him, but I can't give myself to him if he's going to pull that just friends line again.

I towel dry and make my way through the lobby.

Clarity, gone. Tom is here. He's wearing a loose muscle tank and running shorts, and he's dripping with sweat. Explanations are silly. What matters is how badly my body needs his.

"Hey, kid. Good workout?" He looks away, shy.

Tom Steele is shy. With me. That must mean something.

There are footsteps behind us. Drew.

"Why aren't you wearing pants, Wil?" He asks.

Drew's expression is overprotective. He's also clad in work out gear. Must have been at the hotel gym with Tom. Maybe they had a standing work out date. Maybe there's a completely reasonable explanation for why I woke up alone. One besides Tom realizing he made a mistake.

The elevator doors slide open.

I step inside. "Pants would add a lot of drag in the pool."

"She's got you there," Tom says.

Drew shoots him a menacing look. Then he's back to me. "Where'd you go last night?"

"Dinner and a movie. Wanted some time to myself. I'm not used to the constant company." That's close enough to the truth.

Drew looks from me to Tom and back again. "Let's get brunch. Just the two of us."

"Rude of you not to include your sister," Tom teases.

Drew flips him off. He turns to me. "I'll give you twenty minutes to get ready."

The elevator arrives at my floor. I step into the hallway. "Sure. See you then." My eyes catch Tom's. Immediately, my cheeks are burning. I turn away so Drew won't get ideas, and I lock myself in my room.

———

DREW AND I TALK MOVIES OVER PANCAKES AT A COZY restaurant on the other side of town. He still has the same taste—science fiction and super heroes—but Kara has expanded his horizons into classics and independent films.

We linger through coffee refill after coffee refill. I'm

practically shaking from the caffeine overdose when Drew finally asks for the check.

The waitress drops it off with a much too flirty smile. He's completely oblivious to her attention, already pulling bills from his wallet.

I try to steal the little black book. "Let me get it. Please. I got my first paycheck from Hazel."

"No way." He throws down a generous tip, closes the book, and helps me out of my seat. "I need your help."

"With?"

Drew checks the time on his cell. "You have an hour or two?"

I nod. The only thing on my agenda is the show tonight and I have to be there after he does.

His cheeks flush. He's nervous. It must be about Kara. Drew plays his cards pretty close to the vest. Except when it's about her. It's written all over his face, how much he loves her. I want to have that one day. With someone who deserves me.

Whatever this is, I want to help. And I'm infinitely grateful for the distraction.

We walk for a few blocks. The air is warm today. Sunny and bright. There are no signs of last night's rain.

Drew breaks the silence. "You've been hanging out with Tom."

Oh, no. Please don't let this be an ambush. My brother and I are actually getting along for once. Like we're allies and not enemies in the *you should make up with Mom—no way, she's a bitch* battle.

Drew stops at a streetlight and runs a hand through his hair. "I'm glad you're here. Are you?"

"Yeah. Hazel is amazing. And it's nice to see you. To hang out doing little things. TV and breakfast and what-ever. I've been keeping to myself the last few years. I've been lonely." The moment the words are out of my mouth, I know they're true. I've been lonely the last few years. Being around people who care about me is nice. Really nice.

"Yeah." Drew smiles. "The guys can be idiots, but they're sweet deep down. Everyone seems to like you."

Warmth spreads through my stomach. I actually have friends. Or I'm starting to.

The walk sign turns on and we make our way across the street. Drew moves in a little closer. Drops his voice.

"Tom seems to like you."

I'm not sure where this is going, but I'm not optimistic. I clear my throat. "Does he?"

"He's a good guy deep down. If you can get past him being with a different girl every night. Only... Wil, I want you to be happy. I want you to have love in your life. Makes me sick thinking that asshole was the last guy you were with."

It's almost as if he's saying I have his blessing to go after Tom. Almost but not quite.

Drew looks me in the eyes. "He tries to help but it tends to be on his terms. He means well but, given your history, I'm not sure it's the best idea."

I stare back at Drew. "Don't be coy. You're getting at something."

"He's controlling."

I bite my lip. Tom is pushy, yeah, but is he really controlling? It's hard to say. I don't have a great concept of what is or isn't normal. I nod a thank you to Drew. "I'll keep that in mind."

"Do you have a thing for him?"

"We're just friends."

"Not what I asked."

"He's..." I take a deep breath. "He's a really appealing guy in a lot of ways."

"I can talk to him."

"And say what?"

"He's a player, Wil. I'm not saying there's no chance he'll ever have something real, but I don't want him playing you." Drew's hands curl into fists. "If he is playing you, I'll never fucking forgive him."

"Will you hurt him?"

"I'm trying not to go there." Drew looks me in the eyes. "Do you want me to talk to him?"

"No. That's okay. I want to focus on my career right now. And not on guys." It's true. It's also true that I don't quite trust Drew to have the calm, even conversation he's alluding to.

I really do want to focus on my career. Working under Hazel is the kind of opportunity that doesn't come along every day.

I look back to Drew to see if he's buying my explanation but he's staring at something else. A jewelry store.

A smile spreads over his lips. "I know you're not into fashion but you have a good eye for this kinda thing." He lets out a wistful sigh. "I got Kara's ring size from Meg."

My jaw drops. He must be talking about an engagement ring. "You're going to propose?"

He nods. "After her graduation party. With skywriting. I know it's cheesy—"

"Cheesy is good."

We step into the store. It's dead quiet, empty except for the shiny displays. Everything here is gorgeous. What would Kara want? She always looks perfect. Her hair, makeup, nails, clothes always fit the occasion. She'll want something classic. Elegant. But with a little flair too.

I let my eyes lead me. The halo rings are too trendy. Not an angular shape. Something rounder.

There. A cushion cut solitaire draws my attention. Perfect.

Drew is right behind me. His eyes sparkle as much as the gems do.

"You think she'll like it?" he asks.

"We can look around more."

His eyes go to the ring. "No. It's perfect." He waits for the sales woman to approach us then smiles at her. "I want the biggest one you have."

————

A KNOCK ON THE DOOR ROUSES ME FROM MY DAYTIME TV and pancake induced nap.

"Yeah?" I ask the knocker.

"Hey." Tom taps his fingers against the door. "I have something for you. A present."

Tom got me a present? Something tells me it's not a written explanation of his intentions, but I'm intrigued all the same.

I open the door and invite him in. He looks especially yummy in his stage getup. Tight jeans. Tight t-shirt. Messy hair falling in every direction. There's a thin wisp of liner around his green eyes. It does things to me. Makes my knees desperate to buckle.

He sets a bright pink gift bag on the bed.

"I, uh..." He looks me in the eyes. "Pete and I are flying to Los Angeles after the show tonight. We have to take care of some family stuff. We're meeting the band in Minneapolis next week. But I didn't want to leave without getting you this."

I raise an eyebrow. "Should I open it now?"

Right on cue, his pants buzz. His phone is in his front pocket. Very, very close to his—

"Eyes are up here, kid." Tom pulls his phone from his pocket. "I'm late for the sound check. You'd think those assholes could start by themselves for once, given how much time Drew spends tuning his already tuned guitar." He ignores the call and looks me in the eyes. "Open it tonight. Or tomorrow. But not without me."

"You're leaving tonight."

"I'm pretty sure you noticed that buzzing in my pants."

I clear my throat.

"Call me. Want to hear your voice when you see it." His eyes flare with mischief. "You'll like it. I promise."

———

AFTER THE SHOW AND A SOLID HOUR EDITING WITH HAZEL, I'm dead tired. I drag my heels to the bus and collapse in the private room. Technically, it's Tom's turn, but he offered it to me.

I text him a thank you and get to unpacking my suitcase.

The room is clean and bare except for the overflowing dresser drawer. The amount of clothing in it is disturbing, considering that the band uniform appears to be v-neck, dark wash skinny jeans, and sneakers. It's hard to criticize when they always look damn good.

Not that I'm only thinking about one of them in particular.

Not that I'm remembering how he looks without the v-neck, sneakers, and skinny jeans.

My purse hums with Justin Timberlake singing *SexyBack*.

Incoming call from Tom Steele, Irresistible.

I answer the phone. "Hello."

"Hey, kid. You miss me yet?" His voice is light.

I tease back. "It's all I think about. I ran out of ink doodling your name in my notebook. You think I should get my 'Tom Steele' tattoo as a tramp stamp or at the top of my bikini line."

"Depends how much you like doggy style."

My cheeks flush. I try to think about something besides Tom throwing me on the bed and fucking me from behind.

I fail miserably.

"Bet I can guess where your mind went." He chuckles. "We're boarding in fifteen. This is your last chance to open the present without Pete overhearing everything."

"What if I want him overhearing?"

"Don't tell me Hazel convinced you that bassists are where it's at. She's already torn my heart in half."

"I wouldn't step on her turf. Sisters before misters."

Tom's laugh flows through the speakers, filling the room with warmth. It's like he's here. Almost. If he was here, I'm not sure I'd be able to resist touching him.

"It's up to you," he says. "I understand delayed gratification a little too well at the moment."

"Can I ask you something?"

"Don't embarrass easily."

My cheeks flush. Any normal person would find this question horribly inappropriate, but Tom is not at all normal. "Do you have wet dreams?"

"Tsk. Tsk." His voice drips with mock offense. "I ever ask you if you have sex dreams?"

"Something tells me you will." I find the wrapped gift bag in my suitcase, take a seat on the bed, and place it in my lap. "Do you?"

"Yeah."

"About anyone in particular?"

His voice softens. "I'm not sure I should answer that."

I bite my lip. This might lead to him saying *sorry, that was a mistake* but it's a risk I have to take. "Why did you get me off last night?"

He's quiet for a minute. "I wanted to make you feel good."

"Tom. That's barely an answer."

"I'll explain after you open the present."

This better be good. "I'll put you on speaker." I set my phone on the bed and reach into the gift bag slowly.

It's a vibrator.

A hot pink vibrator.

For a solid thirty seconds, I'm speechless. "You're going to have to explain this to me."

"You haven't had sex in six years."

"I'm aware."

"Do you have any sex toys?"

"No." I reach for my phone. I need to hang up this call so I can think straight. This isn't hot and cold. This is Death Valley and Antarctica. This is absolute zero and melting gold.

"I'm sure you're very capable with your hands, but six years is a long fucking time to not feel any desire. Any pleasure." There's no irony in his voice. He's totally earnest. "You deserve better than that. You deserve to feel so good you could die."

"And you're the one who should get me there?"

He's quiet for a minute. "The point of the toy isn't something to do together on long drives. It's so you can take your time figuring out what you like."

My muscles relax. "Why, Tom? Why did you touch me?"

"You wanted me to."

"That's it?"

"No. I wanted to."

I pull my knees into my chest. "What about my feelings?"

His voice softens. "I don't want to hurt your feelings, kid. I care about you."

My stomach clenches. I don't like where this is going.

"I've never done the boyfriend/girlfriend thing before. Never even considered it."

"We don't have to jump to that," I say. "We can be friends who fool around. See where it goes."

"Maybe." He lets out an anguished groan. "This is new for me. I want what's best for you. Not sure that's me."

"How could it not be you?"

"I'm not the kind of guy you should be with."

Tom is usually a pillar of confidence. Does he really believe he's not what's best for me? That he's not the best fucking thing in the world for me? I take a deep breath.

"I'm not going to be around the next few weeks. Pete and I are mostly going to be home with Mom. Next three, four shows we're flying in morning of and leaving for the airport five minutes after the encore." He takes a deep breath. "You should focus on your photography. We can talk once I'm back."

"Is everything okay with your Mom?"

"Not sure yet. I'll tell you once I know."

"I'm going to ask you something," I say. "Will you promise to answer honestly?"

"Yeah."

"What do you want? Right now, in this moment? Even if it's selfish. Even if it's not what you think is best for me or anyone else."

"Besides the ability to teleport?"

"Yeah."

"I want you to use that vibrator to come until you can't take it anymore."

My cheek flush. My exhaustion has my defenses down. It makes me bold. "Do you want to listen?"

He groans. "God, yes."

Chapter Nineteen

I check to make sure the door is locked.

Can I really do this? Can I really masturbate for Tom's listening pleasure?

Self-consciousness threatens to overwhelm me.

"You there, kid?" His voice is heavy, breathy.

It encourages me. I need his groans and sighs in my ears. I need him as desperate and wanting as I am. "Yeah."

"Don't tell me you lost your nerve."

"No. I want to. Are you alone?"

"I can be. Hold on a minute." His side of the call goes mute. A few moments later, he's back. "Done."

"I've never used a vibrator before."

"You want me to walk you through it?"

"Okay. Let me get it out."

The vibrator is about six inches long and a little less wide than a... uh... Can I really do this?

"You okay, kid?"

I nod. But he can't see that. "A little intimidated."

"It's hot as hell that you're willing to admit it. Put the phone next to your mouth so I can hear you groaning."

Oh, God, the way he says that, like my groans are his favorite song. I'm already flushed and wanting. I set the phone on the bed, near my ear.

"Take off your t-shirt," he commands.

I pull my top over my head. There's something intimate about doing what he asks.

"You wearing a bra?"

"Yeah. You want a picture?" I offer.

Tom groans. "God yes, but we don't have time." His breath gets heavy. "Tease yourself. Run your fingers over the edge of your bra. Do it lightly, slowly, like I did with your tank top yesterday."

My eyelids flutter closed as I run my fingertips over the edge of my demi-cup. It's a little awkward at first, but Tom's heavy exhales spur me on. I move slowly.

Yes. Pleasure spreads out from my fingertips, over my chest. It's a start. A tease. I need more. "Tom," I groan.

"Take off the bra."

I fling it to the other side of the room. "Done."

He lets out a soft groan. "Rub your thumbs over your nipples."

I'm not nearly as exact as Tom was. It takes a few tries to find a speed and pressure that makes my sex clench.

I groan.

"Whatever that was, do it again."

The pleasure in his voice does something to me. I play with my nipples until I'm moaning loudly enough to wake up one of the guys.

"Take off your jeans," he says.

I unzip my pants, pull them off my legs, and toss them to the floor. "Done."

"Are you wearing panties?"

"Yeah. Normal cotton ones. They're not very sexy."

"My hard-on disagrees."

"Don't you have another two weeks until you can masturbate?"

"Yeah." His groan is half agony, half ecstasy. "This is more than worth the blue balls." He takes a deep breath. "Grab the vibrator. The settings are on the white handle, in the shape of a heart. Press and hold the one on the bottom to turn it on."

The settings are in the shape of a heart. There's something sweet about that. I remind myself that it doesn't necessarily mean anything, that Tom explicitly backed away from making this relationship anything, even friends with benefits.

Tom takes me through the controls until I'm at the lowest setting of constant vibration.

"Try it over your panties," he says. "It'll be intense."

I test the toy against my inner thigh. It's similar to my phone's vibrate setting only a hell of a lot stronger. Slowly, I spread my legs, working the toy to my sex.

That *is* intense. I gasp.

Tom continues. "Play with it until you find the spot that feels best. That makes your whole body seize up with pleasure."

I shift my wrist, my hips, my pelvis. There. That's it. Wave after wave of pleasure spreads through me. It's intense, fast. My sex clenches, already close to an orgasm.

God, how I want Tom here with me, coming with me. God, how I want Tom. This isn't enough. Nothing is going to be enough until he's mine.

I let myself imagine him here, his hands around the toy, his body next to mine, his lips on my neck. A groan escapes my lips. Yes. There. Almost.

His breath is heavy, desperate. He needs this as badly as I do. It pushes me to the edge.

Pleasure wells up inside me. This thing is damn strong.

Then he groans, and I can't take it anymore. I hold nothing back, moaning and panting as an orgasm overtakes me. Pleasure spills out from my core. I come in spasms.

When I can't take it anymore, I turn off the toy and collapse into the bed. Tom's breath flows through the receiver. It's steady and needy at once.

"That was amazing."

"Thanks."

"You okay?"

"Better than okay."

His line is silent for a moment. "Shit. We're about to board."

"Will you text me when you get in?"

He hesitates. "Sure."

"Tom, I..."

"I gotta go, kid. Sweet dreams."

"You too."

FOR THE NEXT FEW DAYS, TOM AND I TEXT ABOUT nothing and everything. Those little details that make up the day. Running out of eggs in the middle of making breakfast. My attempts at trimming my bangs. A picture of a particularly decadent iced coffee/chocolate cupcake combination. He sends pictures from his morning runs. Play by plays of his mom and Pete's commentary as they watch trashy reality TV. Requests for movie picks that will please his mom.

Then it's the concert, and Tom is barely here.

The next few days, our texts about nothing spread thinner. Thinner.

The next concert, I don't even get a chance to say hello.

I try to give Tom space to deal with whatever it is that's keeping him away. It's good for me to focus on my work. When I'm not assisting Hazel on one of her passion projects, I'm researching opening a boudoir studio. I'm still too shy to ask a model to pose for me but I'm not willing to wait any longer to practice.

So I take self-portraits.

Completely mortifying self-portraits I'm never going to show anyone.

Except that I want to show Tom. I resist for days. I throw myself into work. Until I'm alone in my hotel room, well past midnight, unable to sleep because my thoughts are stuck on him.

I have to call.

"Hey, kid," he answers. "You ring me up this time of night, I'm going to think it's a booty call."

I laugh. Everything feels easier with his voice in my ears. I've missed him. "How have you been?"

"Two flights every four days. Living the dream." His voice drops. "You haven't asked why I've been away."

"Last time I asked, you said you'd tell me later."

"You trust me?"

"Yeah." I really do. "Whenever you decide you want to talk about it, I'm here to listen."

"Do I get to *listen?*" he asks.

Oh. Yes please. "You don't have to bribe me with emotional confessions. I... I liked doing that with you." My cheeks flush. "We're in a hotel today. I'm alone."

"Fuck yes." He lets out a sigh of pleasure. "We should talk first. I'll be incoherent after."

"How are you so comfortable with yourself?" I ask. "I don't think I could ever say anything like that."

"Practice. Try it."

"What specifically?"

"Tell me how you'll feel after you come."

God, I'm burning up. "Um..."

"Anything. Even a single word."

"Good."

His laugh is sweet. "Anything else?"

"Like I wish you were here."

The sound that comes out of the speakers is a lot less sweet. It's a heavy, needy sigh.

I like that. A lot. It's enough to convince me to try this potentially embarrassing honesty thing again. "Like I can't wait until I can hear you come."

"And?"

"Like I want you inside of me."

Tom let's out an anguished groan. "You're a fast learner."

According to the mirror, I'm as red as a tomato. But he doesn't have to know that. I keep my voice confident. "Thanks."

"Better get on task, or I'll be incoherent a lot faster."

"I did another boudoir set."

"Without me?" He teases.

"They're self-portraits."

"Fuck. Show me when I'm back. Not sure I trust myself if I have them on my phone. Still have two days until I'm cleared for action."

He can't trust himself not to masturbate if he has sexy photos of me? God damn, I'm on fire. I better change the subject or I'll be the incoherent one.

"Where are you?" I ask.

"Home. My mom lives in the same house she did when she first fostered me. I have the same Nirvana and Blink 182 posters on my walls."

"Tell me about your room," I say. "I want to imagine you there."

His voice is light. "House is a three bedroom. Nice, comfortable suburban place. My room is upstairs. It's small. Twin bed, plain black sheets and black comforter. Sad little desk I never used 'cause I barely did my homework. Walls are nothing but posters. A few other bands, then all the great George A. Romero flicks."

"Who?"

"*Dawn of the Dead*! The original. It's a commentary on commercial culture. The zombies flock to the mall because they're drawn to it."

"Zombies? It's a horror movie?"

"Technically. But you'd like it. A lot less scary than *Let The Right One In*."

"Maybe. I get freaked out pretty easily. I mostly watch more upbeat classics. *Roman Holiday* is my favorite." I lie back on my bed. "When will you be back for good?"

"After Kara and Meg's graduation. Tried to rearrange our tour dates so we wouldn't be flying nonstop, but Mom threatened to change the locks if we canceled a show to see her."

"Your mom sounds badass."

"She is."

"It must be scary... whatever it is she's going through."

"Yeah."

He wants to tell me. I can hear it in his voice. He just needs a push.

I take a deep breath. "What is she going through?"

His voice softens. "She had cancer when I was in high school. Breast cancer. It might be back. She found a lump last month."

I don't breathe.

"I didn't handle it well then. I want to be better this time. Be strong for her."

"Are you scared?"

"Yeah. Trying not to get ahead of myself. It might be nothing. So far, test results are inconclusive."

"I'm sorry." I don't know what else to say. God, I wish he was here so I could wrap my arms around him, do something to comfort him properly. "Is there anything I can do?"

"No. I'm about to drop. How about a rain check on the phone sex?"

"Yeah. Sure. I miss you." I bite my lip. I hope that doesn't scare him off.

"I miss you too, kid. Whatever happens..." His voice trails off.

"What could happen?"

"Never mind. I'll see you soon."

―――――

THE TONE OF TOM'S VOICE HAUNTS ME ALL DAY.

I get to the concert venue an hour before he's due on the off chance he'll be early enough that we can talk. Or at least that I can comfort him the way he comforted me.

Sitting does nothing to help with the nerves in my stomach. I pace instead. The security guard invites me backstage twenty times. Eventually, I see the light in being inside, and I accept his offer.

There are a few roadies setting up. I wander the tiny backstage area in hopes of finding a proper distraction.

My phone buzzes. I almost jump. It's from Tom. He's on his way.

The airport is only fifteen minutes from the venue.

I spend all fifteen of those minutes pacing. Then another ten.

Finally, the back door pushes open. There are voices. Pete. And Tom. They're laughing about something. God, it's nice to hear his laugh.

But when Tom looks at me, his expression darkens.

Pete clears his throat. "I have to make a call."

Tom looks at his brother. "You don't have to—"

"Yes, I do. Drew and Miles will be here in twenty." Pete nods goodbye and makes his way outside.

We're behind the stage, behind the curtain. Everything around us is black. The walls, the ceiling, the tile floors, the mood.

"Willow, I..." Tom runs his hand through his hair. "I've been thinking a lot. Like we said."

My stomach clenches. There's no way this ends with *and I realized I'm in love with you. Let's make this official.*

"I care about you. A lot. Too much to keep doing this." He holds my gaze, even as his eyes cloud with regret. "I'm sorry if I was leading you on. Wasn't my intention."

"But I..."

He looks away. "It's better if we stick with being friends."

God, did he have to do this before a show? I have to spend the next few hours watching him drip with sex appeal.

At least I haven't eaten since lunch. Nothing to throw up.

He stares at the floor. "Tomorrow is the end of my six weeks, and Miles is making a big deal about taking me out, making sure I break my celibacy."

No. He's not saying these words. No. I take a step backwards. Another.

I hit the wall. "You're calling this off to fuck a stranger?"

"No, kid. That's not—"

"Don't call me that."

"This is going to hurt more if we have sex," he says. "This is what's best for you. For both of us."

"Fuck you. If this is what you want, fine, but I decide what's best for me."

"Willow."

"Why are you running away from this?" I ask. "Tell me. Please. If it's me, if you don't want someone like me, I understand."

"It's not you."

"Then what is it?"

He says nothing.

"Okay. Fine. I understand." I swallow hard. Anything to keep from crying. "Good luck at the show. Hope you enjoy fucking some random woman tomorrow. Hope it's really special."

"I'm not going to—"

"No. No. I want you to enjoy your fucking piercing. We're nothing. You're a free agent. Free to fuck anybody you want."

I turn and rush to the women's bathroom. He says something, but it's not *You're right. I'm an idiot for running away from this. Let me press you against the wall and make it up to you. In fact, I'm going to skip the show. What does a rock song need drums for, anyway? I'd much rather bang you.*

Chapter Twenty

The music is throbbing. Much too loud for conversation. Thank God, because there's no way I can get any words out of mouth besides *what the hell am I doing here?*

I get it. We're just friends. But that doesn't mean I want to watch Tom pick out his next sexual partner.

I'm going to throw up.

I adjust my cocktail dress. It's the sexiest thing I own— tight, short, low-cut enough to show off my chest piece and my cleavage. Not that I got dressed thinking of what would make Tom reconsider.

All the guys are here. I need to keep up my poker face or I'll quickly become the band's new pity project.

At least we're secluded in the VIP area. Traveling with rock stars has its perks. I cross and uncross my legs but nothing helps me get comfortable. These drinks are taking forever.

Tom plops on the couch next to me. His leg presses against mine, the rough fabric of skinny jeans sending shivers of electricity up my spine.

Miles holds up his cell phone to show off the time. Midnight. "There you go, Sticks. You survived. Six weeks. Let's take bets on how long he'll last. Who wants thirty seconds?"

"I'll take thirty seconds." Pete looks at me, staring through me, checking if I'm okay. My poker face must be pretty strong because he turns back to Miles with a light voice. "But we can't trust the honor system. Who's volunteering to watch and time it?"

Tom flips his brother off. "Can I get in on this?"

"Seems fair." Miles turns to me. "You have a guess? Ladies should *go* first, but I doubt Tom will manage that today."

"Uh..." I uncross and cross my legs. Anything to stem the heat building between them. How can my body be raring to go when my heart is ready to give out? My knee brushing against Tom's does nothing to help the situation.

"*Price is Right* rules, or closest?" Drew asks.

"Closest." Miles pulls a hundred dollars out of his wallet and slams it on the table. "I'll give him two minutes." He looks Tom in the eyes. "Don't say I never speak highly of you."

A cocktail waitress arrives with our drinks. Club soda for Miles. A bottle of whiskey and mixers to be shared between everyone else.

Tom pours whiskey on the rocks for him, Pete, and Drew and slides the glasses across the table. He looks at me. "You want one, kid?"

"Please don't call me that," I say.

Tom stares at me with this regret in his eyes. Fuck him and his regret. He's the one running away from this.

I adjust my top for maximum cleavage potential and stare back at Tom. "Whiskey and diet please."

"Since when do you drink?" Drew's expression gets intense and protective.

I shrug as if drinking is something I do all the time.

He and Miles share a knowing look.

"All right." Drew takes a long sip of his whiskey. "I'll stay for one drink, then I'm going to bed. Tom, I'm counting on you to make sure Wil doesn't get drunk."

"That's weak delegating," Miles says. "I'm hurt."

"You too." Drew turns from Miles to Tom. "Just, I know which of you three is usually the instigator."

"You in or not?" Miles asks.

"This is disgusting," Drew says.

"Not hearing a *no*." Miles makes the money gesture with his thumb and forefinger. "Come on, hundred bucks an entry." He looks at me. "I'll even pay for Willow's entry if she's interested."

"Uh..." I take a long, long sip of my whiskey and diet. It mostly tastes of cola and artificial sweetener.

"All right." Drew pulls five twenties from his wallet. "I'll take three minutes."

"Thanks for believing in me." Tom rolls his eyes.

Pete fishes a hundred dollar bill out of his wallet. "Clock starts at the moment of insertion?"

Miles nods.

"Are we talking oral or intercourse?" Pete asks. "Makes a difference."

"What do you say, Tom? Got plans for how you're breaking your fast?" Miles laughs, reveling in the awkwardness of the situation.

"Lady's choice," Tom says.

"Oh? You have anything to say, Willow?" Miles asks.

I have a lot to say but my mouth is sticky. I shake my head and take another sip. The bite of alcohol isn't bad. Even if it warms my throat and chest more than I'd like.

Tom's eyes catch mine. They fill with something I can't place then go to the floor.

Okay, time to finish this drink. It takes two sips and I'm slurping melted ice.

"Fuck it. I'll call it now. Intercourse." Tom slams his drink in one long sip. "I'll take five."

"That's it?" Miles asks.

"A man should know his limitations. If we're taking bets for round two, I'll take twenty." Tom pulls a hundred out of his wallet and adds it to the pile. "Any other commentary?"

"Condom?" Pete asks.

"What kind of idiot do you take me for?" Tom asks.

"You can sneak in some sensation dulling bullshit." Pete smiles.

He's enjoying this way too much.

"Got some that are specially made for piercings. Normal sensation."

"Capitalism at its finest." Miles laughs. "How much do those run?"

"What do you care?" Tom shakes his head. "Never knew you guys were obsessed with my cock. It's flattering, but I don't swing that way."

Pete laughs. "I'll go up to one minute unless you want to call it, Willow."

I pass my drink to Tom for a refill. Okay. Might as well be a part of the action. "I'll take fifteen."

Our eyes connect. Something passes between us. Something intimate and not at all just friends. Almost like he's considering how long he'd take with me.

"Damn, Sticks. The girl believes in you. She tripled the highest bet." Miles looks at me. "I'm not offering any odds. You can bet six and win with 5:31. Bet fifteen and you need 10:01 to win."

The gambling statistics mean nothing to me. "What can I say? I believe in Tom. He can do whatever he puts his mind to." I drink until my cheeks are burning.

Miles collects the money and slides it into his pocket. "That's five hundred dollars for whoever gets closest. Tom is honorable enough to report accurately."

"You guys need new hobbies." Drew slams his drink and pushes out of his seat.

Drew's eyes lock with mine. He studies me, assessing whether or not I'm okay. I guess the answer is yes. Or maybe he's realized I'm an adult, and I'm able to make my own mistakes.

God, being here is a mistake. But being somewhere else, wondering how it's going, would be worse.

"Call me if anything comes up, Wil," Drew says.

I nod an okay.

Tom finishes his drink and pours a refill. He watches Drew walk away then turns back to Miles and Pete. "I can't wait to spend your money."

Miles nods to a blonde woman in a short red dress. "Ask if she'll volunteer. Bet she'd do it right here so we could get an honest timing."

Tom shakes his head. "In your dreams."

The blonde woman looks in the direction of the group. She's making eyes at someone.

"Only two minutes from here to the alley." Miles sips his club soda.

"She's not my type," Tom says.

Miles and Pete shoot him *oh please* looks.

"What *is* your type, Tom?" I ask.

The look in his eyes says *don't*.

But my alcohol dulled inhibitions say *do*. "Really? What kind of girls do you like?"

"Breathing," Miles says.

"Willing." Pete adds.

"Fuck you, assholes. I can't help that I love the female body. As long as we're on the same page about things being casual, I don't discriminate," Tom says.

"But you must have a preference." I take a deep breath. I'm a glutton for punishment. As long as I'm going for it, might as well go for broke. "Tattoos or small breasts or unnaturally colored hair. Something."

Miles looks at me and raises a brow. My drink is nothing but ice again. Funny how that works out.

More liquor is a bad idea. My head is already spinning. I stand up and brush any lint off my dress. I'm here. Might as well make this as painful for Tom as it is for me.

I run my hand through my hair so it's properly *I'm too cool for this* messy. Then I drag my fingertips down my neck and over my chest piece.

Victory. Tom's eyes are glued to my chest. The tattoo then the cleavage then all the way up to my eyes.

"You going somewhere?" Tom asks.

"This is a dance club, isn't it?" I turn and walk with as much hip sway as I can. I can hear the guys muttering something. It's not as if my ass in a tight dress is going to convince Tom to reconsider, but I can't sit on the sidelines watching this go down.

I wait until I'm in the middle of the dance floor to look back to the VIP area. Miles and Pete stay put in their seats. But Tom is on his way over here.

Okay. I'm not spying. Absolutely not spying. I turn my back to the guys and find the beat of the song. There. I sway my hips in time with the music. I scan the crowd for anyone who might get my mind off Tom.

A hand slides around my waist. "You all right, kid?"

Tom. He moves closer. Until his chest is pressed against my back, his crotch against my ass.

"I asked you not to call me that," I say.

He's not hard. Yet. It's wrong that I want to grind against him until he's begging me to help him lose that bet.

His breath is warm on my neck. What the hell is he doing here? He knows how I feel. He's made his stance clear.

"You have a big night ahead of you." I shrug my shoulders to break his grip. "You should probably get to it."

"I want to dance with you."

"Why?"

"'Cause you believe in me." He slides his hands to my hips. "If you're not interested, I'll find someone else. It's a yes or no proposition."

"Okay. Let's dance."

He guides my hips.

I'm not playing nice. I sway with him, arching my back to rub my ass against his crotch. My heels put me at the perfect height to make this *hard* for him.

He leans in to whisper in my ear. "Are you really okay with this?"

I copy his favorite comeback. "You keep dancing like that and I'm going to get ideas."

He shifts his body away from mine. "You know what I'm asking."

Of course I'm not okay. But he knows that. There's no way I'm going to say it again. I turn and stare Tom in his eyes. "Try to make it last. I could use the five hundred dollars."

He stares though me like he's looking into my soul. "You don't look okay."

I can hold this poker face for another ten seconds. No, he's still close. Make that three seconds. Two.

I turn away from Tom. "I hope you enjoy yourself. Excuse me."

One. My facade crumbles. I cut through the crowd before he has the chance to look at me.

The dance floor is throbbing with warm bodies and pheromones. No one who wants company is going home alone. Not that Tom ever lacks for a partner.

I find the woman's bathroom and hide out until my breath returns to normal. I can face this. So I'm crazy for a guy who's about to take a stranger home for anonymous sex? So what? It's not like I'd fall to pieces over a little thing like my heart breaking.

After twenty minutes, I give up on solitude and go in search of Miles or Pete. They're sitting on the couch, whispering about something. Their expressions flare with concern when they spot me but they still wave me over.

I plop in the spot between them and try to tune in to the conversation about independent film. But my eyes have a mind of their own. They find Tom. He's dancing with a short, dark-haired woman. She paws at him, already more than willing.

"You have a favorite TV show, Willow?" Miles asks.

"*Murder, She Wrote.*"

Her hands slide around his neck. She rises to her tiptoes to whisper in his ear. He nods and looks over at the couch.

Miles waves him towards the door.

Pete clears his throat. "You ever see *Monk?*"

"No. I'll have to check that out." I play with the hem of my dress, willing my eyes to stay on my knees.

They refuse. Tom nods back to Miles. Even though he's fifty feet away, his eyes catch mine. He stares through me again. It's like he's opening up my head and dissecting my thoughts.

But he's not. Because he's turning and he's leading that girl out of the club.

I listen to Pete and Miles discuss cozy mysteries for five minutes. Their words fly through my ears. Tom is going home with that woman.

My eyes sting. Something warm and salty rolls down my cheek.

Fuck. I'm crying.

I can't cry here.

I blink my eyelids together. The hotel is right around the corner. It's a three-minute walk. I can make it three minutes.

"Excuse me." I push off the couch. "I'm really tired. I'm going to crash in my room."

"I'll walk you," Miles offers.

"No. I need some time to think." I wipe my eyes and turn back to Pete and Miles with my best *everything is great* smile. "Thanks for offering."

"You sure?" Miles asks.

"Positive. Have fun." I turn before they can object further.

It's difficult to cut through the crowd with every ounce of strength fleeing my body. Finally, I make it to the street. It's a warm night. Humid. By the time I'm in the air-conditioned hotel lobby, my hair is sticking to my skin.

There's no sign of Tom. It's better that no one will see me in this sorry state. I skip the elevator—too much chance I'll run into someone—in favor of walking the four floors to my room.

My bed beckons me. I turn off the lights and throw myself on the mattress. Okay, this is it. This is all the crying over Tom I'm going to do. I might as well make it count.

I curl into a ball and give in to the tears rolling down my cheek.

I'm about to collapse when there's a knock at my door.

I'm lucky people care enough to check on me. At the moment, it's hard to muster any gratitude.

With great effort, I push myself off the bed, make my way to the door, and look out the peephole.

It's Tom.

Chapter Twenty-One

Tom knocks again. "Willow. It's me. Open up."

"Only if you're dropping off my winnings."

He's quiet for a moment. "No, I..."

No, I only made it two minutes or *No, I'm waiting to see what time we can get?*

He taps his fingers against the door. "I can scream my half of the conversation but someone will call security."

I unlock the door. "How was it?"

He slides it open another two inches. "You mind?"

"No. Come in." I step backwards.

Light fills the room as Tom steps inside. He presses the door closed with his back. His eyes connect with mine. He can tell I've been crying. It's written all over his face.

He swallows hard. "I didn't fuck her."

"Why not? She was pretty. Big boobs. Nice ass."

"Maybe. Barely looked at her." He takes a step towards me. "I didn't have any intention of fucking her."

"But you... you left with her."

"Needed to get the fuck out of there so I could think. Told her I wanted a cigarette."

"You don't smoke."

"She didn't know that." Tom presses the pad of his thumb against my cheek. "You've been crying."

"No."

"That's the worst lie I've ever heard."

I shake my head.

"Yeah." He brushes stray tears from under my eyes. "You were crying over me?"

"That's quite the accusation."

He stares back at me.

"Are you really that full of yourself?"

"I am. But you were." He slides his hand behind my neck. "You've been crying a lot."

"Not a lot."

"How much have you cried before that this isn't a lot?" His voice is soft, sweet.

"Too much." I go to step backwards but the damn wall is in the way. "We're supposed to be friends. I can't take this hot and cold thing anymore."

"I've been thinking about you nonstop since we talked. Not sure if you noticed but last night was the shittiest I ever played."

"Tom. No... If this is another upswing on the fucking sine wave that is your feelings towards me, then go now. If you're going to wake up tomorrow and realize this is a mistake and that we should just be friends, then go now. You're playing with my heart and I'm not going to take it anymore." God, I'm talking myself out of having sex with Tom. But it's necessary if I want to live through this tour. "If you're here for anything other than giving a relationship an honest shot, then you need to leave."

"I want to be with you." He slides a hand around my waist. "But I've never done that before. Might not be any good at it."

"That's okay. I'm not very good at it either."

He brushes his fingers against my cheek. "I don't know what to do here, kid. Nothing has ever made me hesitate."

I stare back into Tom's eyes. "You want me."

He nods.

"I want you. We'll figure the rest out. I promise."

"I've never cared about anyone this much. I... I'll hate myself if I break your heart."

I slide my hand around his neck. "You won't. Not on purpose."

"How do you know?"

"Say this goes bad and you break my heart because you're dealing with your own shit. That will cut me to my soul. But running away now would hurt worse." I press my fingertips into his skin. "I've spent the last few years running away from anything that might hurt me, and all I've got is an empty life. I don't want to run. I want you." I arch my back to press my crotch against his. "Please, Tom. I can't bear waiting another second. I need you."

He stares back into my eyes, and I know he understands me. He feels it too, needs me too.

"I'm going to kiss you," I say. "I know you don't normally—"

His lips press against mine before I can finish my sentence. Yes. Better than in my dreams. Better than anything.

Just a peck and Tom pulls back to look at me. There's so much in his gorgeous green eyes. Desire, affection, need.

He kisses me again. Any hint of reservation is gone. He sucks on my lower lip until I sigh with pleasure. His tongue slips into my mouth, swirling around mine.

He tastes good. Not like the three shots of whiskey I watched him drink. Like spearmint toothpaste. Like Tom.

He got ready for this.

He got ready for me.

I don't catch my breath until our kiss breaks.

His eyes meet mine. Different than before. Hungrier. He brings his hand to the bottom of my dress. I spread my legs to guide him.

Slowly, he drags his fingertips up my thigh. Almost. They skim the edge of my panties.

"Please," I breathe.

He presses his lips against my ear. "I love the way you say that. It's fucking sexy."

I arch my back to press my sex against his hand. "Please."

He kisses me hard. His tongue slides into my mouth, exploring it. He's damn patient as he strokes me over my panties.

I tug at his hair. Now. I need all of him, now. I drag my fingertips over his chest, his neck, his ears.

He groans.

Yes, the ears. I run my fingertips over his earlobes with a feather light touch.

Tom pulls back. He grabs my hands and presses them hard against the wall. "Let me lead, kid." He slides my panties to my knees. "I want to savor this." He drags his fingers up the inside of the thigh. "I want to feel every second of your pleasure."

My sex clenches. I want him leading. I trust him with my body. And that's everything.

Tom takes his sweet time unzipping my dress and sliding it to my feet. He drags his fingertips up my calves, my thighs, my hips.

He unhooks my bra and slides it off, one shoulder, then the other. His eyes go wide at the sight of my breasts. Like it's the first time he's ever seen a woman naked.

Or maybe it's the best time.

His touch is light over my stomach, my chest, my collarbones. He catches my bottom lip with the soft pad of his thumb. I slide his digit into my mouth and suck gently. His eyelids flutter closed.

He drags his hand back down my torso then cups my hip, holding me upright. A good thing because the moment his fingers skim my clit, my knees buckle.

His touch is light. My body throbs in protest. More.

His lips make contact with mine. He strokes me harder. Harder.

Harder.

I shudder. Yes. There. I groan into his mouth instead of speaking. He keeps the same speed. The same rhythm.

Drummers, they know how to keep a fucking beat.

Tension builds as he strokes me. When I can't take the rising bliss any more, I pry my lids apart. Watch the expression of fascination on his face. His eyes are wide, transfixed. Right now, I'm the most important person in the world. The sexiest woman in the world.

My eyelids press together. My hands find his shoulders and tug at his t-shirt. Then under it. There's something right about our skin connecting. I want my fingers on every inch of his body. His fingers on every inch of mine.

God, Tom.

Conscious thought melts away. The flutter of his lips against mine. The sigh of pleasure as his fingers find the perfect rhythm. The arch of my back bringing our bodies together.

Pleasure wells up inside me. It knots tighter, tighter, harder. I break our kiss to cry out. How is it possible for anything to feel this good?

God, the way he's looking at me. It makes it hard to stand.

With his next touch, the knot releases and pleasure spills through me. My sex pulses as I come.

He pulls his t-shirt over his head, and presses his bare chest against mine. Every nerve in my body lights up at once. He's against me. Just him. Just me.

Tom presses his lips against my neck and shoulders. Kissing, sucking, biting gently. His fingers tease my sex. Slowly, he slides one inside me.

Yes. God yes.

His eyes connect with mine. He's watching me, watching my reactions. I'm so wrecked with need that I barely manage to nod. He pushes deeper then slides another finger inside me.

My body tenses. It hurts for a moment then it feels really fucking good.

I take my time exploring the hard muscles of his chest and stomach as I work my way down his torso. Tom's eyes flutter closed. He lets out a low groan as I cup him over his jeans.

The look of bliss on his face is the best thing I've ever seen.

He pulls his hand away, reaches into the back pocket of his jeans, and pulls out a condom. He shimmies out of his jeans. "Tell me if it hurts."

I nod.

His boxers join his jeans on the floor.

Almost.

Tom's eyes go straight to my chest as he rolls the condom on. He cups my breasts as he presses his body against mine. His hard cock presses against my stomach. Not quite where it needs to be.

He brings his hands to my ass, kissing me as he kneads my flesh. We're close to where we need to be. Almost.

He lifts me, holds me against the wall. The muscles of

his arms flex against my flesh. I should feel scared. That he'll drop me. That this will hurt. That everything will somehow go wrong.

But I'm not scared.

My eyelids press together. My breath hitches. I hook my legs around his waist, spreading as wide as I can, giving myself to him.

I want to be his. Want him erasing the memories of anyone else.

Tom's breath is slow, even. He shifts, his cock nudging against my sex. Almost.

Almost.

He groans as his tip strains against me.

My sex stretches around him. I dig my nails into his shoulders to contain the overwhelming sense of being filled. One delicious inch at a time, he enters me. His eyes darken. His breath hitches. He nips at my neck, his groans vibrating against my skin, filling my ears.

Deeper.

Then it's too deep. Too much. My teeth clench. My neck tenses.

He stops. Cups my neck.

I take a deep breath. I want all of him inside me. Every damn inch. I bring my lips to Tom's, slide my tongue into his mouth. He holds me upright with one hand. The other goes to my breasts, teasing my nipples until my muscles relax.

Tom looks me in the eyes, watching my expression as he slides all the way inside me. I can feel every inch of him, the way my body stretches around him. We're two puzzle pieces, finally locked together.

The world is right.

A groan escapes his lips. He moves slowly, unbearably slowly, thrusting deep inside me and pulling out again and again. With every thrust, the discomfort fades, replaced by pleasure. He's in control. I'm safe with him. As his.

My eyelids press together. It feels too good to do anything but moan. His lips find mine. Our kiss is as deep and slow as his movements.

We're locked together for minutes. Not fast. Not even a little. He's gentle as he fills me with long, slow thrusts. Again and again and again until I'm close enough I'm shaking.

He plants kisses along my jaw, my neck, my shoulder.

Tom Steele is a patient, gentle lover.

Who the hell would have guessed?

I shudder.

Almost.

I arch my hips to push him deeper.

God, he feels good.

He thrusts into me with those same slow, gentle movements. Minutes pass. I'm lost in some world where everything feels good.

My sex clenches. Tighter and tighter and tighter. It's the slowest orgasm in the history of the world.

I keep my eyes glued to his until I can't take it anymore. My lids press together. One more thrust and I tumble over the edge. I come in spasms, pulling him closer, tighter.

He stays inside me until I'm still. His grip tightens against my hips. Our bodies come untangled as carries me on the bed. My back hits the mattress. My legs splay open.

He brings his body on top of mine. His arms plant outside mine. I spread my legs, arching my back to give myself to him.

His tip strains against me. I bite my lip, not sure if I can take him at full force. He's big.

Tom brings his hands to my hips, not holding me, but cradling me. He presses his cheek against mine.

"I've got you," he whispers.

He does. I only barely nod. Tom teases me with his tip. Again and again. And again. Until I'm desperate for all of him. Now.

With one swift movement, he thrusts inside me. It's deep. Hard. My eyelids close. My fingers dig into his skin. I give in to the bliss spreading through me. My hips move of their own accord, matching his movements, pushing him deeper.

He groans as he moves faster and harder.

Another orgasm rises up inside me. My sex clenches again and again as I come. It pulls him closer, deeper.

Tom's grip tightens around my hips. He goes harder. Deeper.

Within moments, he's there, groaning into my ear and digging his fingers into my skin as he comes. I soak in every second of his orgasm. The way his breath goes erratic, the way his voice goes higher, the way his body shakes against mine.

He presses his lips against my neck, untangles our bodies, and does away with the condom.

I fall onto my side, my thoughts slowly drifting back into my head.

Then Tom is back on the bed, his arms around me, his lips against my neck. And I realize I'm done with thoughts for the night. All I need to know is how good he makes me feel.

How badly I want to be his.

Chapter Twenty-Two

T here's a warm body pressed against mine. Breath on my neck. A heart pounding against my back. Not my heart but Tom's.

He's still in bed with me.

Every organ begs me to stay next to him, to soak in the comfort of his arms for as long as possible. Every organ except my bladder.

Damn, I have to pee. I'm careful about unwrapping his arms without disturbing him. Still, he stirs. Mutters something incomprehensible. He looks gorgeous asleep. But not like an angel. Even surrounded by the soft glow of light peeking through the curtains, he looks like trouble.

The curtains are only open a sliver and there's still all this light. It's far too bright to be a.m. I should be used to the sleep all day, party all night rock star lifestyle by now.

I allow myself one long moment to gawk at Tom lying on the bed on his stomach. Strong shoulders, sculpted ass, muscular legs. God, he's yummy. But the heat building between my legs only makes this whole I have to pee situation worse.

I lock the bathroom door, pee, brush my teeth, start the shower. There's noise in the main room. Must be Tom getting up. And his voice. He's on the phone. Ah, please let that be something trivial. Something that won't force life to come crashing down around us.

There are footsteps then a knock on the bathroom door. I open up for Tom.

He's still naked.

It would be rude to do anything but gawk. I take my time checking out his just as amazing front— from the messy hair to the defined abs to the hardening cock. God, he's already getting hard.

I am naked.

But still.

"Eyes up here, kid."

"I have other areas of interest."

"Do tell."

"Think they're pretty obvious." With great effort, I meet his gaze. "Who was that?"

"Room service. You need your strength."

"Why is that?"

He slides his arm around my waist, pulls me into the main room, and points to the bed. "There for starters." He points to the messy table. "There." To the armchair in the corner. "Definitely there." He nods to the shower. "Seems you already have the right idea here."

Oh.

"It's past noon but I talked the cook into making us eggs. Special request."

"Uh-huh."

He's naked. I offer him my toothbrush so I'll stop gawking. He takes it, one eye on me as he brushes his teeth.

"I've never been in a shower with someone else before," I say.

He rinses his mouth and sets my toothbrush back on the counter. "Don't do it too often. Condoms don't always play nice with water." Excitement flares in his expression. "Actually. Give me a sec."

He steps out of the bathroom. Wait here or get started without him? I'm already desperate for his touch. Desperate for our bodies to join again. This is more than care but I'm not sure how much. It's been ages since I've had any feeling for a man that wasn't indifference.

Tom is back in a hot second. He hands me a folded piece of paper. His eyes meet mine. He motions *go ahead*.

It's an STD test.

He's clean.

"I haven't been with anyone since before—" He motions to his still erect cock.

I check the date. Three days ago. I look back into his eyes. "You got this for me?"

He nods.

"But you called this off at the show."

"Was trying to convince myself I could want something else."

"What else?"

"Something less complicated. That wouldn't end with one of us hurting." He presses his lips into my neck. "You want me to get a condom?"

"You trust me?"

He nods. "Even with my hands here." He slides his hands over my chest to cup my breasts.

"I'm clean. I got tested after everything with my ex and again six months after." I lean into his touch. "I have an IUD. Got it just in case... anything happened again."

"Just in case?" He lowers his voice. "Oh."

"It's not exactly a sexy conversation."

"No, just—" He leads me into the shower. "Not enough blood in my brain for me to think quickly."

I move under the flow of the showerhead. I'm already flushed. The warm water threatens to overheat me. I switch places and watch with rapt attention as water streams down Tom's perfect body.

His hands go to my shoulders. His lips go to my ear. "You've been through so much pain. With your parents. Your ex."

I press my back into his chest. Being this close isn't just sexy. It's intimate. Safe. We're in a magic bubble where nothing else can hurt us. "You have, too. You just don't let on."

He tilts my head towards his shoulder and presses his lips to the spot just behind my ears. "I've never felt like this before. Like the only thing I wanted was to take someone's pain away."

There isn't much space to move around. I let Tom lead. He positions me under the water then takes his sweet, sweet time wetting, shampooing, and rinsing my hair.

"I know there's nothing I can do to erase the past." He conditions and rinses my hair. His hands trace a slow path from the back of my neck to my sides. "But I can even the score with a hell of a lot of pleasure."

Tom presses me into the wall. The weight of his body sinks into mine. We're both sopping wet, slippery in just the right way. I let my eyes close so I can focus on Tom dragging his fingertips down my chest. It's different than when we're dry. Slicker. Smoother. The pleasure is diffused through my entire torso.

His hands explore my sides and stomach and back. They make their way back up my torso and curve around my breasts.

Tom rubs his thumbs over my nipples. "Look at me, Willow."

His eyes are filled with desire. My knees threaten to buckle from the intensity of it.

"I have a hypothesis to test here." He draws slow circles around me. "I'm going to need your feedback."

"Yes" I say.

"Yes, what?" He shifts so his cock presses against my belly.

"Your hypothesis. The one about small breasts being responsive, right?"

"You're a budding scientist."

He flicks his fingers over my nipples until I'm panting. So much for diffuse pleasure. Every touch sends a shock wave straight to my core. I reach for something to steady myself.

"This is a very good experiment," I groan. "We should probably repeat it every day."

"For science?"

I nod.

My hand brushes against the firm muscles of his stomach. He feels good all slippery and wet. I've been attracted to men, admired them from afar, but I've never craved my hands on their skin. Even before Bradley.

They had nothing on this.

His body is already my favorite thing in the world. The way he shudders as my hands make their way down his torso. The way he presses his cheek against mine and sighs right into my ear.

My hand slips below his belly button. There. It brushes against his cock.

He grabs onto my hips and presses me against the wall.

I keep my touch light as I stroke him from his base to

his tip. His eyelids flutter closed. His lips part with a sigh. His pleasure is my pleasure. Better than my pleasure even.

I rub my thumb over his tip, testing his reactions as I play with the barbell on top. It's snug against his glans. Barely moves when I touch it. But that doesn't stop him from shuddering and pressing his lips to my ear.

"You keep doing that and I'm gonna come." His voice is breathy and desperate.

"That's the idea."

I tease him the way he teased me, rubbing my thumb over every inch of his tip until he's shaking. My, do I like this apadravya of his. He groans with pleasure every time I touch it.

"Willow." Tom slides his hand around my ass and holds on tight.

I rise to my tiptoes to bring my mouth to his ear. The ceramic floor is too slick for me to keep my balance. I slip.

Tom catches me and holds me against the wall. "You need to work on your balance, kid. Some yoga or rollerblading or something."

I laugh. So much for being the cool, suave sex expert. I can still drive him out of his damn mind. I look up at Tom and slide my free hand up his stomach and chest.

"Later. Right now." I drag my fingertips up his neck. "I need to feel you come on my hand."

"Fuck yes."

"Show me."

He takes one hand off my hips. "Sure you can balance on your own?"

I nod.

Tom places his palm on the back of my hand and uses it to guide my movements. Long, slow strokes get faster, harder.

I use my free hand to play with his earlobe. Every

brush makes him shake or shudder a little more. He groans, releasing my hand from his guidance to press it against the slick tile wall next to my shoulder.

He stares deeply into my eyes. "Don't fucking stop."

No way in hell would I stop. I stroke hard. He kisses me aggressively. His tongue slides against mine as he groans into my mouth. I can feel his sigh of pleasure reverberating across my cheeks and down my chest.

The way he's shaking and groaning—he's almost there.

I keep my pace, even as he pulls his lips away from mine to let out a deep, animal groan.

"I'm gonna come." He slams his hand against the wall.

I can feel him pulsing. Can see the ecstasy in his eyes and lips. There. He comes, spurting against my hand and onto my belly.

"Fuck, Willow." He wraps his arms around me and holds our bodies together. "Haven't enjoyed a hand job that much since I was fifteen."

"Is that a compliment?"

"You're fucking amazing." He slides his hands around my neck. "That better?"

"It's a start."

He nudges me towards the showerhead. The water flows over my head and chest. He turns me, bringing my back against his chest. Tom rubs a bar of soap between his hands. Then his soapy hands are on me.

"That's fucking naughty, distracting me like that." He sucks on my earlobe.

"Told you I wasn't nice."

"You really are dirty." He kneads my breasts. "Better get you clean."

I laugh. "I'm not sure I trust your intentions, Mr. Steele."

"You shouldn't." He presses his lips to my neck. "You like it, huh?"

"Like what?"

"The piercing."

I rub the bar between my hands and take my time soaping his chest and back. When I'm thoroughly satisfied, I tilt my neck to whisper in his ears. "I love it."

Chapter Twenty-Three

After a quiet brunch, Tom leaves for the band's afternoon TV appearance. Kara and Meg's graduation is tomorrow. We're flying back to Los Angeles tonight.

Around dinnertime, a limo picks me up at the hotel. The guys are already inside. Already bantering.

It's a real party machine. Tom sits next to the mini-bar, guarding it.

No one else seems interested in the mini bottles of liquor, but that does nothing to lessen Tom's guard dog stance. He keeps one hand on top of the handle. The expression on his face says *don't even try it.*

"Shit, really thought you'd lose the stick up your ass after you came. What happened? Don't tell me that woman turned you down. She looked like she was gonna drag you to the manager's office and throw you on the desk." Miles drifts into a memory.

Pete has one eye on their conversation. The other is on his phone. He shakes his head like he can't believe how ridiculous his band mates are.

Drew, on the other hand, is not even remotely here. He stares out the tinted windows, lost in thought.

Miles reaches for the liquor cabinet, taunting Tom. It earns him a slap on the wrist. His next taunt earns him a slap on the forearm.

"Whiskey dick? You were pounding those shots. Happens to the best of us. Or so I hear." Miles smiles.

Tom rolls his eyes. "I had sex with a woman last night, yes. I came once. She came three times. Do you need any more details?"

Miles is sarcastic. "Sounds like it was a lot of fun, all that joy in your voice."

There's no way he could possibly know he's talking about me, but the comments stings all the same. The sex was good. There's no way he was faking the groans that made it into my ears.

But it's been hours now. Maybe he's reconsidering.

Tom's eyes catch mine. He turns back to Miles. "It was fantastic. Wish I was with her instead of you assholes."

"I've never seen you with a girl unless you were on your way to or from her bed." Pete slides his phone into his pocket.

"Fucking her," Tom corrects.

Miles follows Tom's gaze to me. He shakes his head and makes eye contact with Tom. "Enough suspense, you tease. Tell me you only made it one-minute-thirty-one seconds. Meg will enjoy dinner more if she knows your loss is paying for it."

"Sorry guys. Got carried away. She looks so fucking sexy coming on my hand. Completely forget I was supposed to time it." Tom's eyes connect with mine.

My sex clenches. He's talking about me. About us having sex. It's our dirty little secret.

"At least ballpark it," Miles says.

Tom smiles. "At least twenty minutes."

Pete shakes his head. "I've never heard you last twenty minutes before."

"You listen that closely?" Tom asks.

Pete shrugs, not at all shy.

"Shit. Twenty minutes. After two months? I don't buy it." Miles pulls five one hundred dollar bills from his wallet. "I'll take your word for it, but only cause Willow is the underdog."

"If I was going to lie, wouldn't I lie to win?" Tom asks.

"Your ego means more to you than five hundred dollars," Pete says.

"Closer to five hundred thousand dollars," Miles adds.

They look to Drew for a comeback but he's still in a daze.

"What's wrong with Denton?" Pete asks.

"What?" Drew blinks, his attention returning to the limo. "I don't care how long Tom spent fucking that Goth chick. Stop asking for my opinion. I've got more important shit on my mind."

Miles looks at Tom like he's expecting the drummer to get involved.

Tom shrugs. "Maybe we should leave Guitar Prince alone."

"You've never left anyone alone in your life," Miles says.

"Shut up and pay Willow." Tom shifts back in his seat, spreading his legs, inviting me between them.

If only we didn't have this damn audience.

"Congrats." Miles hands me the stack of cash and nods to Drew. "You know what his problem is?"

"I have a guess," I say.

"You three ever mind your own business?" Drew pulls a

ring box out of his pocket and stares at it with a blissful sigh.

Eyes go wide with enthusiasm. The mood mellows into a series of *good lucks*. After I issue mine, I turn my attention to Tom. There's something in his eyes. I can't place it. He catches me staring and motions to his jeans. To his phone. He pulls it out and taps something.

Oh, he's texting me. I pull my phone out of my purse as inconspicuously as possible.

Tom: How was your afternoon?

Willow: Busy doing edits for Hazel. She's a taskmaster. You?

Tom: Busy thinking about what I'm going to do to you when I get you alone. Still dying to spread your legs and taste you.

My cheeks flush. I check for an audience. Nothing. Miles and Pete are swarming Drew with attention. My brother is the color of a tomato.

There's a buzzing in Tom's hands. His eyes flash with mischief. He must think it's from me. That or he's sexting some other woman. The mental image makes my stomach clench.

"Fuck." He dials a number and holds the phone to his ear. "How long... Can you get it down to three hours? Okay... Don't apologize. Shit happens... I'll figure something out." He hangs up the phone but keeps his eyes and fingers on the screen. "The flight is delayed. Could be four hours or eight."

Drew's eyes flash with concern. "I'm not missing Kara's graduation."

"I know." Tom taps his screen with concentration. "There's two tickets on the red eye but they're both in coach."

"Get the fucking tickets," Drew growls.

Tom looks to Miles. "You too?"

Miles nods.

A few more taps and the crisis is averted. Damn, that's fast. Tom really has his shit together. He gives Miles and Drew a series of instructions. They'll take the limo. We'll give the chartered flight two hours to nail down a departure time. If it stays indefinitely delayed, there's a flight with empty seats leaving at the crack of dawn tomorrow. We should arrive in time for the last half of Kara's graduation party.

The limo pulls over on a side street to drop us off. I get out first. Drew grabs Tom on his way out and whispers something in his ear.

Tom shakes his head. Drew must be getting overprotective.

Tom slides out of the car and nods goodbye to Drew. "I wouldn't expect any less from you." His fingertips brush against the back of my hand on their way to his pockets.

Drew looks at me. "Call if you have any issues."

I nod. "Good luck. I hope she says *yes*."

Drew groans and slinks back into his seat, his brows screwed with concern.

"Fuck, kid, that was harsh." Tom nudges me. "The man is already in pieces over this."

"I was trying to be encouraging."

The limo pulls away.

Pete waits until it's a dot on the horizon to address Tom. "You know what you're risking here?"

"Yeah," Tom says.

The brothers share a knowing look. I'm out of the loop again. I guess being family has its perks.

"I have something to take care of. Text me when you know the flight details and I'll meet you at the airport." Pete looks me in the eyes. "He really last twenty minutes?"

I'm sure my expression gives everything away.

Pete laughs. "Good for you." He nods goodbye then turns and leaves.

"Is that going to be a problem?" I ask.

"Nah. He doesn't even talk to me." Tom slides his arm around my waist. "Come on. I have plans for what I want to do with you."

"With me or to me?"

"First one, then the other."

———

TOM IS KNEELING AT MY FEET. IT'S A BEAUTIFUL SIGHT, close to perfection. Only we're both fully dressed and we're surrounded by a dozen families. I'm having dirty thoughts at a roller rink. I need to get a grip.

This place is the antithesis of sexy. Disco blares from the speakers. Multi-colored string lights flicker on and off. Hell, half the people here are dressed in bell-bottoms.

Yet, my thoughts stay in delicious places.

Tom ties my left skate tight. His fingers skim my exposed calf. I thank whatever inspired me to wear a skirt. Jeans would make it much harder for him to touch my bare skin.

Tom looks up at me with mischief in his eyes. He slides his fingers up the inside of my leg, over the hem of my skirt, and back down my right leg. He takes his time lacing my right skate then he pushes himself to his feet. Well, to his skates.

He's balanced perfectly.

"When did you learn to roller skate?" I ask.

He takes my hands and pulls me to my feet. "I'll tell you after you get around the rink twice."

"My balance isn't that hopeless."

"Good." He brushes his lips against my ear. "I'd love to distract you."

"You're a naughty boy."

He cups my ass as he slides his arm around my waist. "You like it."

"No comment."

"Come on. I don't want to miss the end of *Staying Alive*. My disco moves are legendary."

With one hand attached to mine, Tom skate-steps backwards to the entrance of the roller rink. He's totally effortless.

I take careful steps. I gave up my attempts to rollerblade when we moved to San Francisco. The hills made the once fun activity terrifying. I was always wobbly.

The floor of the rink is some squishy rubber thing. I'll be okay if I fall. I won't get hurt.

Taking steps is easy. Gliding is not. I squeeze Tom's hand for balance but I'm still wobbly.

Tom skates circles around me. The show-off has skills. He's damn cute with his skinny jeans tucked into retro skates.

"I won't let you fall." He sets his hands on my waist with a light touch. "Trust me."

He's talking about skating, I know, but the words cut all the way to my soul. I do trust him. It's a good thing because he's already got a vice grip on my heart.

Left leg first. I pick up my foot and try my best to slide as I place it back on the rink. That buys me about two inches. I try with my right foot. Three inches this time. I can do this. I go faster.

Faster.

Shit. My foot goes down wrong. My ankle doesn't twist. It can't. The skates are so tight that my entire leg twists. Only I don't fall face first.

Tom catches me without missing a step.

He squeezes tight. "You okay?"

I nod.

"Then hop to it, kid."

"Hopping is out of the question."

"Glide to it." He shifts backwards to give me enough room to skate.

Okay. I can glide to it. My movements start cautious. Each time, I move a little faster, glide a little farther. I get halfway around the rink before I trip. This time, I regain my balance. Well, with Tom's help.

He presses his lips to my neck. "Not sure I'll be able to distract you much at this rate."

"You're very distracting."

"This is nothing." He brings his hand to my shoulder and slides it over the neckline of my blouse.

I grab onto the edge of the rink so I'll have some chance of keeping my balance. "What is that?"

"A one."

"What's a ten look like?"

"That will get us arrested." He cups my breast over my top. "You're not wearing a bra."

I nod.

"That's naughty, teasing me like that." His thumb brushes over my nipple, pressing the fabric of my top against the bud. "I'm going to have to tease you back."

"Please do."

"Fuck, do I love the way you say that." Tom nips at my earlobe.

He rubs his thumb over me. Just once and he brings his hand back to my hips. Pangs of desire shoot to my sex. My body cries out for more. Now.

Okay, no playing nice. I try to shift my ass against his

crotch but the roller-skates make it difficult. Words will have to get me there. "Please."

"Mmm." He moves closer, kisses his way up my neck and over my ear. "This is a four."

"You have a real mouth on you, Mr. Steele."

"Not yet, kid. That will take us all the way up to an eight." He shifts, bringing our bodies to a roller rink appropriate distance.

"I've never... no one has ever done that to me."

He lets out a low groan. He brings his mouth to my ear. "It's like this. Only—" He slides one hand under my skirt and presses his palm against me.

My sex clenches with anticipation.

The warmth of his breath sends shivers down my spine. He sucks on my earlobe. Gently. Then harder. Then he's scraping his teeth against it. His tongue slides over the outside of my ear. Then just inside its first curve.

Holy shit. That's going to be intense.

Tom brings his hand back to my waist. He shows my other ear the same attention. Then his lips are on my neck, sucking and nibbling and kissing with that same perfect finesse. When he finally releases me, I'm panting.

This is a family place. I can't jump his bones right here. No matter how badly my body is begging me to unzip his jeans.

Skating. I am skating. I am not fucking Tom in public in front of forty or fifty witnesses.

I pick up my foot. Place it down. I'm more stomping than skating. With my next step, I glide. The motion is smooth. Like how seamlessly our bodies fit together—

Shit. I stumble, landing on my hands and knees. It's not too bad.

Tom kneels next to me. He smiles and brushes my hair

away from my eyes. "What happened to your concentration?"

"This guy who likes to torture me by getting me all worked up and making me wait."

"He sounds hot."

"Pretty hot."

"Pretty?" Tom helps me to my feet.

"Incredibly hot." I look into his eyes. "But he's far too aware of it."

"Vanity is one of the worst traits a person can have."

I laugh. "Besides arrogance?"

"Of course." He slides his arms around my waist. "Is he nosy too?"

"Very."

"Why is it that you put up with him?"

I press my hand against Tom's stomach. "I'm using him for his body."

"I'm sure he understands, being that obsessed with his appearance." Tom smiles.

I press my lips into his. He pulls me closer, kissing back with intensity and warmth. This is one hell of a good time, but it's also more.

His feelings pour into me. They're everything.

He pulls back and plants a kiss on my forehead. "At this rate, we're going to miss the flight."

"Is there any word on that?"

"Don't pretend like you aren't aware of everything that happens in my jeans."

"Mr. Steele, I'm not sure what you're referring to. A lady never gawks." I take a few skate-steps.

"No word yet." He places his hands on my hips, guiding me. "As soon as I hear, I'll book us a limo to the airport."

"A limo?"

He nods. "I'd explain, but it's at least a three."

Warmth fills my belly as I laugh. It's easy being with Tom. Like nothing else in the world can hurt me.

I roll my shoulders to loosen my muscles. "Okay, Master Roller Skater, let's do this."

"Let's do this, what?"

"Please."

He groans.

———

WE SPEND THE BETTER PART OF AN HOUR MAKING SLOW laps around the rink. By the sixth or seventh, I can skate without his hands on my hips or my hand on the railing. Tom tries and fails to teach me how to spin. I fall on my ass over and over again. Between the squishy floor and the way his eyes light up as my legs spread, it's hard to complain.

One more try. I hold onto his hand and attempt to twirl. No go. My left leg trips over my right. Again, I fall. This time, I land in Tom's arms.

He adjusts my balance. "You this willing to try new things when you're naked?"

"I'm not usually willing to try things."

"Why not?"

"Too much risk of getting hurt."

"What's different?"

"You." I press my body against his. "I want to do everything with you. Sexually or otherwise."

"You're stroking my ego pretty hard, kid."

A laugh escapes my lips. "I love when you call me that."

"You asked me to stop."

"Because you hurt me, Tom, running without an explanation. I didn't want a term of endearment if you were going to turn off your affection at the drop of a hat."

"It wasn't anything about you. It's me... Nobody has ever cared about me."

I stare back at Tom. "There are probably a thousand girls in love with you."

"With my stage persona, sure. Who wouldn't love that guy? He's rich, cocky, talented as fuck. Hot as hell. But that's not me. Not all of me."

"I care about you."

"Now."

"Why would I stop?"

He looks away. "You'll get tired of me. Realize I'm not that playful guy who can show you the world. That I've got my own shit to deal with."

I shake my head. "You're already showing me the world."

I stare deeply into Tom's gorgeous green eyes. There's a sadness in them. But of course there is. He's still waiting to hear if his mom is going to live or die.

"How did you get so good at skating?" I ask.

"Ophelia was in a roller derby league. She always took me and Pete to her practices. Eventually, I got tired of sitting by myself and I learned to skate."

"Him too?"

Tom nods. "Not as good as I am, of course."

"Of course."

I follow him to the rink exit. "Does she still do roller derby?"

He shakes his head. "She had to stop a while back..." His eyes cloud. "Never picked it back up."

"When she was sick?"

Tom nods. He squeezes my hand. "Life is gonna intrude on this soon enough." He leans in close enough to whisper. "Right now, I don't want to think about anything besides how good you taste."

The sounds that escape my lips are in no way words.

"Heard this amazing idea about breaking into the manager's office and getting on my knees."

I. Uh. It's really fucking hot in here. I nod. "Okay."

"Only okay?"

"Please."

He steps out of the rink then helps me onto a bench and out of my skates and into my shoes. Most of the pain is gone from his expression but there's a hint of it in his eyes.

"You have to promise something," I say.

"Don't think I've ever promised a woman anything."

"I'll pop your cherry."

Tom pulls me to my feet. "You keep saying naughty things and I won't be able to promise to spell my name."

"It's only three letters."

"Even so."

"Promise that you'll tell me about it later. About your mom and your family and being in foster care."

He nods. "I promise we'll talk on the plane. After I wear you out."

Chapter Twenty-Four

T om is a champion lock picker. All it takes is his credit card and thirty seconds of effort and the door marked *Manager's Office* is open. He leads me inside and flicks the light on.

The lock clicks behind us.

I broke into an office with a rock star.

I'm not sure what happened to the old version of Willow—the one who kept to herself and poured all of her attention into her photography—but she must be gone, because there's no way she would have done this.

Tom's hands slide to my hips. He presses me into the door, the weight of his body sinking into mine. He's so fucking warm. And he smells so damn good.

Our lips lock. Need pours between us. Desire. And something more, something deeper. At the moment, it's hard to place anything that isn't *oh hell yes*. I dig my hands into his messy hair. Sigh into his mouth. Rub my crotch into his until the friction has me groaning.

He kisses his way down my neck and over my chest. His fingers go to the buttons of my blouse. He undoes them one at a time, his fingers lingering over my exposed skin, until I'm all the way unbuttoned.

My blouse hangs at my shoulders, my breasts exposed to him.

"I like you not wearing a bra." He flicks his tongue against my nipple. "How can I convince you to make it a habit?"

"Keep doing this."

His mouth closes around my nipple and he sucks hard. The pressure is so intense my knees buckle.

"How's that?" He groans.

"Yes. I'm convinced. To do something. I forget what."

He moves to my other breast and teases it just as mercilessly.

"To swear off bras." He sucks on my nipple.

God, yes. Sensation overwhelms me. No one has ever paid my body this much attention, and he's fucking amazing.

"As long as I'm an edgy photographer, I can get away with that."

"You decide what you want to focus on yet?"

"I'm not sure I know how to spell my name at the moment."

"It's a lot more than three letters." He laughs, then he's right back to drawing circles around my nipple with his tongue.

A groan escapes my lips. "What happens if I go without panties?"

"Fuck, kid, you're giving me ideas." He pushes my skirt up. His palm presses against my sex. "I better demonstrate."

"Please do."

He groans as he slides my panties to my knees. "Say that again."

"Please." I kick my panties off my feet.

"Please what?" Tom flicks his tongue against my nipple until I'm panting.

"Just please."

I press my palm against the door to steady myself. The words echo through my brain. *Please, please, please.* Please, don't break my heart. Please, fall in love with me. Please, let me fall in love with you.

He traces the lines of my chest piece with his tongue. "I know you got this cause your heart was broken." He kisses me between my breasts. "But I still think it's sexy as all hell."

"Tom, please." I tug at his hair.

"The way you say that is fucking sexy." He kisses his way to my belly button then positions himself on his knees.

"You think I'm that sexy?"

"Fuck yes."

His lips tread lower. Lower. He traces the lie of my hipbone with his tongue. Almost.

He slides his hand up my thigh and over my sex. "This. How wet you are—"

I groan.

"That's fucking sexy." He slides his hand up my torso and teases my nipple until I'm groaning. "And that." He sucks on my inner thigh. "And this."

God, he's close.

I take a deep breath. "Tom, I..."

"I've got you, kid. All you have to do is relax and breathe." He flicks his tongue against my skin. "If you like something–" He takes my hand, places it on his shoulder, and guides me through a squeeze.

Okay. I can do that.

My eyes close as his mouth moves closer. Closer. I try to

push any insecurity out of my head. Relax and breathe. I'm breathing. I deserve partial credit.

His tongue flicks against me, and I forget everything else. My name. W-I-L. Oh. Fuck. That hardly matters.

Intense doesn't begin to describe it. His mouth is warm and wet and he moves with all the precision in the world. Hard flicks send shocks of pleasure through my torso. Soft licks build slow waves of ecstasy. My knees nearly buckle when he sucks on my lips. Holy hell.

I squeeze his shoulder. Yes. More.

Tom slides his hand around my hip and under my ass. He adjusts my leg, hooking it over his shoulder, spreading me open. He sucks on my labium until I'm wrecked with pleasure, until I'm clawing at his shoulder. Then he's at the other, moving with that same finesse.

My groans build until they're much too loud for our semi-public venue. I don't care. Arrest me. Better to go to jail for the next one hundred years than to hold back anything.

I reach for Tom's hair, pressing my fingers against the back of his head. Who knew it was possible for two people to be this close? For one person to matter more than anything else in the world.

He licks me up and down, teasing my clit with a single flick of his tongue each time. Again and again. Until I can't take it anymore.

"Please," I groan. "Please make me come."

He responds by sucking on my clit. This time, my knees do buckle. Tom pulls away. He shifts to his feet and looks me in the eyes. "You okay making a mess of that desk?"

I should care that I'm fucking up a stranger's office, but I don't. Not even a hint.

I nod. "Yes. Now. Please."

He pushes everything off the thick desk and sets me on

top of it. He guides me onto my back and spreads my knees. His lips trail up my leg. Close and closer. Until they're on me again. My eyes flutter closed. His tongue flicks against my clit, and the world clicks into place.

Fireworks everywhere. These beautiful bursts of color and light. Like a movie. Like a daydream. Like everything.

"Don't stop." I squeeze his shoulders as hard as I can.

He works me with that same rhythm, same pressure. Yes. There. I settle into the ground. Dig my heels into his back. Tighter and tighter. One more flick and I scream.

All that pressure releases as I come. An orgasm washes over me. I'm not sure I even know my name at this point. A plant of some kind. A tree. Who cares?

Tom looks up at me, the pride of accomplishment spread over his beautiful face.

"Don't have to ask if you liked it." He climbs onto the desk, kisses his way up my stomach and chest. Until he's positioned on top of me. "You okay to go again?"

"Is it you fucking me?"

He nods.

"Yes please."

He pulls his t-shirt over his head, unzips and unbuttons his jeans. "You want me to wear a condom?"

"No."

Tom strips to his boxers. His eyes meet mine. "I've never had sex without a condom."

"Really?"

He nods. "Never been in a monogamous relationship."

Relationship.

I like that word.

I love that word.

He slides his boxers to his feet.

I gawk. Every inch of him is yummy. His pierced cock is no exception.

241

Tom doesn't give me much time to ogle him. He nudges my knees apart, lifts my ass, and sets my ankles on his shoulders.

"Is this another attempt to teach me some balance?" I groan as his fingertips brush against my nipple.

"No." His other hand slides under my ass. He brings our bodies together, his cock nudging against my sex. "Just want to be as deep in you as I can."

God, yes.

He enters me slowly. It's different without the condom. Closer. He pulls back until he's only barely inside me, then thrusts into me again. Again. Again. Each time, I feel more full, more whole.

By the time he sets me back on the desk, I'm dizzy with pleasure. I let him lead. I'm too overwhelmed to do anything else. He feels so good inside me. So right.

His fingers dig into my hips, encouraging my move-ment. I rock in time with his guidance. Oh. Yes. There. The metal balls of his apadravya hit me just right. One of them anyway. It rubs against my G-spot, sending wave after wave of pleasure through my torso. It's a good thing I'm already on my back. I can barely keep my legs against his chest.

I stare back into his eyes. It's intimate, intense. This isn't fucking. It must be making love. Or whatever comes right before love.

Feelings threaten to overwhelm me. I shift my legs off his chest and wrap them around his waist. "Kiss me. Please."

He lowers his body onto mine, kissing me as he adjusts my legs. We're pressed together. It feels right, how close we are, how he taste of me, how his tongue claims my mouth.

He moves deeper. Faster. My orgasm builds quickly. It's

fast, intense. I come as he thrusts into me. My whole body is shaking.

I grab onto Tom's hair to pull him closer. He kisses harder. There's intention in it, need, everything.

He breaks our kiss to moan against my neck. I need more of that. Yes. The ears. I bring my mouth to his ears, licking and sucking until his moans get louder and more desperate. Until his motions are just as hard and desperate.

"Fuck, Willow." He sucks on my neck.

There. I can feel his body shaking, his cock pulsing as he comes inside me. When he's spent, he collapses on top of me. It takes minutes for our breath to return to normal.

Tom shifts off me. I find a box of tissues and clean up the best I can.

He gets into his boxers and jeans and checks his phone. "Two hours until departure."

"Did you have anything to do with the flight getting delayed?"

"If I could feel anything but satisfaction, I'd be hurt," he teases.

"Got rid of Drew and got us a few hours alone."

"I wish I had." He pulls his t-shirt over his head. "But that was sheer luck."

I re-button my blouse and get into my panties.

Tom taps a few things into his phone. He slides the device into his pocket and helps me up. "Come on. There's a lot to talk about."

I nod.

"And a lot I want to do to you on the way to the airport."

Chapter Twenty-Five

This limo is a little smaller and a lot less party central. No booze, no mood lighting, no stripper poles. It's plenty of room for to two to sit. Or lie.

"Pizza with vegetables on it?" Tom scrunches his nose like he smells something bad. "Really?"

"If you don't want it, get something else on your half. Just not meat. It touches."

"Okay. Red peppers, artichoke hearts, and broccoli it is." He shakes his head but taps the order into a takeout app on his phone.

"You'll like it."

"That's my line." Tom pulls me onto his lap and nods to the moon roof. "We're not in an 80s movie. Fight your urge to get up and look around."

"I don't think it's possible to be around you and have an urge to do something besides jumping your bones."

"That's an urge I can get behind. Or in front of. Or under. Or on top of."

"Or all of the above?"

"I like the way you think."

Tom presses a button to slide the roof open. The dark blue evening light falls over us. The city is too bright for stars but the moon is big and beautiful.

I lean back on the bench seat and stare at the sky. Minutes pass without conversation but the silence is comfortable.

Tom really has no idea how romantic he is. How sweet he is. He's cocky about his looks, his music, his fucking, his role as bossy band protector... about a million things. But, somehow, he can't see how lovable he is.

His hand slides into my hair. "Don't fall asleep on me."

"I'm not on you. I'm on the bench."

"Don't fall asleep until I make you come at least two more times. I hate to let a beautiful woman down."

"You can make me come," I murmur. "Just don't wake me."

"Won't be doing it right if you sleep through it."

A fair point.

He scoots closer, shifts me so my head is in his lap and he's looking down at me. "You really want me to wake you with an orgasm sometime?"

"Sometime." I stare back at him. "Not yet but sometime."

There's understanding in his eyes. He doesn't need it explained. That kind of thing is the next level of trust.

"You can wake me with sex anytime."

"You won't feel used if you wake up to me riding you senselessly?"

"Mmm. I lost my train of thought." Tom pulls me up and into his lap. He presses his lips into my neck. "Have you eaten anything since breakfast?"

"No."

"Then don't fall asleep until after dinner." He checks the time on his phone. "You skip a lot of meals?"

"When I'm preoccupied." I dig through the mini-fridge for a bottle of water. "I don't need someone reminding me to eat. I'm a big girl. I can feed myself."

He shakes his head. "Afraid I can't agree to those terms, kid."

I bite my lip. Part of me is touched by his concern. The other part is terrified of a not-quite-boyfriend asserting control over any part of my life. "I'm sure you have good intentions, but I need you to back off about looking after me. That's how things started with Bradley. At first it was little things—don't wear that dress, don't stay out late after your swim meet, don't walk home by yourself at night—until it become big things. Skipping class. Ending friend-ships. Running off from my family."

"I won't push you, won't try to control you. But there's nothing you can say to convince me not to take care of you."

Okay. That part of me that's touched is winning. I nod.

The limo pulls to a stop. The driver's door slams open and shut. A few moments later, he pulls open our door and slides something into the backseat.

A pizza box. That was fast.

Tom pulls it open and tears off a slice and offers it to me. "You really should eat. You need your strength before I exhaust you."

I take the steaming slice. It's topped with broccoli, red peppers, and artichoke hearts. He got the whole pizza the way I like it.

Tom nods goodbye to the driver and takes a bite of a slice. "That's not as bad as I was expecting."

"It's good."

He peels off a piece of broccoli, tosses it in his mouth, chews and swallows. "It's decent."

I dig into my slice. It's better than good. It's fucking

amazing. Cheesy and chewy and bursting with the rich flavor of red peppers. I talk with my mouth full. "It's great."

Tom pulls a packet of hot sauce from the box and tosses it to me.

Yes, pizza and hot sauce. I used to love eating pizza with hot sauce. It's been a million years since I've enjoyed a meal this much. It's been a million years since I've enjoyed anything as much as I enjoy being around him.

I tear open the hot sauce and douse my slice in spice. "Thank you. For the pizza. And—"

"Don't worry about thanking me for the orgasms, kid. More than happy to oblige."

My cheeks flush.

"And there's more where that came from." He nods to my slice. "As soon as you're done eating."

———

I come four times in the limo. True to his word, Tom gets behind me, in front of me, under me, and on top of me. By the time we arrive at the airport, I'm completely out of energy. Thank goodness we don't have to go through security. Hanging out with a rock stars has its perks. The private jet is a new one.

It's amazing. Room for about ten people, big cushy seats, a widescreen TV with a massive collection of films. It's almost a shame that it's well past by bedtime.

The pilot, a slight man with a charming British accent, introduces himself with an apology for the delay, then gets into the cockpit. We're scheduled to depart in half an hour. Pete is yet to arrive but has sent word he's on his way.

I get cozy in a corner seat, ready to sleep until we land. But there's something about Tom's expression that won't allow me to relax. He's on edge. Worried. About his brother or about something else?

"You okay?" I ask.

"Yeah. Just... should have asked Pete where he was going. He wouldn't have told me, but... I was a little distracted."

"You really love him."

"He's my brother."

"That doesn't have to mean anything." I shift closer to Tom. "I don't love my parents. Not anymore."

His gaze goes to the window.

He must have been through a lot ending up in foster care. I want to know everything there is to know about Tom but I'm not sure either one of us is ready to go back to those dark places.

I change the subject to something easier to discuss. "How did we end up on a private jet?"

"It belongs to the label. We're probably their third or fourth most popular artist. We only get offered it when the VP is in a giving mood."

"Who gets it first?"

Tom shrugs. "Some pop star who sings about being a bad girl."

"All pop stars sing about being bad girls."

"Not Taylor Swift."

"You're a fan?"

He shakes his head. "Not my kind of music. You?"

"If fits a certain *men are shit, they need to stop doing me wrong* mood." The words echo in my head again. *Please don't break my heart.*

"The VP and I have had some tense conversations. Don't think he likes anybody in the band except Pete, and that's only cause he wants in Pete's pants."

"Oh. He's gay?"

"Bisexual. In his case, it means he has twice the potential sexual harassment victims. Gives other bisexual people a bad name."

"Did you fight about that?"

Tom shakes his head. "Our manager."

"The asshole?"

His face lights up. "You remembered?"

"Of course."

"A few years back, he was involved in our day to day. Back then Miles partied pretty hard. Mostly slamming vodka shots and fucking a different girl every night. Seemed normal. We were all excited to be playing big enough shows to feel like rock stars."

"I can't imagine you as anything but a rock star."

Tom smirks. "I always had the ego and the drive. But I had those moments during our first tour when we were packed into a van, playing for two-dozen bored people, sleeping on the floor, eating fast food off the dollar menu. Moments where I asked myself if it was worth it."

"Was it?"

"Yeah. Didn't really have much to go home to. Just my mom. She would have told me to suck it up and get back to chasing my dreams. Not to be cruel but because she knew I'd never forgive myself if I quit."

"She sounds amazing."

"She is." His expression hardens. Back to someplace ugly.

I clear my throat. We can't go there yet. "So, you were partying like rock stars and..."

"It became pretty obvious that Miles had a problem. And it only got worse once the label rented us this mansion in Hollywood and Miles got caught up in the party scene. Aiden was always pulling Miles out of meetings for some BS reason or another. One day I caught them doing coke.

Aiden's, of course. Miles was never really into being up but then he'd do anything to not be in his head."

"How come I've never read a tabloid story about Miles using? Or going to rehab?"

"You follow gossip?"

"There could be something about Drew. I'd be a bad sister not to follow it."

Tom laughs. "You won't believe me."

"Try me."

"A few almost popped up but I persuaded the journalists to change the conversation."

"To?"

"Those leaked nude pictures."

"You leaked them to keep your friend's addiction a secret?"

"And to fuel my massive ego. Turned out to be a great move."

"I never looked at them."

He raises a brow. "We have wifi on the plane."

"I'll keep that in mind."

He smiles. "After I dealt with the press, I asked Aiden, very nicely—"

"I don't buy that for a second."

"Threatening to break someone's legs when you want to kill them is nice."

I laugh.

"Asked him nicely to stop with the coke. When he didn't, I pulled strings—"

"Was that more fighting and threats of violence?"

"Mostly. Might have involved some blackmail too."

"Might have?"

"I owe it to the blackmailed to keep that a secret," he teases. "Nothing could get him fired. He's somebody's fuck up nephew. So I had a polite conversation with Aiden—"

"Polite conversation?"

"Very polite."

"Did you hit him?"

"Just once. I know you hate violence—"

"The asshole was enabling your friend. You were upset. It happens."

"You shouldn't cut me slack, kid. I like that you stick to your principles. Won't forgive myself if you sacrifice them for me." Tom looks into my eyes. "Told him he could keep the title and the money, but I would take over his job. And that if I saw him again his nose would be broken so bad he'd never snort shit again. Coward got lost right away. Only shows up when it's strictly necessary."

"That must be a lot of work."

Tom shrugs. "He never did it right anyway."

"Why don't you take credit for running the band?"

"What's it matter who takes credit? Miles would have done the same thing for me. Once he got clean and got his head out of his ass." Tom runs a hand through his hair. "I should have confronted him sooner. I let him go on using for ever."

"He's an adult. You didn't let him do anything."

"Knowing someone needs help and doing nothing is just as bad as being the asshole pushing drugs on him. I knew Miles was gonna die, sooner or later, if nobody stepped up."

"You really believe that?"

He looks at me like I have two heads. "Of course."

"Not many people think that way."

"It's nothing. Should have given him an ultimatum a lot sooner. Truth is, I didn't want to threaten him with expulsion from the band. Miles is the face of Sinful Serenade. We wouldn't be where we are if girls didn't go apeshit for his tortured voice and his pretty blue eyes."

"But you did give him an ultimatum."

"Eventually. He still hates me for it. But that's better than him dying in some hotel room by himself." Tom's expression hardens.

He has no idea how much he's willing to sacrifice for his friends.

"You are a good guy," I whisper in his ear.

"Just getting shit done."

He really believes that.

But I don't. "When Miles was using, who was the person who pushed him to get clean? Was it Drew or Pete or was it you?"

"They wanted it too."

"But were they willing to let Miles hate them for it?"

"We were all in agreement. When he was fucking shit up with Meg too. We all agreed we couldn't watch him destroy himself. It was nothing. Selfish even."

"Do you really believe that?"

Tom shrugs.

But he's not selfish. Selfish guys don't make sure you come three times for every one time they do. Selfish guys don't order pizza they don't like to make you happy.

And selfish guys don't risk their livelihoods to help a friend in need.

I try to think up some way to convince him but I'm interrupted by Pete's arrival. I cross my fingers that he'll be perfect evidence of how much Tom does for the band, for his friends.

No luck.

Pete's got a black eye and bruised knuckles.

Chapter Twenty-Six

The plane is silent. Pete and Tom stare at each other but say nothing.

We taxi, take off, and get all the way to cruising altitude before either of the Steele brothers breaks the silence.

"I'm going to sleep. Do whatever you want to do, just keep it on that side of the plane." Pete brandishes a pair of noise-canceling headphones.

"Three questions," Tom says.

"Fine."

"You kill anyone?"

"No." Pete untangles his headphones.

"Assault?"

"He threw the first punch. He won't press charges and nobody took a picture. Shit won't end up online. You can back off."

"I don't care about the gossip."

Pete shakes his head like he finds this implausible.

Tom looks his brother in the eyes. "Who was it?"

"Kyle."

Tom's brow screws in confusion. "Thought you guys were still tight."

"Things change."

Tom's voice softens. "What happened?"

"She's been fucking him."

"What?"

"For six months, give or take." Pete's expression goes cold. "He met to beg me for forgiveness."

Clarity fills Tom's eyes. "That's bullshit."

"Why is that bullshit?" I immediately regret the words. I shouldn't get involved. This is personal and I'm not part of the family.

Pete looks at me. "Anyone ever do you wrong?"

That's an understatement. I nod. "Yeah."

"Man or woman?" Pete asks.

"Man," I say.

"Did he ask you to forgive him?" Pete asks.

I nod.

"How did you feel? Like he was really sorry and hoped his apology would help you move on? Or like he was full of shit and wanted you to absolve his guilt?"

I've never thought about it that way, but no one has every apologized to me like they really wanted me to move on. It's always an attempt to absolve their guilt. "The latter."

"Did you forgive him?"

"No, but I told him I did."

"You shouldn't have. You should have let the guilt eat away at him until he couldn't fucking breathe." Pete directs his gaze to the window. "You earn forgiveness. You don't get engaged."

Concern creeps into Tom's expression. "You're fucking with me."

Pete's voice is flat and lifeless. "Nope."

"What could she possibly see in Kyle?" Tom. asks. "You're richer, hotter, funnier, smarter—"

"They're in love." Pete's voice fills with disdain. "They couldn't help it."

"She cheated on you?" I ask.

He nods.

"I'm sorry," I say.

Pete expression is blank. "Should have ended it a while ago."

"She doesn't deserve you," Tom says.

But that's not what Pete needs.

I shift into the seat next to Tom and whisper into his ear. "Reminding him of that is only going to make it hurt worse."

Tom swallows hard. He brings his mouth to my ear. "Gotta do something."

"You should leave him alone," I say.

"You guys know I can see you, right?" Pete shakes his head. "If you're gonna whisper, whisper about the things you want to do to each other. I'm fine. Tom, you should worry about yourself for once."

"I don't worry," Tom says.

Pete rolls his eyes. "Hope you're taking this seriously. Cause Denton will fucking kill you if you're just playing around."

"I know."

"One hundred percent chance he leaves the band if you fuck this up," Pete says.

"I'm not a possession or a child. Why don't I get a say in this?" I fold my arms over my chest. I hate that I'm pouting, but I've had enough of being protected.

"You want a say, talk to your brother. How would you like him fucking your best friend and keeping it a secret from you?" Pete asks.

A fair counter-argument.

"Pete." Tom's voice wavers.

"It's fine."

"You were with her six years. How can it be fine?"

"I don't need your help, Sticks." Pete pulls his hoodie over his head and turns to face away from us.

It's about as final as it gets.

Tom gets out of his seat and goes back to pacing. He can't stand doing nothing. That much is obvious.

The feeling spreads to me. It sucks having your heart broken. It's worse when you can't admit it, to yourself or to someone else. I look around the small plane for something I can do to help. I find a set of pillows and blankets. It's not much but it's something.

I sit next to Pete and offer him one of each.

He nods a thank you. "Do me a favor and keep Tom busy. Even if it means fucking him. I've got a massive headache and his voice is driving me bonkers."

"Sure."

"He likes you a lot," Pete says.

"How can you tell?" I ask.

"He didn't offer to kill Kyle."

I laugh. "You have a good sense of humor about things."

"Didn't have much of a choice growing up." He turns his back to me. "I'd offer to talk to Drew but we've never really seen eye to eye about anything."

"That's okay. Just keep this a secret until I figure out how to tell him," I say.

"As much as I like to fuck with Tom, I'd never betray his trust." Pete nods.

Tom is on the other side of the plane. On a love seat. I go to him, slide my hands around his shoulders and press my lips into his neck.

"He'll be okay," I say.

Tom nods. "Wish he wasn't taking after me, getting into fights. My mom is gonna kill me."

"I want to hear more about her."

"I'm not sure I want to talk right now."

"Then hold me for five minutes. Please."

A small groan escapes his lips.

Ah, it's the magic word. I whisper in his ears. "Please."

"You keep saying that and I'm gonna get hard."

"That isn't a problem for me."

"You know Pete likes to watch. Or at least to listen."

I shrug. "So let him listen."

"Damn. You really are naughty." He brings his body behind mine. "Never held anybody this much."

"Is it bad?"

"No." His voice is a whisper. "Different."

My eyes flutter closed. It's late. It would be easy to fall asleep in Tom's arms. It would be just as easy to give in to the lust building between my legs, kick off my panties, and pull him on top of me. But I can still feel the uneasiness in his body. He needs somebody. He might not realize it, but he does.

I won't let myself believe he needs me. Not yet. Not even if I already need him.

"Are you going to see your Mom while we're in Los Angeles?" I ask.

"Yeah. Day after tomorrow. She lives in Tustin. It's about an hour drive from our place in Hollywood. I wanted to go straight there but she's really insistent about us not giving up anything for her. Even Kara's graduation party. All due respect to Kara—she's a sweet girl—but Ophelia's a lot more important to me." His voice wavers. "Of course, in her infinite stubbornness she told me she'll be out all day, with her ex. The one who hates me. Supposedly, she'd prefer me not being there anyway."

"Do you believe her?"

"Yeah. She'll do anything to get her way. But it's not out of malice. She always knows what we need."

"Sounds like you."

"I learned a lot from her." He nods. "Should have seen us fighting over me dropping out of school. Wasn't like I planned it. Just didn't take her getting sick too well. She was the first person who thought I was something other than a piece of shit."

There's something about his voice, a vulnerability. I squeeze his hand, offering whatever comfort I can.

He's quiet for a minute. When he breaks the silence, his voice wavers. Like he's not sure if he should share his secret. "My dad was never in the picture. My biological mom was a drug addict who let her boyfriend beat me when he came down from his high. A teacher picked up on it when I was eleven, then the state stepped in. Must have been in four or five foster homes before Ophelia. All the families were the same. Thought I was some no good punk. I was. Got into fights with the other kids, hit people, got suspended. Only thing I didn't do was drugs."

I turn to face him. There's an ocean of pain in his eyes. It sinks into my skin, as real as my own. I never want him to hurt again. That's impossible, I know, but I need to be there the next time he hurts, to ease his pain however I can.

I wrap my arms around Tom. It must do something to comfort him because his posture relaxes. He leans into my touch.

"Ophelia was the first person who saw past that. The only person. I didn't know how I could ever live in a world that didn't include her. I went on some stupid drinking and fighting tear to convince myself I'd be fine without her."

"What happened?"

"Didn't work. I held it together at home but I was a wreck the rest of the time. Would say I was going to school but I'd go to this practice space instead and I'd play until I was too tired to feel anything." He rubs his cheek against mine. "When she found out, she refused to let me take her to the hospital for her treatments until I got back in school. Refused to update me on how she was doing. Threatened to write specific instructions into her will to ban me from the funeral. She's always had a dark sense of humor."

"She didn't want to be a burden to you."

He nods. "Only time in my life I ever compromised was getting my GED to please her." He pulls me closer. "If the cancer's back, that's it. They don't have a way to treat it."

"That must be terrifying."

"Yeah."

"Can I come with you?" I ask. "When you see her?"

"I appreciate the thought, kid, but it's not a good idea."

"Why not?" I bite my lip. "I care about you. I want to be there for you."

Tom shakes his head. He pushes off the couch and plops in a seat by himself. "I'm gonna try and get some sleep."

He pulls a blanket to his chest and reclines his seat.

And that's it.

End of conversation.

Chapter Twenty-Seven

After the flight lands, we take a cab to Tom and Pete's place in Hollywood. It's a huge house, the kind that belongs on an episode of *Cribs*. The main room has a tall ceiling and a curving staircase straight out of *Sunset Boulevard*. There's a big backyard behind it, complete with a shining blue pool.

It's Southern California celebrity perfection.

Pete excuses himself to his room. Tom sits me on the couch and presses his lips into my neck.

It's as soft and sweet as it was yesterday but it feels different. Fuller and emptier at once.

"I'll make coffee." He steps backwards. "We have an hour before we have to leave. You can take the shower down here or the one in my room."

"You have a shower in your room?"

Tom smiles smugly. "I got the master bedroom."

"How did you pull that off?"

He shrugs nonchalantly. There's no pain in his eyes. Is he hiding it from me or from himself? I try to convince myself that he's feeling better because of my epic comforting skills, but the suggestion falls flat. His mom might be dying. That kind of pain doesn't go away because of a hug and a nice night of sleep.

I find the downstairs bathroom and take a long, hot shower. I'm not ready to face the onslaught of feelings that come with being in the same room as Tom so I take my sweet, sweet time changing into my party dress and doing my makeup.

I'm almost finished when there's a soft knock on the door.

"Why do I feel like you're avoiding me?" Tom asks.

"Just getting ready."

"You want coffee? We have almond milk."

"Okay."

"It's already waiting on the counter." He taps the door. "There's plenty of snacks in the fridge if you're hungry. Our housekeeper makes sure the kitchen is full of food whenever we'll be home."

I press my fingers into the door at the places he's tapping, so the thick plaster is between is. "No. I'm not hungry."

"Is there something exciting in the bathroom or are you ready to admit you're avoiding me?"

I don't know what to say here. I unlock the door and step into the main room.

Tom is all cleaned up in slacks and a button down shirt. Damn, does he look good cleaned up. Just as sexy as he does in his usual tattooed bad boy jeans and t-shirt.

Tom's eyes scan my body. "You look fucking hot."

"Thanks."

His gaze goes to my chest. "Tell me you're not wearing panties either."

"Either?"

"You're not wearing a bra."

"How do you know?"

"Your nipples are hard."

"It's cold."

"It's almost eighty degrees outside and the windows are open." He gives me a thorough once-over. "Don't tell me. It will be even harder not to touch you in front of Drew." Tom shakes his head. "Never thought I'd be this disappointed to go to a party."

"You really like having sex with me."

"Fuck, yes." Tom pulls me into the kitchen and hands me a cup of coffee. "Why does that sound accusatory?"

"It's not."

He looks at me carefully. "You want eggs?"

I nod.

"Well, you'll have to wait until we can pick something up. I can't cook for shit."

I laugh. "You're a tease."

"Thank you."

I take a long sip of my coffee. It's good—dark, nutty, creamy, and sweet at once—but that doesn't make this easier. "Why don't you want me to come with you to see your mom?"

Tom runs a hand through his hair. He doesn't say anything. There's all this pain in his eyes. Confusion too. "Need some time to think."

"About what?"

"Can't exactly explain it."

"I don't want to add to your frustration," I say. "I'm sure there's a lot on your mind, with your mom. I don't want to make that harder for you."

"You don't, kid."

I stare back into his eyes. They're earnest. But then why doesn't he want me there? I take a deep breath. My lack of sleep isn't helping me find clarity in the situation.

"We can talk about this, about what it is, after you see your mom."

He looks at me for a while. "If you're sure that's what you want."

I'm already loving the idea. I don't want to add to *my* frustration either. I want a fun night with Tom in Los Angeles. I want everything to feel easy and effortless again.

I finish my coffee and set the cup on the end table. "Positive."

He presses his lips to my neck. "If I see you frowning, I'm going to use every tool at my disposal to get a different expression on your face."

"Like..."

He runs his hands over my chest. "This." Then down my sides and along the hem of my skirt. "This." He pulls me closer so his erection is pressed against my crotch. "This."

"This?" I press my lips into his.

"No. Like this." He slides his hand around the back of my neck and pulls me into a long, deep kiss.

I see fireworks. Even as I pull back and open my eyes.

"Oh," I breathe.

There are footsteps upstairs.

"We don't have twenty minutes," Pete says. "Either make it a quickie or find another ride to Kara's."

I laugh.

Tom shakes his head, but he untangles our bodies.

———

THE PARTY IS IN FULL SWING WHEN WE ARRIVE. KARA practically bounces over to us. Hard to tell what her legs are doing under her royal blue dress. She always looks picture perfect, but today she's especially glowing and glamorous.

"I can't believe it, but I actually missed you two." Kara smiles.

She pulls Tom into a hug before he can escape. He grimaces. Slowly, he accepts the hug. Pete doesn't take it much better.

Kara turns to me. "How are you doing, Willow?"

"Good. Except for the jet lag," I say.

She takes a long look at me. "Hmm. Yes. I bet it was the flight keeping you up late." Her gaze goes to Tom. "Not anything else."

Tom shrugs *who me?*

Kara nods *yes, you*. She shakes her head in a teasing way.

"Congrats on your degree," Pete says. "We got you something—"

Tom cuts in, handing her a blue gift bag stuffed with yellow paper. "You'll like it."

"Aw, thanks guys. It's even in my school colors." Her expression fills with affection. "You didn't have to do that."

"We did." Tom winks. "Drew can thank us later."

Kara blushes. "Oh, lord. Tell me it's not inappropriate."

Tom feigns innocence.

Kara peeks inside the bag. Her cheeks turn red. She pulls the gift from the bag, showing off a naughty teacher lingerie set.

"Don't worry. We got Meg one too. Had to special order a doctor outfit. It's all naughty nurses." Tom folds his arms with outrage. "Can you believe the sexism?"

Kara throws him some serious side eye. She points to a table stocked with food and drinks. "Be a gentleman for once in your life, Tom, and pour my girl Willow a drink."

Tom stays put.

Kara puts her arms on her hips. "Go." She nods to Pete. "You too."

The boys do as they are told. Tom motions for me to follow. I take my time filling a plate with snacks. There's a lot of food here. Fruit, veggies, chips, cakes and cookies, a platter of sushi. I fill up on avocado rolls and watermelon.

Tom's hand brushes against mine. It sends a jolt of electricity straight to my core. My body wakes up with all kinds of demands about where and how it wants him.

"You want a drink?" He holds up a bottle of tequila. "There's only tequila, but the way Kara and Meg moan over their grapefruit and tequilas, you'd think that was the drink called a screaming orgasm."

"No, I'm okay."

"You sure?"

I nod.

He sets the bottle down. "Then I'll hold off."

"You don't have to stay sober for me."

"I know." He runs his fingertips over my lower back as he leans in to whisper. "I have better uses for my mouth."

Oh my.

"Guessing I can't talk you into sneaking upstairs." His fingers brush my ass, over my dress. "You're not wearing panties, are you?"

"I'm not."

He lets out the most delicious groan.

My mind fills with all sorts of beautiful ideas. How is it I'm tempted to sneak upstairs? I shouldn't be this willing to bend to my body's demands. Not when there's so much at stake.

But damn do I want Tom pressed against me, those delicious groans of his filling my ears as he comes.

Fuck, it's hot in here. Black was a poor choice. Even if

this dress is the sexiest thing I own. Even if it's what I was wearing that night when Tom and I had sex and the world finally made sense again.

My cheeks flush. But not from Tom's words or his proximity. No. There's this strange feeling in my stomach. Someone is watching. I scan the room. Sure enough, Kara has her eyes on us. She's talking to an older woman in a suit—must be her mom—but she's looking at us.

She raises a brow.

I shrug, denying whatever it is she's accusing me of.

She turns back to her conversation partner and excuses herself gracefully. Shit, she's walking this way.

Tom nods a goodbye and makes himself scarce. As if that will help dampen the flames of suspicion. Oh well, Kara isn't the type to snitch. Even if her loyalty lies with Drew.

She grabs a plate and fills it with grapes. "You and Tom are hanging out a lot."

I pour myself a large glass of fruit juice. "Why does that fascinate everyone?"

"Tom has never hung out with a girl in his life. Besides me or Meg and that's only when the other guys are around."

I shrug. Nothing to see here except a girl in a slinky black dress and fuck me heels drinking her apple juice.

"I'll be with you guys the rest of the tour." She looks me in the eyes. "Meg too."

"That will be fun."

She leans closer. "I'm on your side. Whatever you're doing and whatever you decide. Drew has gotten better with his, ahem, caveman violence. He has good intentions, but he's especially prone to overreacting when it comes to you."

"Yeah."

"I don't think he'd kill Tom, but it could be ugly if it catches him off guard. Do you understand me?"

"Yes." I understand her, and I understand Pete. I understand that I am somehow responsible for Drew's inability to accept that I am an adult woman with desires. "With all due respect, Kara, Drew freaking out over me having consensual sex is not my problem."

Her eyes turn down. "I'm sorry. You're right. I don't have any siblings. I don't really know how much you guys tell each other." She press her lips together. "I worry about Drew. He gets kinda tense dealing with the celebrity thing for three months straight. I know he doesn't want be that guy everyone else is on edge around."

I will myself to stay righteous, but her concern for Drew is touching.

"As a favor to me, be careful. Tell him before someone else does," she says.

That's a fair enough request. "Okay."

Her eyes go to my chest. Huh? Is my brother's girl-friend checking me out? That's totally bizarre.

"You're brave, getting a tattoo on your chest," she says.

Oh. That makes more sense. "Thank you. It felt right, getting it over my heart."

"It looks great." She lowers her voice. "Can I ask you something completely inappropriate?"

I nod.

"How is Tom? I've always wondered."

First Pete, now Kara. At this rate, everyone will know Tom and I are fucking by tomorrow night.

"Sorry. That was rude." She takes a step backwards. "As good as his cockiness would suggest?"

"You know how he plays like a crazy, frantic animal? And he pushes people around like he's a wrecking ball?"

Her eyes fill with interest. She nods *go on*.

"Nothing like that." I take a long sip of my drink. "He's tender. Attentive. I'm sure some of it is that I... he has to be careful with his new piercing."

"His what?"

I whisper a quick breakdown of Tom's piercing in Kara's ear.

"Holy fuck." Her hand goes to her mouth. "Is that good?"

"Amazing."

"Never would have guessed."

"Never would have guessed what?" Drew steps up to us.

He's wearing a suit and his hair is slicked back. I haven't seen him in a suit since my high school graduation. That was probably the last time my parents, Drew, and I were all in the same room.

"Mmmm." Kara tugs at his suit jacket. "I could get used to you wearing this thing."

"You can't distract me, Kendrick."

She strokes his tie as if to prove how thoroughly she can distract him. It works remarkably well. Within moments, he's panting.

She looks back to me. "Meet us for brunch tomorrow. Around noon. I'll text you the address."

"You staying here, Wil?" Drew barely gets the words out.

Okay. It's a safe enough time to tease him. "No, I'm going to pick up some guy and go back to his place."

"Very funny." He growls.

Kara sucks on his earlobe and the growl turns into a purr.

She releases him and pushes him towards the action. "Excuse us."

He follows her like a puppy following his owner.

271

God, they're cute. It's remarkable how good she is for him. Drew is a different person around her. Not the sullen, quick to anger loner who avoids everything besides his guitar, but a guy who cares about his friends. I hope she says yes. I can't imagine him ever being okay without her.

My gaze goes to Tom. A college-aged woman, must be one of Kara's friends, gushes at him. She squeezes his arm and my stomach clenches. He's already got my heart. But is he going to smash it or piece it back together?

His eyes catch mine. He motions to the stairs as if to suggest *should we*? God, am I tempted. I shake my head *no* anyway and try my best to mingle.

Kara's friends are nice but I'm not really the party type. After a solid hour of introductions and small talk, I find a seat on the couch by myself. It's bright. Sometime in the mid-afternoon. I lean back and soak in the sun. Only so much gets through the windows. Well, Drew wouldn't want me to hold back. I unlock the door to the backyard and step outside.

The small pool shines in a brilliant shade of aqua. I sit down, slide out of my heels, and dip my toes in the water.

Deep breaths do nothing to clear my head. My feelings for Tom already go far beyond like. There's no rush to label things. In theory. We're monogamous. We'll be together, more or less, the rest of the tour. And I can go wherever I want after that. I can even set up a studio in Los Angeles.

There's no reason why I need a label, but I want one. My feelings burn a hole through my gut. He might never love me. When I give him my heart, he might smash it into a million little pieces.

There are footsteps coming towards me. Then Tom's voice.

"Hey, kid. Cooling off?"

"Yeah."

"Drew and Kara left a while ago." He sits next to me and runs a hand through my hair. "I convinced Pete to take a cab back home."

"Oh."

"You want to go out or you want to go back to my place?"

I push myself to a seated position and look Tom in the eyes. All those feelings well up inside me. But I'm not ready to hand over my heart yet. Not right now.

Right now, I'm only giving him my body.

"Depends," I say.

"On?"

"Do you really wear a speedo?"

"Better."

I slide into my shoes and push myself to my feet. "That, I have to see."

Chapter Twenty-Eight

That is much better than a speedo.

I lean back in my lounge chair so I can gawk properly. The soft orange glow of sunset falls over Tom's shaggy hair, his broad shoulders, his sculpted abs, the tiny scrap of fabric posing as a swimsuit. A thong swimsuit.

He turns to show off his toned ass. He's like a sculpture, all hard and defined. And he's on display for me.

"Do you wear that in public?" My words are punctuated with deep sighs of pleasure. It's hard to talk when he's wearing such a small amount of clothing. There's no way he dons that on the beach. It would cause a mob scene. Even without his celebrity.

"I have."

"Did you get arrested?"

"No." He takes a step towards me. "Garnered a lot of attention."

"I'll bet."

"Willow, my eyes are up here."

"Uh-huh." My gaze stays glued to the so-called swimsuit. Why do men wear board shorts? This is much better than a pair of board shorts.

"You're going to make me feel like a piece of meat."

"I'm a vegetarian."

"Not sure that's relevant, kid."

Finally, I look up into Tom's gorgeous green eyes. They're wide, enthusiastic. He delights in teasing me. Can't say I have any cause for complaint.

I manage to hold his gaze. "If you were a piece of meat, I wouldn't be interested."

"Is that so?"

I nod. "I lo—like you for your personality."

"I didn't realize my personality was between my legs."

I laugh. "Not many people do."

"Is that where your personality is?"

I nod.

He kneels in front of my lounge chair and pulls my legs towards the edge. "Better investigate this claim."

He runs his finger up the inside of my calf, slowing as he reaches my inner thigh. My body hums from his touch. I don't stand a chance.

Tom pushes my skirt up my thighs, one inch at a time. "You *aren't* wearing panties." He pushes the skirt to my waist. "Fuck, I love it when you're naughty." He nibbles on my inner thigh.

He moves closer. Closer. So fucking close but not quite there. Yes. This is exactly what I need. No thinking. No tomorrow. Just his body and mine creating a lightening storm of pleasure.

I dig my hands into his hair. "Please."

"Say it again."

"Please, Tom. I need you."

So much for just our bodies. The feeling crashes into

me. I need him. I need him every way it's possible to need a person.

I love him.

Easy to love someone when his head is planted between your legs, but I don't have a single doubt I'll feel the same way tomorrow.

I reach for something that won't overwhelm me. "What if Pete comes home?"

"He won't."

"But what if he does?"

"He won't. But if he does then he'll see me making you come. Hmm..." He pushes my dress up my torso and over my head. "Let's try for three times.""

"Right now?"

"Unless that gets in the way of your plans." He flicks his tongue against my nipple. "We can take this to my room if you're feeling shy."

"Tom, I—" I bite my tongue. Nope. Not saying that yet. Not with us nearly naked. "I need you."

He groans into my skin. His kisses lower. Lower. Then his mouth is on me. Pleasure spreads to my fingers and toes. I'm already so keyed up I want to scream. I'm not sure how I'll survive three orgasms but I'm more than game to try.

I press my fingers against the back of his head, spreading my legs to give him as much access as he needs. The intimacy of it overwhelms me. We're close. It's like I really am giving myself to him.

He works his way up my sex, plants one feather light flick against my clit, then back to the bottom to start again. And again. And again. I lose track after ten. I'm already throbbing with desire.

"Tom, please." I rock my hips to press against his face. "I need to come."

He teases again. Again. Three. Four. Then his tongue is on my clit. No more teasing. He works me with hard, fast strokes.

I squeeze his shoulders and he goes harder. Faster.

"Yes," I breathe. "Please don't stop."

He licks me again and again. Until the pressure in my core knots tight and unfurls in a deep, intense orgasm. I groan his name again and again as I come.

Tom drags his lips up and down my inner thighs. My whole body shudders with after shakes. I'm so fucking sensitive that his teeth scraping against my skin is enough to make me groan.

And then he's licking me again. I relax into the lounge chair, spreading my legs wider. For a split second, my eyes flutter open. Everything about this is fucking beautiful. The light of the sunset dancing off the pool. The clean concrete. The flowers that line the backyard. The almost-a-mansion house behind us.

Tom looks up at me, this delicious mix of desire and mischief and satisfaction in his eyes.

My lids press together. It's too much to take. The rest of the world falls away until I'm nothing but the pleasure building inside me. More and more until I overflow with another orgasm.

This time, Tom doesn't relent. He sucks on my clit until I'm screaming. I dig my hands into his hair as he works me. It's intense. Almost too intense. But not quite.

My orgasm is hard and fast. One knot of tension, then it's all unraveling, flowing through me.

I pull him off by the hair. I expect a complaint but he smiles with the pride of a job well done.

"Three seemed about right." He presses his lips against my knee.

"You're amazing." I sink into the chair, still lost in a daze of bliss.

"I know." He kisses his way down my shin, over my foot. "Come on. I need to get wet."

"I'm not sure I can take any more sensation."

I pry my eyelids apart. When I look back to Tom, he's already gone in the pool.

His swimsuit on the concrete.

————

WE SWIM IN CIRCLES AS THE SUN SETS. ORANGE BLEEDS across the sky, casting the house in a beautiful glow. It sinks lower, the sky goes red, then the sun is gone, swallowed up by the horizon, and everything is a serene shade of indigo.

It's quiet here. Much more quiet than what I imagined.

Tom slides his arms around me. We're still naked, and he's still as sexy as the day is long, but there's more to the gesture than heat. There's affection. Love.

The words already want out of my throat. But I can't say them now, not with all this weight hanging around his shoulders. I press my eyelids together and soak in the feeling of Tom's chest against my back, his neck against my cheek. His skin is soft but his muscles are hard. I can feel them flexing against me as he shifts his weight, as he breathes.

Love might chase him away. Might end this for good. And then I'll have to spend the next month as miserable as I was at the last show. The pictures I took were total shit. I can't do that. I can't waste this opportunity.

Okay, I'm scared. I'm looking for excuses. I'm the one who told him this relationship was worth the risk of getting hurt. Maybe the words can wait. Maybe they don't matter as much as being with him.

"You're off someplace," Tom says. "Good or bad?"

Both. I turn around and stare into his gorgeous green eyes. Can my gaze say it for me? I try. *I love you.* Nothing in his expression changes. It's that same intense affection.

Screw the eyes. I let my lids flutter together and raise to my tip toes to kiss him. His lips are chapped from swimming all afternoon. He tastes like chlorine. And like Tom.

His kiss is that same intense affection. When it breaks, I can barely breathe. That wasn't enough. I need to tell him. *I love you, Tom.* I practice it in my head, but I can't do it. Not today.

Not tomorrow.

Not until after he knows whether or not his mom is going to be okay.

It's an excuse, I know, but it feels right.

Tom cups my cheek. "You hungry?"

"Yeah." Now that I think about it, I'm starving.

He leads me to the pool's steps and helps me out. "Let's order something. You want Indian or Thai?"

"Let's cook."

"Not sure we have much actual food. Mostly it's snacks. There hasn't been much cooking since Miles and Drew moved out."

"They used to live here?"

"Yeah." Tom leads me into the kitchen. He nods to the ceiling above the fridge. "Technically, that's still Miles's room." He points to the ceiling on the other side of the room. "And that's still Drew's. Our label rented this place for us way back when. Whoever was in charge of kicking us out forgot to do it."

"You live here rent free?" I ask.

He wraps his arms around me. "Yeah."

"Damn. Rock stars get all the breaks."

"You can stay here. If you decide to move to Los Angeles after the tour."

I look up into his eyes. "Really?"

"Yeah... till you find your own place."

Oh. I don't expect him to invite me to move in with him. We've only been in a not even official relationship for a few days.

I break his hug. Damn, where is my dress? I can't have this conversation naked. I excuse myself to the living room, find my suitcase, and change into the first acceptable outfit I can put together—a skirt and a tank top, underwear but no bra.

Tom follows me into the living room. He leans against the wall, utterly comfortable with his lack of clothing, and stares at me.

"What's going on, kid? What are you thinking?"

"You're naked."

"I can see how that would be distracting."

Yes, that's it. I'm distracted. Nothing more. I nod.

"Asking me to put on my clothes for once. That's new." His lips curl into a smile. "But anything for you."

He's teasing. The mood is light. I can't ruin that. It feels good joking with Tom. Everything with Tom feels good.

God, I love him so much. It eclipses everything.

Tom's eyes connect with mine. His gaze is penetrating. Maybe I was wrong about my eyes. Maybe he can see how much I love him.

"You sure you're okay?" he asks.

I nod.

He accepts my answer and makes his way upstairs to dress. I use the time to dig through the kitchen. It's clean and stocked with pots, pans, oils, spices. Aside from a little fruit and several different kinds of dairy and non-dairy milk, there's nothing in the way of fresh food. We'll have to go to the store if we want to cook anything beyond a TV dinner.

Tom's footsteps make their way down the stairs, across the living room.

"Hey." He presses his palms against the kitchen counter. "What do you want to cook?"

"You don't have any food here."

"There's a place at the bottom of the hill. We can get whatever you need."

I need you. I nod. Okay. "Pasta."

"What kind?"

"With tomatoes. And garlic. Pasta pomodoro." I stare into Tom's eyes. "I need to have it. I need to cook it with you. I need us to have it together."

"Sure."

"No, Tom, I..." *I love you.* "You don't understand. I... I love... I love pasta. I can't live without it. I hate going a single day without it."

He stares back at me. Understanding fills his eyes. "I love pasta, too."

"Yeah?"

His expression softens. "Yeah, but I've never made a point of eating it regularly. Of planning like that. Arranging my life around anything."

"Tom, I..."

He takes my hands and pulls me into a slow, deep kiss. It's there in the way he kisses me. Neither one of us can say the words, but right now, I feel them.

When our kiss breaks, he pulls me into a tight hug, presses his palm against the back of my head, holding me against his chest.

"I've never... made pasta before," he says. "Not sure if I can."

"That's okay. We can learn together."

Chapter Twenty-Nine

There are eight million kinds of pasta at the natural foods store nearest Tom's place. He teases me about my indecision over noodle types.

"There is a recipe for pasta pomodoro." He holds up his phone to show off said recipe. "We can follow it."

I shake my head. "I cook from the heart."

"Then lead the way, Mistress Chef."

Okay. I can do this. Fresh spaghetti works. We still need basil, garlic, tomatoes.

I lead Tom to the produce section and take my time picking out ingredients. He hangs by the cart, watching me with a wide smile.

This could be our normal. We could live together, go grocery shopping every Tuesday night, sit at the table planning a menu together. It wouldn't have to be fancy. It could be half TV dinners and takeout, but it would be ours.

I get caught up in the fantasy of a life with him as we make our way to the register, to the car, back up to his place.

I'm not exactly an expert chef, but I do my best to take him through the dish step by step. Boil the noodles and set them aside. Coat the heated pan with olive oil, add minced garlic, tomatoes, pasta, basil. Every few minutes, he stops to pull me into a kiss, to whisper something in my ear, to tease me about being bossy.

He makes a salad. Sets the table. It's fucking normal, having dinner with Tom, like a real couple. Like this is forever.

After we finish eating, we cuddle up on the couch. It's his idea to watch *Roman Holiday*. He holds me the entire time, but he keeps his attention on the film.

It's overwhelming how good this feels. I don't snap out of my trance until I'm in the bathroom after the movie, splashing cool water on my face in the hopes of finding clarity.

This can be forever.

This needs to be forever.

———

WHEN I GET BACK TO THE LIVING ROOM, TOM IS GONE.

His clothes are not. There's one shoe on the couch. Another in front of the stairs. A sock a few steps above it. I follow his garments all the way up the stairs and down the hallway, to the open door of a bedroom.

Manners first. I knock.

"Yes?" he asks.

"May I come in?"

"Please do."

When I go to push the door open it gets stuck on something. A pair of boxers. Oh. He must be...

He's sitting on his bed naked.

It shouldn't be this remarkable given how many times we've been together but it is. He's magnificent.

He holds up his hand to show off something hot pink. The vibrator.

"Wasn't that in my suitcase?" I ask.

He nods. "Wanted to use it on you."

I bite my lip. That is a wonderful idea but invading my privacy is unacceptable. "Tom, I—"

"Don't appreciate me looking through your stuff?"

I nod.

"Was thinking with my cock. Won't do it again."

That's it? He's not objecting or calling me ridiculous or insisting it was for my own good. He's just respecting my boundary and moving on.

Somehow, I manage to pull my eyes away from his body to take in the room. It's so Tom. Just flashy enough with a disco ball on the ceiling, a sleek modern armchair in the corner, star decals all over the walls.

"You think that's something. Look at this." He reaches for the side table and presses a button.

The lights turn off except for the one on the disco ball. The star decals glow in the semi-dark. An R&B slow jam plays.

Tom tugs at something tied to the sleek white head-board—bondage restraints.

I almost trip over my feet and I'm standing still.

He smiles. "You okay, kid?"

"You're into bondage?"

"From time to time."

"You tied up or you tying up?"

"Either way. I'm game for almost anything." He pats the spot next to him. "As long as you're into it."

"I don't know about those."

"That's all right. It's not my main thing." He pushes himself off the bed and slides his arms around me.

"What's your main thing?"

"Making you come."

I squeeze him. It's the only way to balance. "Me specifically?"

He nods. "I've never been with somebody I cared about before. It's different. Better."

My cheeks flush. My whole fucking body is on fire. I untangle myself from his arms and plant on the bed. Now I don't have to balance. But these clothes are damn confining.

Tom sits next to me. He pulls me onto his lap so I'm straddling him and pushes the straps of my top off my shoulders. "If you don't want to use the vibrator, tell me. I'll get you something else." He runs his fingertips over my thighs. "My hands are at your disposal at the moment but I'm afraid I can't let you take them home with you."

"No, I do."

"Have you been using it?"

I shake my head. "Just my hands."

He unhooks my bra. "Did you think about me?"

"Yes." A lot. "Have you thought of me?"

"Haven't had too many chances to fuck myself but I thought of you every time." He pulls my top over my head. Pushes my skirt off my hips. "I've never wanted anyone the way I want you."

"Never? You've been with a lot of women."

"Barely cared enough to learn their names." He lays me flat on my back and slides my panties to my feet. "Never been with anyone more than three nights. Usually bored by the second. It's not as awful as it sounds. Always make sure a woman enjoys herself—"

"You don't have to apologize for your slutty past."

"It doesn't bug you?"

"No. The past doesn't matter unless it's still haunting you."

He brings his body next to mine. His mouth to my ear. "Then why is there a sad look in your eyes?"

"I don't want to talk about it."

"Then I'm not gonna fuck you."

I take a deep breath. I can't explain all of it. Not yet. "I know this might not work out but I'll be crushed if it's because you get bored of me."

"Couldn't." Tom takes the cylindrical vibrator and wraps my hands around the handle.

"How do you know?"

"Some things you just know."

I swallow hard.

He presses his lips against my neck and props himself up beside me. "You should be more concerned about waking up and realizing I'm no good."

I stare back into his eyes. How can he believe that? "Is there any way I can convince you that you're wrong?"

"Come for me."

I laugh. "Why do I get the feeling I'm being manipulated?"

His thumb presses against a button and the device roars on. "You are. Do it anyway."

"If you admit you're a good person."

"A good fuck."

"A good guy."

He looks me in the eyes. "You'd really rather get me to admit I'm a good guy than come?"

I nod.

He runs his fingers over my jaw. "I can see that, through your eyes, I am a good guy. That's all you're getting." He drags his hands over my neck and between my breasts. "Now, I want to watch you enjoy your gift."

"Sounds more like a gift for you."

He pinches my nipple gently.

Lust shoots straight to my core. I sigh with need. "Please."

He groans. "Never stop saying it like that."

This is a nice gift. But it's not what I want. Tom is what I want, and I'm not above using the tools at my disposal. "Please fuck me."

"After."

"Please."

He sucks on my earlobe. "If you're not feeling it, I'll take over."

"Please," I breathe.

He lets out a low groan but stays put on his side, watching over me.

I take a deep breath, unsure how to position myself. I've never been a performer. Certainly never masturbated for someone's viewing pleasure. I press my lids together as my legs splay open. Okay. I'll try the toy.

No teasing. I press the vibrator against my clit. Damn. It's intense. Pleasure shoots through me.

Tom is watching with such rapt attention. It does something to me. I feel it everywhere.

I try to hold his gaze, but between the vibrator and all the need in his eyes, it's too much. My eyelids press together. I reach for Tom. Get the shoulder.

I drag my hand down his muscular arm, all the way to his wrist, and I place his hand over mine. "Please take over."

He groans as he shifts into position behind me. His chest presses against my back. His hard cock presses against the flesh of my ass. Desire shoots through me. I need our bodies joining. I need intimacy with him however I can get it.

Tom holds my body against his with one hand. With the other, he takes the vibrator and runs it over my clit. The motions of the machine are the same but it feels better when it's his hand, when it's us together.

Tension builds between my legs. Not yet. I shift my crotch back to break contact with the device. "Please, Tom. I want you inside me when I come."

"Fuck yes."

In one smooth motion, he lifts my leg and thrusts into me. I'm putty in his hands, only moving when he directs me.

He keeps the vibrator pressed against my clit as he thrusts into me. It's harder and faster than it's been before. He's as desperate as I am.

Sensation overwhelms me. I stay pressed against him, melted around him. The room is disco lights and R&B but mostly it's our breath and our moans and the sweet sound of his body pounding into mine.

An orgasm rises up inside me. "Tom," I groan as I come. My sex pulses around him, pulling him closer.

He doesn't change a thing. He thrusts into me with deep, steady strokes. Again and again. The toy stays pressed against me with the most delightful buzz. Within moments, I'm coming again. My spasms are so intense I forget to breathe. It feels like I'm going to push him out of my body. But he only moves deeper. Closer.

"You feel so fucking good," he groans into my ear.

I gasp. It's the only thing I can do.

"Too much?" He sucks on my neck.

"One more."

He moves faster. Harder. He moves the toy away for a moment. Damn, I need the break. My body is almost spent but I can't give out until I feel his release. Tom. God, Tom. The world feels so right when we're pressed together. So wrong when we're apart.

He brings the toy back to my clit. Waves of bliss shoot through me. I've only got a handful of seconds before I'm coming again.

"Not yet." I push the toy away. "I want you to come with me."

"Not sure you're gonna make it." He shifts the vibrator away. "But I'll try."

He repositions our bodies, me flat on my stomach, my legs spread, him on top of me. He thrusts into me. His mouth goes to my shoulders and neck, sucking, kissing, biting gently. He's still attentive, like he's never going to lose control.

A few more thrusts, and I'm too close to think anything at all. I bite my lip, trying to hold off my orgasm. It's no use. The tension knots. It's too much, too intense. I need to come. Immediately. I arch my hips to match his movements, to push him deeper.

There. My orgasm is one hard pulse of pressure and then I'm unraveling. My legs shake as I come. I squeeze the sheets, screaming anything that will fall off my lips. Mostly his name.

My body goes slack. I collapse. Spent.

Tom presses his lips to my ear. "Fuck was that hot." He shifts off me, lying flat on his back.

No way I'm letting him go unfinished.

I push myself onto my hands and knees and bring my body over his. I wrap my hand around his cock. "Can I help you with this problem?"

"You don't have to be that polite," he groans.

"No? Doesn't turn you on—" I suck on his earlobe

until he's groaning and thrusting into my hand. "To hear me ask, Tom, may I please suck your cock?"

"Fuck," he groans. "Say it again."

I'm too wound up to get self-conscious. I whisper in his ear. "May I please suck your cock?"

He groans something completely incomprehensible.

I kiss my way to his chest and stop to flick my tongue over his nipples. "Will you come in my mouth?"

"You want me to?"

"Please."

"You're gonna kill me." He brings his hands to my hair. "God, yes."

I plant kisses down his torso. I've never enjoyed giving head before. Certainly never made a special request. But I want to make Tom feel as good as I do. I want to be in control of his pleasure.

The piercing is a little daunting. I take my time getting into position. I push his legs apart, sit back on my heels, and press one hand against his hip. Once I'm confident in my leverage and my balance, I lower myself closer.

There. I wrap my hand around his cock and flick my tongue against his tip. He tastes like me. Because he fucked me so thoroughly. It spurs me on, but I'm not feeling merciful.

Teasing earns teasing.

I flick my tongue against him. Again and again. Until he's groaning and clawing at the bed. I try different speeds. Faster. Slower. Harder. Softer. I lick my way around him, stopping to give his piercing thorough attention. It's even more fun like this. He shudders whenever I flick my tongue against it. He claws at my hair. His groans are desperate and needy.

Still, I tease. I tease until I can't take it anymore.

He sighs when I wrap my mouth around him. He

presses his hand against the back of my head, guiding me gently. I take him deeper. Deeper. When I can't take anymore, I use my hand like an extension of my mouth, stroking him.

I do it again. Again.

"Harder," he groans.

God, the way that pleasure sounds on his lips. It echoes around the room, filling me with satisfaction.

I suck harder. Harder. Until he groans loudly enough to wake the people down the street. I keep up my motions until his hands knot in my hair.

Deep groans escape his lips. "I'm gonna come."

He tugs at my hair. Gently at first. Then rough enough it hurts.

I hold Tom in my mouth as he comes. He's salty and sweet at once. I like him in my mouth, feeling his orgasm, tasting it.

When he's finished, I push myself up and swallow hard.

There's a world of wonder in his eyes. He blinks, dumbfounded.

He pulls me onto the bed and wraps his body around mine. He runs his fingers through my hair. "Haven't got carried away in a long time."

"I liked it." I nestle into his body.

"You knocked me out. Only have about ninety seconds of consciousness left."

"Sleep. You have TCM and Netflix. I'll be entertained."

I go to shift off the bed but Tom pulls me next to him.

He wraps his arms around me, pulls my body into his. "Don't go."

"Okay."

"No." His voice is soft, mumbled, halfway to sleep. "Don't leave me."

"I won't."

"You promise?"

"Yeah." I press my lips into his forehead. "I promise."

Within minutes, his muscles go slack, his breathing slows. He's asleep. I close my eyes and let my body find slumber.

This could be my life.

It really could be this perfect.

Chapter Thirty

I wake to an empty house. The glory of this place is utterly lost on me. The sunshine, the warm air, the crystal clear aqua pool—it's all lost on me. I can barely smell the chlorine. Barely taste my coffee. It's not that he's gone. Not exactly.

He must be worried. Scared. My stomach refuses to settle. I'm scared for him. I shoot him the most low-key *I'm absolutely not checking on you* text I can muster.

Willow: Hey. How is everything? Call me if you need to talk.

No response.

No response while I kill time watching a movie.

No response when I dress, pack my suitcase, and take an Uber to Kara and Drew's brunch spot. They're both ecstatic when they arrive. Kara takes every opportunity to show off her engagement ring. But she's much more excited by the fresh ink on her shoulder. A key. And Drew has the matching lock on his shoulder. When they press against each other, the key and the lock connect.

And here I thought they couldn't get more adorable.

I muster up enough enthusiasm they don't interrogate

my mood. Don't get me wrong. I'm happy for them. It's just hard for the happiness to get through all the dread in my gut. For Tom or because of him? The only thing I'm sure of is how much I need him.

Drew and Kara spend the entire day showing off Santa Monica, Venice Beach, and Marina Del Rey. The loose collection of cities west of the 405 is called the Westside and it's beautiful. Everything is clean. The sun shines big in the bright blue sky. The air tastes of salt. The breeze blows over the streets, tempering the heat.

Even with all the nerves in my stomach, I fall for the city. I want to be here. Near my brother and all the people who are becoming my friends.

It's the perfect place to set up a studio.

But not if things get messier with Tom.

Still no response.

Still no response at dinner.

Or when we get ice cream after.

Or when we go back to Drew's place and pick out classic romance *Sabrina* from the many streaming options. My brother, the good fiancé. He doesn't object to watching something about feelings.

Halfway through the movie, my phone buzzes in my pocket. I nearly jump out of my seat.

Tom: Results are inconclusive. Mom has to have another test in a few weeks. It should be right after we finish the tour.

Willow: Are you okay?

Tom: Yeah. You alone?

Willow: With Drew and Kara.

Tom: Too bad. I was going to send you a naughty picture.

Willow: Do it anyway. Please.

Tom: Thinking about it.

Willow: They got a couple's tattoo. It's disgustingly cute.

Tom: Tsk. Tsk. You should be happy for your brother, kid.

Willow: I am.

Tom: Would you ever get a couple's tattoo?

Willow: With you or with someone else?

Tom: With Brad Pitt. Of course with me.

Willow: Depends.

Tom: On?

Willow: If this is forever or not.

Drew clears his throat. "It's rude to text during the movie, Wil."

Kara whispers something in his ear, capturing all his attention. "If you want some privacy, you can take the spare room, sweetie." She motions upstairs. "Just ignore the guitars. In fact, if one is lying on the floor, go ahead and kick it."

"Insolent today, Kendrick. I'm gonna have to punish you for that." He whispers in her ear.

She laughs.

Yes, privacy sounds like a capital idea. For them as much as for me. It must be nice, loving someone that openly and honestly.

"Yeah. Thanks." I push myself off the couch. Sorry, Humphrey Bogart but you've got nothing on Tom Steele.

I don't look at my phone until I'm alone in the spare room, my back pressed against the door for extra security.

Tom hasn't replied to my not quite a question. Not with words.

The only thing on my phone is a picture message:

Him, from the neck down, completely naked.

So much for thinking anything besides *oh hell yes* for the rest of the night.

———

TOM AND I TALK ABOUT NOTHING FOR HOURS.

The next day, we're back on the road, on the tour. The bus is louder with Meg and Kara around. But sometimes it's not. Sometimes it's quieter, sometimes one of the happy couples goes off to a bunk or to the bedroom and soaks in the glory of just being together.

And I sit with Tom, close enough to feel all the warmth of him but not close enough that I have to explain this to anyone, and soak in the glory of being with him.

I get lost in the rhythm of the tour. Hazel works me hard. Every night we're stopped, she has a new project that requires my assistance. She talks to me about my interest in a studio, guides me through my options. Encourages my boudoir aspirations enough that I actually manage to do a shoot with a model. Then it's two. Then three. Then half a dozen. Little by little, I get comfortable working with strangers.

I go on a photography tear. When we're stopped with nothing to do, I take headshots or portraits of anyone who will get in front of the camera.

The pictures are good.

Really good.

Like I can really do this.

Like my life could really be setting up a studio in Los Angeles, near Tom, near everyone.

If he loves me too.

If this is forever.

There are too many possibilities, and I don't get much of him. There's always someone around. I'm tired. He's busy trying to catch up on all the stuff he does besides playing the drums like a God damn machine. We're two ships passing in the night, barely time for a kiss or a hug or an occasional screw in my hotel room, late at night, after everyone is asleep.

The days blur together. Two weeks. Then three. We curve around the South West. Then we're in San Diego.

Today is the last show. The last day of knowing where I'm going to be or what I'm going to do.

Now I have to figure out what the hell I'm doing with my photography.

With Tom.

With the rest of my life.

———

THE GUYS ARE MORE RELAXED TONIGHT. IT IS A RELIEF, knowing this is the last show for a while. Can't say that I spend much time taking in Pete, Drew, or Miles's mood. Behind the camera, the world makes sense. My feelings for Tom don't overwhelm me. Even when I'm photographing him. He's an amazing subject. This look of concentration spreads over his face as he loses himself in the music. His arms flail with frenetic energy. But they're precise. Exact. Sweat drips off his torso. During a break in the set, he stands and joins Miles at the mic. Mostly to show off his body. Some to goad Drew and Pete out of their clothes.

It works! It never works. Pete really is attractive. I can see why Hazel teases. His body is easily as good as Tom's. The curving lines of a tattoo peek out from the waist of his skinny jeans. It's not just a thigh tattoo. It's over his hip too.

That's yummy.

I spend almost a whole ten seconds looking at something that isn't Tom.

Can't say I'm particularly moved by my brother stripping. But I know other women will be. Especially with the way he's blushing. I capture his awkwardness. And the way the audience groans with adoration when he shows off his new tattoo.

The show blurs together. I get lost in my photography. The concert thing gets old, night after night, but there's something amazing about capturing the energy, the mood, the facial expressions.

I snap out of my trance in time for the encore. Thank God we're almost done with this touring thing. I'm exhausted. I barely hear the outro, the guys soaking in the adoration of the audience.

They make a dramatic exit. The lights go down.

And that's it. Show's over. I can't hide behind my camera anymore. I can't throw all my energy into surviving the tour anymore.

I have to figure out what the hell I'm doing with my life.

Hell, I have to figure out what I'm doing tomorrow. It's Ophelia's test. And I'm still not sure if I'm invited. Every time it comes up, Tom and I end up out of our clothes before we can discuss it.

Thankfully, Hazel demands my presence immediately. I take one last look at the sweaty crowd leaving the packed venue—it's been a hell of a ride—and make my way to her backstage editing nook.

"You've come a long way, Willow." She compares a set of pictures from our first show to a set from last night's show. "How do you feel?"

"Exhausted."

"Don't tell me you're skipping the end of tour party." She hooks up my camera and uploads the pictures. Her eyes stay on the computer. "You're too young to hide."

"I'm not hiding from anything."

"Hmm."

Hazel takes me through the evening's set. She points out her favorites and gives me tips on places to improve. Then we do the same with her photos. She's taken half as many pictures but there are twice as many keepers. One day, I'll be that good.

"Show me some of your personal projects, sweetheart." She nods to my camera. "Every time I see you, you look exhausted. Tell me it's because you're busy shooting pictures and not because you're sleeping off hangovers."

"I don't really drink. But there's nothing on my camera. I wiped my memory card last night. Here." I take over on the computer and show off a Dropbox folder of my recent portraits. It's a mix of standard actor headshots, moody editorial pieces, and a hell of a lot of boudoir.

"These are fantastic." She points to a headshot of Pete with a mysterious look on his face. "I can admit my bias towards the subject, but you'll get actors knocking down your door if you can get Pete to show off this much emotion." She navigates to a sweet yet sultry boudoir shoot of an inexperienced model. "You captured her shyness without letting it bleed into fear or insecurity. This is great work."

"Thank you."

"I have an offer for you. A job."

"What?"

"In two weeks, I'm doing this all over again with another band. The tour will be six months with a few breaks. I'll spend most of those doing editorial work. I'd love to have you as my assistant again."

Hazel Alexander wants me to continue as her assistant. It's the most flattering thing I've ever heard. But six months is a long time away from everything. From Tom. If there is even a *me and Tom* after I tell him how I feel.

"I understand if you've had enough of the rock star lifestyle," she says. "But I can bump your salary by about fifty percent."

"Can I think about it?"

"Let me know by the end of the week. Whatever you do, you'll do great." She looks away at something. "Just make sure it's what you want. Men never put their ambitions aside for you."

"Huh?"

She motions to something behind me. Tom is leaning against the wall.

He nods hello, not at all shy about spying.

"Enjoy the party." Hazel nods goodbye to Tom, packs up her computer, and takes the back exit.

Once we're alone, Tom slides his arms around me. He smells good. His hair is wet. His shirt isn't his usual sweaty, discarded v-neck but a sleek white button-up thing. He showered and changed. For me.

"Never been this excited for a tour to end." He presses his lips to mine. "I haven't had enough of you."

"Me either." The need inside me pours into him as I kiss back. God, he tastes good. I break our kiss and bury my face in his chest. "We shouldn't be making out here."

"Can't help myself." His voice is breathy, needy. "What were you and Hazel talking about?"

"I'll tell you once some blood is back in my brain."

Chapter Thirty-One

I t's not a party as much as an extra fancy hangout session. The band, plus significant others and a few roadies, laugh, eat, and drink in a hotel suite. There's no fancy bartender. Just a row of liquor and mixers and a plentiful supply of mostly healthy snacks.

No one comments on Tom and me arriving together, but Meg throws him some pretty serious side-eye.

She pushes off her boyfriend's lap and moves towards us. Usually she wears flats but today she's in heels that put her about an inch above Miles and several inches above Tom. It's intimidating, how tall she is, how confident she is, how she's going to be a doctor.

Miles is so supportive when he talks about her. I can only hope Tom is as supportive of what I want.

"You've never showered after a show before." She looks him up and down. "Do you have a date or something?"

"Shit. I thought Miles told you about our plan to double team you," Tom teases.

Miles laughs.

Meg blushes but stays strong. "In your dreams."

"You know I don't date," Tom says.

"Things change." Meg's eyes drift to me. "It could be nice, taking someone special out after a long day—"

"And making her come until she begs for mercy." Miles pulls his girlfriend onto his lap. He presses his lips against her neck.

She's putty. It takes her a full minute to pull away from Miles enough to talk to Tom. "Whatever you're doing, I hope you're treating her..." She looks at me. "Whoever that is. Well."

Is subtlety a lost art? I can't exactly blame people for tiptoeing around me and Tom's relationship, but this is clomping.

"Babe, that was the worst hint I've ever heard." Miles teases his girlfriend. "You're lucky everyone knows that Tom and Willow are fucking. Everyone except Drew."

Tom shoots him a death glare.

Miles laughs. "Not as much fun the shoe being on the other foot, huh?"

"I wasn't *that* obvious." Meg motions to Kara and Drew cuddling on the couch then turns to me. "As long as Guitar Prince is busy, how is Tom?"

"I'm right here," Tom says.

"Please. You'd not only ask that, but you'd subject us to some truth or dare bullshit just for the excuse." Meg folds her arms over her chest. "So..."

"Must be good if she's sticking around," Miles says. "It's not for his wit."

"I don't know. Tom's pretty good-looking once you get past his personality," Meg teases.

"Come on." Tom glances at Drew as if to check if the coast is clear, and slides his arm around my waist. "I need to talk to you."

"Enjoy the *conversation*." Miles winks.

We find an empty space in the kitchenette. There's something about Tom's expression. Something bothering him. Of course there is. Tomorrow, he's going to find out if his mom is going to live or die.

"Can I come tomorrow?" I'm too tired to hold anything back. "I want to be there for you."

"Yeah." He runs a hand through my hair. "I want you to be there."

"Really?"

He nods.

"Tom, I—" I barely bite my lip in time to keep the words in my throat. The man has enough on his mind.

"You okay, kid? You and Hazel looked pretty serious."

Okay, that's something I can discuss. "She offered me a job. Being her assistant on her next tour. It would start in two weeks and I'd be gone most of the year."

"Is that what you want?"

I study his eyes for a sign to his reaction. There's no telling if he wants me to stay or if he's totally apathetic. "It's a good opportunity."

Tom's voice gets stern. "That's not what I asked."

There are footsteps coming towards us. Tom practically jumps backwards. He gets busy filling a glass with ice and whiskey.

False alarm. It's only Miles.

He takes one look at our startled expressions and shakes his head. "Take it from someone who's been there. This is going to blow up in your faces sooner rather than later."

"Asshole," Tom mutters.

"Love you too, buddy." Miles fills a glass with water and returns to the main area.

Tom scans the room. He motions to the bathroom in the bedroom. "Let's get some privacy."

Okay. That works. There's another bathroom in the main area. We should be pretty safe. I lead the way, planting on the marble sink while I wait for Tom.

He slips into the room quietly. His eyes meet mine. "You want to tell me what's wrong?"

"No."

"It's not actually a request."

"Aren't you worried about your mom?" I ask.

"Of course." He moves closer. "But one thing at a time." He brushes my hair from my eyes. "Something is bothering you."

"No."

He pushes my t-shirt up an inch and runs his fingers over my stomach. "I have ways of making you talk."

I swallow hard.

He plays with the button of my jeans. "Why won't you tell me?"

"Because." *Because I love you, idiot.* I swallow hard. Is it possible he doesn't see that?

"You want to take Hazel's job offer?"

"Maybe."

"I'll miss you." He kisses from my ear to my shoulder. "But we'll figure it out."

"What is it we'll figure out, Tom?"

"This."

"What is this?"

"You're changing the subject." He shifts away from me. "Tell me what it is that's wrong."

I don't want to tell him. I don't want to do anything but get in control of my senses again. My feelings are so overwhelming. I can't explain them with words. But the way our bodies fit together... it's there. He must feel it too.

"I'll tell you." I pull my shirt over my head. "After you fuck me."

He stares into my eyes. "Tell me first."

I can't tell him first. Telling him might scare him off. And I'm not going to give up my last time with Tom. Even if it will hurt as much as it feels good.

Okay. No more playing nice. I unhook my bra and slide it off my shoulders. "Please."

"Willow," he groans. "I'm not gonna fuck your pain away."

"Why not?"

Confusion forms in his eyes. "You mean more to me than that."

"Then fuck *your* pain away." I run my hands through his hair. "Look me in the eyes and tell me you're not scared."

"I'm not running away from my feelings this time."

"Which feelings?"

"Any of them."

I bring my hand to the back of his neck. It feels damn good to touch him. I need the upper hand again. "What do I mean to you?"

"Can't exactly explain—"

"Then show me."

That, he understands. He unbuttons his shirt and shrugs it off his shoulders.

I unzip my jeans and slide them to my knees. "I need you. Do you need me?"

"Always."

He presses his lips to mine. Maybe he can't explain it either. That's okay. I don't need words to show him how I feel about him.

My feelings pour into my kiss. *I want you. I need you. I love you.* Everything I can't say.

I've got no patience today. I drag my hands over Tom's shoulders and down his chest. He's so hard, so strong, so safe. My hands go for his jeans but I need to keep this slow. To keep it making love.

There's the thinnest layer of perspiration on his skin. He's worked up for me. I slide my tongue into Tom's mouth. Dig my hands into his hair. He slides my panties off my feet. Unbuttons his jeans. Breaks our kiss to whisper in my ear.

"I'll make this fast." Tom slides his arms around my hips, bringing me to the edge of the counter. His eyes go wide as he aligns our bodies.

His expression is damn beautiful. The desire as his cock nudges against my sex. The relief as he fills me.

God he feels good. The intensity threatens to break my silence. The words form on my lips, demanding my attention. When I can't take it anymore, I kiss him hard and deep.

He's just as needy. I can feel it in the way his tongue slides against mine. The way his fingers press against my hips. The way he thrusts into me with long, slow movements.

I wrap my arms around his shoulders for support and press my chest against his. Our bodies are practically merged. It's not just sex. It can't be. Not with the way he's kissing me, the way he's touching me.

I press my fingers into his skin, soaking in all of him that I can. My lungs don't fill until our kiss breaks. His eyes catch mine and I know I won't be able to look away until we're finished.

It's just as hard to breathe with him staring into my eyes.

Everything else fades away. The world is Tom. His soft skin. His hard muscles. His ragged breath. His deep groans. All the pleasure and affection in his gorgeous green eyes.

Pleasure builds in my core. More and more until it commands me to close my eyes, to look away, to do anything to temper the emotions welling up inside 'me. I fight it.

Tom doesn't look away. He stares back at me, running his fingers along my chin and jaw. He must feel the way I do. That or he's pretending. And I can't even stomach that thought.

He shifts. His pubic bone rubs against my clit.

Yes. I sink my fingers into his skin. "Come with me. Please."

He groans. His lips press against mine and my eyes flutter closed.

My tongue slides into his mouth. My hands dig into his hair. We stay glued together, moans reverberating down our throats. Tension knots inside me. Yes. Almost. I kiss harder. Bring my body closer to his.

His nails dig into my skin. His shoulders shake. I try to hold back my orgasm. It's no use. My sex clenches. Again. Again. Then I'm coming, pulsing around him.

It pulls him closer. Urges him on. He doesn't break our kiss. Only gets more aggressive with his lips and his tongue as he comes. As he fills me.

We stay pressed together for a long moment. My senses shift into focus.

There's no holding back anymore. I can't stop myself from saying it. "Tom, I—"

I'm interrupted by a woman's giggle and the bathroom door swinging open.

Kara.

"Oh, my God." She shrieks.

I grab a towel to cover myself. Tom pulls his jeans on. But it's not fast enough. Kara steps backwards. She trips over something.

Drew's converse clad foot. He looks down at her. "What the—"

Then he's looking at us.

There's no talking my way out of this. I'm in a towel. Tom is barely in his jeans. He's got that just fucked look about him, and I'm sure I'm no better.

Drew's expression flares with anger. "I'm going to fucking kill you."

Chapter Thirty-Two

Kara plants herself in front of Drew. He seethes but he stays put. There's no way he'd ever risk hurting her.

"Please step aside," he growls.

She turns back to him and presses her hands against his chest. "You're not hitting him."

Drew glares at Tom. "Okay. Please move so I can speak to Tom privately."

She tugs at his t-shirt. "You really want to betray my trust by going back on your word?"

"I won't." Drew looks back to Kara. "I won't hit anyone."

She motions to her engagement ring. "I'm not marrying a man with a violent temper, Drew. I don't care how much it will break my heart not being with you." Her voice softens. "You're better than this."

The same anger stays on his face, but his posture shifts from alpha dog *I'll fucking kill you* to a slightly less menacing *I'm thinking about killing you but I'm not willing to risk the jail time.*

Still, Kara stays put in front of him.

Drew clenches his fists. His eyes are laser glued to Tom. "Do you love her?"

"What?" Tom steps backwards.

"It's not a trick question," Drew says.

"Baby, did you like Tom dragging our shit in front of everyone?" Kara rubs Drew's biceps. She leans closer and whispers something in his ear.

"Seems fair, doing it to him now." Drew turns his attention to Tom. "Do you?"

Tom frowns. "I don't know."

"You better fucking figure it out. Because if you love her, fine. But if you're using your player bullshit on her." Drew squeezes his fists so tight his veins bulge. "I won't kill you. I won't hit you. But I sure as hell won't ever look at your smug face again. I don't give a fuck about contractual obligations. I'm not going to show up at some event. I'm not going to pose for some god damn magazine cover. And I'm sure as hell never getting on a stage or in a studio next to you."

"Drew." Kara reaches for his hand.

I can't watch them destroy something this important to them and pretend it's about protecting me.

I swallow hard. Here goes nothing. "No."

Drew looks at me. "Excuse me?"

"This isn't something Tom did wrong. He's been honest with me. He's always treated me well. He's not like Bradley. He'd never hurt me that way. Everything we did, I wanted. I asked for."

This does nothing to calm Drew. Instead, his temper flares. He rolls his fists, his glare turned up to eleven.

Men, they don't listen to reason sometimes.

I continue. "I'm an adult, Drew. I can decide who I fuck. You don't have the right to threaten a guy for sleeping with me."

Drew glares at Tom. He turns and stalks out of the room.

There are muffled questions in the main room. The front door slams shut.

Okay. Drew is pissed. Business as usual.

Only he caught me and Tom with our pants down.

Not as normal.

"He's been on edge lately. There's no excuse but—" Kara shakes her head. "I'll talk to him."

"No." I pull my towel tighter. "This is between me and Drew."

She looks at Tom with accusation in her eyes. "Pretty sure it's more involved than that."

"Maybe. But I need to set Drew straight on a few things."

"Hold on." She motions *one minute* and steps into the main room.

It leaves me and Tom alone. Sort of.

He turns to me and runs a hand through his hair. "Willow, I—"

I cut in. "Whatever you're going to say, don't. This was my decision. I asked you to fuck me, not the other way around. I'm the one who was reckless." I bite my lip. "I don't need protecting from your raging libido. I know what I want. I want you."

"I don't know, kid. Probably best if I get lost for a while."

My heart sinks. Please don't let Tom dump me after all this. I'm wearing a fucking towel. It's too humiliating. "You're the only one who knows your feelings."

A knock on the half-open door interrupts.

Kara's even voice fills the room. "I have the key. Are you decent?"

"Yeah."

She pushes the door open. She shoots Tom a stern expression then turns to me. "Are you okay?"

"I don't know. But I need to do this now." I look to Tom one last time. In case it's the last time he wants anything to do with me.

Kara hands me a room key. "Last room on the right, 817. Call me if you have an issue, and I'll talk him down."

"Okay."

She motions *go* to Tom. When he does, Kara steps into the bathroom. She wraps her arms around me in a tight hug.

"I'm sorry about this. Falling in love isn't always convenient." She steps back. "But you always know, deep down, if it's worth all the heartache."

She nods goodbye and closes the door on her way out. I try to listen for her conversation with Tom as I get dressed. I could almost swear she says something about making his life miserable if he breaks my heart.

She's going to make one hell of a sister-in-law.

———

Even though I have the key, I knock on Drew's door. As far as I can tell, nothing breaks or slams. He's not punching a wall or kicking a chair. The only sound is footsteps.

"Yeah?" he asks.

"It's me."

Nothing.

"I have the room key. Thought I'd be polite." I run my fingers over the slick plastic key. Okay. No sense in waiting. Let's do this.

Drew opens the door before I can unlock it. There's

still anger and frustration in his expression, but there's a softness too.

"It's none of your business who I date," I say.

Drew stares back at me. "You really believe that?"

Technically, it's not his business. But I can't argue that I didn't intentionally deceive him. "I was afraid how you'd react. That you'd go apeshit like you did with Bradley."

"I'm not seventeen anymore."

"You just threatened to quit the band." I press my hand against the door. "I don't want to be the hussy who ruins your careers. And it's not fair putting that on me."

"It's not about you, Wil. Tom made me a promise."

"Fuck Tom."

"You already did. Pretty recently from the looks of things." There's no humor in his voice.

Apparently, this is not a joking matter.

Okay. Deep breath. I'm not backing down. I press the door closed and find a seat on the armchair in the corner. "Ever since Bradley, you've tried hard to protect me. But I'm not a thing that needs protecting." I sit up straight and make eye contact. "I know you have good intentions. I know you want the best for me. But you need to let me live my own life and make my own mistakes."

He takes a spot on the bed across from me. "Wil, you're the only person who knows how fucked up our family is. The only person who will ever understand. You remember that trip to Hawaii?"

I nod.

"Supposed to be mom and dad reconnecting, but they fought the entire time."

"And when I freaked out, you convinced me to sneak away. We spent the whole day snorkeling without parental supervision."

"That was a pride I'd never felt before, getting you

away from the situation that was making you cry." His smile fades. "It killed me when you ran off with that asshole. I was supposed to protect you from all that bullshit. Certainly supposed to protect you from guys like him."

"Tom isn't—"

"Let me finish." Drew stares into my eyes. "I'm sure you remember what a tool I was in high school, all caught up in being popular and cool and—"

"Winning Homecoming King?"

He nods. "I saw the signs. The bruises. The fear. You'd always gotten freaked about Mom and Dad fighting, but once you were with that asshole, it was different. You froze." His gaze goes to the floor. "It broke my heart finding you at his place, knowing how he'd hurt you."

"It broke my heart too. What he did. And worrying that you'd gotten yourself killed defending my honor."

His eyes fill with frustration. "I promised myself I'd never let anything else happen to you."

"Nothing has happened to me, Drew. I had sex with Tom. I wanted him. I asked him. And he was fucking fantastic. Caring. Attentive. Always made sure I came."

"These details are not making me feel better."

"I'm an adult. As long as we're both on the same page, what's the harm in me and Tom having sex?"

Drew stares back at me. "Are you in love with him?"

"Yes."

"Have you told him?"

"No."

"Go fucking do it." Drew rises to his feet. "That's the only way you'll know if it's real."

What? My head is swimming. "I thought you were against the whole thing."

"I am." He offers his hand. "But I'm not blind. I've

seen the way he makes you laugh. Fuck, you haven't laughed like that since last time I face-planted on my skis. And that must have been ten years ago.

He motions for me to grab his hand. When I do, he pulls me up. And he hugs me. It's not an awkward, stilted hug but an affectionate one.

"I want you to be happy, Wil. I love you. I don't trust Tom as far as I can throw him, but if you trust him, if you love him—I'm not going to get in the way of that." He walks me to the door. "I can't promise I won't hurt him if he is playing you."

"No violence."

Drew nods. "There are other ways to make his life miserable."

"Don't leave the band, Drew. It's everything to you."

"You want to be free to fuck whoever you want, fine. I'm just as free to associate with whoever I want."

There's no arguing that point. "Will you get another tattoo with me? If he does break my heart?"

"Not sure." He opens the door and nudges go. "Might be hard to get tattoos together if I'm convicted of murder."

He smiles.

He's joking, thank goodness.

"That's not funny," I say. But I laugh anyway. "I can't believe you're my favorite brother."

"Can't believe you're my favorite sibling." He one-ups me. His expression gets serious. "Good luck."

"Thanks."

I take a deep breath as I walk back to the party.

The door is still open. The room is quiet. No doubt, everyone is waiting to see whether or not I survived my conversation with Drew.

I step inside and scan the room. There are a lot of

worried expressions. On some of the roadies. On Meg and Kara and even the usually aloof Miles.

None of that matters.

There's no sign of Tom.

And from the way everyone is looking at me with pity, there's no way the news is good.

Chapter Thirty-Three

Time passes slowly when half a dozen people are trying and failing not to stare. The clock on the wall suggests that it's only been ten seconds. Feels like ten hours.

There are no sounds in the bedroom or in the kitchen around the corner or in the bathroom.

There's no sign of Tom.

No one assuring me that he's on a beer run. Come to think of it, I never see beer. Everyone jumps straight to liquor.

Might not be a bad idea, enough whiskey to dull my thoughts.

"Tom, um, he said he wanted to give Drew some space." Kara steps forward. "Why don't you catch a ride with us?"

Yeah, I'm sure he said that.

Pete motions *come here* to Kara. She does. He whispers something in her ear. It wipes the worry from her expression. Mostly.

The bassist shifts away from the crowd. He makes eye

contact with me. "I'm going to stay the night at the hotel. You should too."

"Please tell me you're not offering rebound sex," Meg says.

"Tom would do it," Miles says.

"True." She nods.

"No, sorry, Willow." Pete motions for us to leave. "I'm sure you'll cry yourself to sleep over missing out, but I'm not offering to fuck you."

"Thanks for clarifying that before I got my hopes up," I say.

"Now let's get out of here." Pete throws warning glances at everyone in attendance. "Last thing you need is attention."

I follow him to my hotel room in a total daze. How could Tom bail without a single word? I check my phone for any sign of contact—a text, a tweet, an Instagram photo. Nothing.

Pete not so gently orders me to change into my pajamas and brush my teeth. He's just as bossy as Tom is, but it's a much calmer way. His deep voice is soothing. I can't imagine what possessed his ex to leave him for anyone.

Don't get me wrong. I'm far too head over heels for Tom to even fathom being interested in Pete. But he is interesting. Sexy, deep, playful and mysterious at once.

When he catches me checking texts on my phone, he plucks it from my hands and turns it off.

"You're going to drive yourself crazy checking that thing all night." He sits on the bed next to me. "It's not you, Willow. Mom, Ophelia called during the show. She's getting scared. Tom went to be with her."

"Oh."

"I'll knock when I pick you up tomorrow. Ten a.m. How do you take your coffee?"

"Almond milk and plenty of sugar." I pull the covers over my shoulders. "Why are you picking me up?"

"You're coming with us to see Mom."

"I'm not sure that's a good idea."

"It's your decision." Vulnerability fills his eyes. "I don't know what happened with you and Tom. Where you guys are. He might not realize it, but he needs you. The way he acts around you... I've never seen him care that much about anything besides the band."

I bite my lip.

"You have to put yourself first. If you don't want to be around him, I get that. I won't push you. But he needs you tomorrow."

"What if he doesn't? What if he left because he doesn't want to be with me?"

"I'll make it up to you."

"How?" I ask.

"Rebound sex."

I laugh. "You're not..." I study his expression. He's stoic. It's hard to tell when he's kidding. "You're kidding, right?"

He nods. "If you do dump Tom, be gentle. Not for his sake. For mine. For some reason, I love the asshole."

There's an ocean of concern in his voice. I don't buy his cool facade for a second. He really cares about Tom. It's obvious how much they mean to each other.

"He's your brother," I say.

"Must be it."

"And he's not an asshole. Usually."

Pete pushes off the bed with a nod goodbye. "If you need anything, I'm in room 816." He steps backwards. "Well, almost anything." He winks on his way out the door.

THE DRIVE IS A BLUR OF NERVES, COFFEE, AND JAZZ MUSIC. I don't bother asking whose car we're driving or where it came from. All my attention goes to keep down my half a bagel breakfast. We might find out Tom and Pete's mom is dying. I know I'm not part of the family, might never be part of the family, but I'm still terrified for them.

Traffic is light on the five freeway. We take an exit somewhere in Orange County. It's a few streets to the big, clean hospital and its wide parking lot. It almost looks like an office building with its big windows and its turquoise exterior.

The inside is nice. Well lit. The walls are cream, the signs bright blue. Pete checks something on his phone then presses his hand against my upper back to lead me through the hallways. I'm almost glad I'm with him and not Tom. I don't think I can handle Tom touching me at the moment.

We stop in front of an open door. There are voices. Laughter. A woman's throaty chuckle. And Tom's bright laugh. I know it well by now. Even with everything all screwed up, his laugh makes the world feel light and effortless.

I follow Pete into the room. Tom's eyes catch mine. They're filled with surprise. And something else. He's nervous.

"Didn't think you were coming, kid." He shoves his hands into his pockets.

"Damn. I was hoping she was Peter's new girlfriend." The woman on the hospital bed laughs. She pushes herself up and extends her hands. "I'm Ophelia."

She's in her late fifties, maybe a little older. Her short hair is electric blue. She's not particularly tall or broad, but she's a presence.

Pete jumps in. "Mom, no one calls me Peter."

"Unless they follow it with Parker." Tom laughs.

"Don't tease your brother. He looked handsome in those thick black glasses." She smiles. "Why wouldn't you want to be Spider-Man, honey? He's one of the least obnoxious of those super heroes."

I shake her hand. "I'm Willow."

"Drew's little sister," Tom adds. "You remember Drew?"

"Please, Thomas. You think I'm going to believe that you're spending time with a beautiful woman, and you aren't sleeping with her?"

Tom cringes. "Is this the time?"

"Sex is life, sweetheart. It's always the time. I've fucked plenty of beautiful women. It's not going to shock me that you're sleeping around," Ophelia says.

Fucked women? "You're gay?" I cover my mouth with my hand. Shit. It's not like she has spots. But no one mentioned it.

"Yes. A good thing too. Men can't handle a nipple-less fake tit."

Pete and Tom turn various shades of red. Ophelia motions to their embarrassment as if it's proving her point.

"I'm sorry, sweetie," she says. "This isn't appropriate getting to know you conversation. I'd love to blame the twelve hours without food or water or the pre-surgery jitters, but—"

"She's always like this," Tom says.

"I hope you're not that rude to your girl... what are you kids calling it nowadays?" she asks.

I bite my tongue.

Tom is equally unable to get words out.

Pete and Ophelia exchange a knowing look.

She raises a brow. "Peter, you should keep a better eye on him."

Pete laughs. "He moves too fast."

"I'll bet." Ophelia shakes her head. She looks to me. "What do you do, sweetheart? You don't strike me as the groupie type."

"I'm a photographer," I say.

"Any good?" she asks.

"Don't be rude," Tom says.

"No, it's fine. I'm pretty good," I say.

"She's going to start a business. Doing headshots. And boudoir." Tom smiles.

He looks proud. He shouldn't be speaking for me, but he looks so fucking proud.

Everything is light again. I press my heel against the wall for balance.

"Boudoir, really? How much do you charge? I'd love to immortalize my one good tit."

Pete and Tom turn even darker shades of red.

I jump in before one of them dies of embarrassment. I like Ophelia. A lot. "I'd be happy to do it as a gift to your family. Tom and Pete have been really great to me. But there's a good chance I'll be out of town for the next six months."

"Oh?" she asks.

"I was offered a job as an assistant photographer on another tour. It starts in two weeks," I say.

Tom's expression darkens but he doesn't say anything.

"With Hazel?" Pete asks. "That's great, Willow. She's a legend."

"You should schedule a session with her before she leaves," I say. "She's dying to shoot nudes of you. I bet she'd do it just for your personal collection."

Pete smiles smugly.

Ophelia is not at all embarrassed. "You should, Peter. It's important to be proud of your body, even when it's..." The joy falls off her face. She reaches for a tissue. "Excuse me."

Both the guys rush to her side to comfort her. She waves them away.

"Stop fussing." She folds the tissue into a tiny ball and drops it in her lap.

I press my back against the wall, unable to come up with any words of comfort that don't feel hollow. Tom and Pete shift the conversation to easier topics, memories of silly fights and non-sexual band antics.

I add to the conversation when I can. Mostly, none of the attention is here in the room. We're all off someplace full of dread and worry.

By the time the nurse arrives to finish prepping Ophelia, we're down to discussing crime TV shows. *The Closer* is a favorite of Ophelia's. I've never seen it, but Tom assures me I'd like the take no shit lead detective Brenda.

"Five minutes, Ms. Steele." The nurse steps out of the room.

Ophelia keeps up a strong facade but the worry is written all over her face. She pulls Tom close enough to whisper. I'm not family. I need to give them space.

"Excuse me. Good luck." I take a step towards the door.

"Thank you, sweetheart." Her face floods with relief. "Will I see you tonight?"

"Depends on how well Tom treats me this afternoon." She smiles.

Chapter Thirty-Four

Ten minutes later, the nurse takes Ophelia to surgery. Tom and Pete go with her. I play with the pockets of my jeans to keep my mind occupied. She seems like a wonderful woman. I hope she's okay.

The mood is tense when the brothers arrive. Tom paces up and down the hall, tapping his feet frantically. Pete sits next to me, his dark eyes filled with concern.

He looks to me. "You want something to drink?"

"Coffee," I say.

"Sure." He pushes out of his seat and nods to Tom. "Why don't you sit down?"

"Not offering me a drink?" Tom taps his fingers impatiently.

Pete shoots Tom a stern look. It's heavy with the weight of mutual history. Whatever it is, it works. Tom nods and plants in the chair.

He's no more relaxed. He taps a beat against his thigh. His eyes go to the bright walls. They fill with deep concern.

"Don't take Hazel's offer," he says.

I swallow hard. "Why?" Half of me wants it to be

because he needs me nearby. The other half wants to punch him for the presumption that I'd rearrange my life for him.

"It's not what you want."

Oh. It's not about us at all. If there is an *us*.

Tom makes eye contact. "You want to set up your own studio. You're good enough. You must have enough money after what Hazel was paying you. I learned a lot about business acting as de facto manager. I can help with anything you need."

"I don't want to talk about this right now."

"Then when? I heard you and Hazel talking. She wants an answer in two days."

"You shouldn't eavesdrop."

"You were avoiding me. Tell me why."

I press my lips together. "I don't want to talk about that now."

"Then what the fuck do you want to talk about, kid?"

"I don't know." I swallow hard. "Pete convinced me that you needed me to be here. Maybe he was wrong."

I go to push myself out of my seat but Tom stops me.

He runs his thumb over mine. "He was right. I need you here."

Now or always? Is this forever? I want it to be forever.

Deep breath. "I'm not sure I have the energy to start a business."

"Don't do that."

"What?"

"Run away from your ambition. You're smart. Talented. You work hard as hell. I know you can do it."

"Good for you, Tom, but you don't get to decide what I do."

"Not what I mean."

"What the fuck do you mean?" I pick up his tapping

habit. Coming here was a bad idea. My emotions have been running high all month. Then yesterday... I can't do the supportive friend thing. Not around Tom. It's too hard wanting to be his everything.

"I was showing Mom your photos last night." His voice is soft, sweet. "You're an amazing photographer. You could be shooting magazine editorials if you wanted."

His expression is earnest. He really believes that.

"I'm thinking about it," I say.

"I'm not going to let up on this one." He squeezes my hand. "You don't have to be shy. You need more models for your boudoir. I volunteer."

A laugh breaks up the tension in my shoulders. "Do you?"

"Absolutely."

"And you'll sign a model release?"

He nods.

"What if I sell the photos to TMZ?"

"Won't be anything anyone hasn't seen before."

I motion to his crotch. "What about your piercing?"

Tom smiles. "I trust you."

"Do you?"

He nods with all this openness and affection.

My heart beat speeds up. My thoughts crash into each other. One thing at a time. Waiting for Ophelia to get out of surgery is nerve-wracking enough without adding heart-break to the mix.

———

PETE DOES A THOROUGH JOB DISTRACTING US. FIRST THE coffee. Then he breaks out a deck of cards and teaches a trick taking game. He's masterful. Tom and I have to team up against him to keep him from running away with it.

We have lunch in the cafeteria. No one is paying much attention to their food. Still, we play round after round of the card game. For a while, we're laughing, teasing.

Around two, we find spots in the waiting room. No more laughing, no more joking. No levity at all. Pete sits by himself. There's something scary about how calm his expression is. Like he's raging under the surface.

Tom isn't hiding anything. He paces back and forth, frantic. Nervous. I can't watch him this upset. I have to get up and wrap my arms around him.

He softens. Slows. He squeezes me and runs his hands up and down my back. We stay close for minutes.

"Thank you for being here." He whispers in my ear.

Then he pulls back, and he's as good as gone. The nerves swallow him whole. He leans against the wall, tapping his toes or his fingers.

"I'd kill for a drum kit right about now," he says.

"Would it be inappropriate to make a joke about how you're welcome to bang me?"

"Yeah." He smiles. "But Mom would love it."

"You are. Welcome to bang me."

He shakes his head. "Not right now, kid. Not with everything..."

"Yeah."

But he does wrap his arms around me. I'm scared too but it feels amazing knowing I can bring him some comfort.

When Tom releases me, he stays close. He keeps his hand intertwined with mine.

We stay like that until a woman in scrubs comes up to us. She nods to Tom with familiarity.

"Where's your brother?" She asks.

Tom motions to the nearly still Pete. It takes the bassist

a minute to move—he must be terrified. Slowly, he makes his way to us.

The woman looks Pete in the eye. "Your mother is in recovery. The surgery went well, but she'll need some time under supervision because of the anesthesia."

No one breathes.

She looks to Tom. "She's going to be okay. The tumor is benign."

"She's okay?" Pete asks.

The doctor nods. "The cancer isn't back. That doesn't mean it will never come back, but for now, it looks good."

Tom's hand squeezes mine. "Thank you."

"It should be about an hour before you can see her. The nurse will call you when she's ready." The doctor nods a courteous but emotionless goodbye and returns to her work.

Tom releases my hand. He turns to his brother. They exchange a meaningful look. Then they're in one of those guy hugs where they're barely touching.

Pete steps back. "I'll make the calls." He motions to the hospital entrance. "Get some fresh air."

Tom swallows hard. "Pete—"

"Go."

Tom takes my hand and leads me through the lobby. "Not used to taking orders."

"Is he always that bossy?"

"Yes." Tom laughs. "Bossier. Don't tell me you're interested."

"Intrigued maybe," I tease. I'm desperate to lighten the mood as quickly as possible.

We step through the first set of double doors. Then the second.

All my senses fire at once. The air smells of salt. The sun is warm. Beautiful blue flowers line the walkway.

And Tom's hands are on my skin.

He pulls me into another hug. No, it's more than a hug. It's an embrace. His body presses against mine. My cheek presses against his neck. He smells good. He's warm.

When he releases me, he looks into my eyes. There's so much relief in his expression. It's my relief. All the happiness he's feeling flows into me like it's my own.

It *is* my own.

I stare back at him. "Tom, I love you."

Chapter Thirty-Five

The wind rustles the bushes. The freeway hums with the steady flow of traffic. A car pulls into a parking space and its engine turns off.

Tom stares at me.

Silent.

My heart pounds against my chest. It's so loud and he's so quiet.

I pinch myself to check that I'm awake. Still in the sunshine, on the concrete outside some clean Orange County hospital.

Still breathing.

"You should probably respond, or I'm going to start to believe what Drew said about you playing me," I say.

Tom blinks. "You can't love me."

It's like I'm punched in the gut. Air rushes out of my lungs. I have to dig my heels into the concrete to manage any balance. How can he believe that, much less say it?

Still, he stares at me, silent.

"I do love you," I say.

"You just think—"

"I don't think anything. I know I love you. I feel it everywhere. I can't breathe without feeling how much I love you. It knocks me over. Hell, look at me. I can barely stand up straight and I'm wearing Keds. There's no thinking involved."

"Willow..."

He looks sad. Like he pities me. My stomach clenches. Anything but pity. Even hate.

"I..."

I stare back into his eyes with as much strength as I can muster. "I want to stay and help with your mom, but I can't be around you unless I know you love me, too."

"No one has ever loved me before."

"That's not true. Your mom, Pete, they both love you so much. Drew and Miles, too."

He stares into my eyes. "You can't go. I'll be worried sick."

I take a step backwards. "I love you, Tom. I want to be your friend. But I can't do it right now. It hurts too much not being your everything."

"I don't know what to say."

"That's a first."

He half-smiles. "Willow, I want to. I do. But I—"

"Please don't finish that sentence. Just think about it and, whatever it is, tell me later." I step backwards. "You should be with your family right now. I'll see you—"

He reaches for me. "Don't go."

"I have to. If you care about me at all, you'll respect that."

"I do care about you. I just—"

"Stop. Please."

He nods with understanding.

My eyes sting. I squint, turn away from the sun. It doesn't help to keep the tear from rolling down my cheek.

The automatic doors swish open behind me.

"Tom, the nurse needs your—" Pete's voice drops as he spots me. He clears his throat. "Your number. Go give it to her."

"Not the best time," Tom says.

Pete shoots him a stern look.

Tom makes eye contact with me. He opens his mouth. It takes half a minute for him to speak. "I'll let you know how Mom is doing."

I shake my head. "Pete can do that."

Tom's expression sinks. "Don't do this, kid. I can't stomach losing you right now."

There's no stopping the tears from rolling down my cheeks. I choke back a sob. "It's not like that. I just—"

"I understand." Tom looks at the ground. His expression fills with frustration, but he nods, and he makes his way back into the hospital.

"You want me to drive you home?" Pete asks.

I shake my head. "You should be with your mom."

"I'll call you a car."

———

IT'S LATE AFTERNOON WHEN I ARRIVE AT DREW'S PLACE. I check my makeup with my cell phone camera. There's some smudging but my eyes are no longer *I've been sobbing* red.

Drew answers the door. His expression fills with concern. He takes my suitcase and pulls me into a hug. "Do I need to kill him?"

"No."

"Should I make an appointment with my tattoo artist for tomorrow or do you need more time to pick out a design?"

"How about the day after tomorrow." I try to laugh but it comes out as a muffled sob.

"Crash and Coco Bandicoot?"

This time, the sound I make is more laugh than sob. Fifty-one/forty-nine but I'll take a single percentage point. "No thank you."

"You do have a thing for blonds."

I swat Drew. "You're not making this easier."

"Mario and Luigi?"

"Who gets Mario and who gets Luigi?"

He points to himself. "Green Yoshi." Then to me. "Pink Yoshi."

"You're fucking with me."

"Maybe." He shrugs. "Spyro the Dragon and Toothless?"

"They're not from the same universe."

"Says who?"

I laugh. "No video game characters."

"Toothless and Hiccup."

"If I get Toothless."

"No way! I want Toothless. How about Batman and Batgirl?"

"Now, I'm sure you're fucking with me."

He laughs and leads me inside. "Come on. I'm teaching Kara how to make shrimp scampi. You can oversee the veggie version."

"Okay."

"You sure I don't need to kill him?"

"Positive."

———

My contribution to the cooking process involves suggesting vegetables then plopping on the couch by myself.

Drew and Kara take turns cooking and attempting to console me. I stream *How To Marry a Millionaire* and get lost in the back and forth between the charming movie stars.

Dinner doesn't have a taste. My thoughts fill with concerns about Ophelia. And about Tom. His words were as good as a rejection, and I'm still worried about him. I dig my phone out of my purse, but Kara steals it.

"Don't text with a broken heart, sweetie." Kara turns my phone off. She motions to the couch. "Let's play a game."

"Yeah, how about *Crash Team Racing*? I'll let you pick the first track," Drew says.

They're trying but all I can feel is the pity in Tom's eyes when I told him I loved him. Like he thought I was pathetic for loving him. Like he thought I was a fool.

A game is a good idea. Anything besides thinking. I take a spot on the couch while Drew digs out an ancient PlayStation. There are only two controllers, so Drew and Kara take turns facing off with me. Drew and I used to play this game all the time when we were kids. I pick it up quickly. Him too. Kara not as much, but she laughs every time she accidentally drives off the edge.

We play for hours. Until we all know the game backwards and forwards. I try to leave but Kara insists she needs my help baking a cake. My help consists of sampling batter and instructing her to add more chocolate chips. It's something. A cake with insufficient chocolate isn't worth eating.

When we're finished, I excuse myself to the spare bedroom and collapse on the dark comforter. The room is sparse. No decorations on the walls, no clothes in the closet, no goodies in the dresser. The only thing in here is one of Drew's guitars and God knows I don't want to face him if I accidentally break it.

My computer is somewhere in my suitcase. There's no way I'll be able to resist the lure of checking on Tom through email or any of the half a dozen social media sites he manages for the band. Then there's his personal accounts. People who ask him to pose for a picture or sign an item of clothing tagging him... There might be a new picture. A clue to how he feels.

I'm already working myself into a tizzy. The computer is a bad idea.

I spend an hour pouring over the photos on my camera. Almost everything is wiped clean except for the last Sinful Serenade show. It's just as unwise looking at a dozen pictures of Tom that I took, but I try my best to look as a photographer and not a girl in love.

The pictures are good. The concerts are fun. Hazel is smart and talented. Working with her again is a great opportunity. But there's something lacking about it. There's nothing of me in these photos. They don't command me the way portraits or even headshots do.

Then again, I'm not sure how much energy I can muster to throw myself into photography sessions. I need to lick my wounds.

At this time of night, I might as well sleep on it. I find my pajamas in my suitcase, brush my teeth, wash my face. When I get back to the spare room, Kara is sitting in the bed holding a tablet.

She motions *come here*. "Close the door. This is our secret."

I do.

"Drew has no idea this exists. He never looks at gossip sites." Her expression gets bashful. "It's embarrassing how often I do." She navigates to something on the tablet and hands it to me. "This went live about an hour ago."

There's an article on a well-known gossip site. *Tom and*

*Pete Steele Fighting Over the Same Woman? Love Triangle To Break
Up Alternative Rock Band Sinful Serenade.*

There's a picture of me and Tom talking outside the
hospital. And another of Pete consoling me after Tom
walked away. What kind of asshole takes pictures of people
outside a hospital?

The article is mostly conjecture about how I'm a home-
wrecker, well, band-wrecker. There are other questions too,
about why we're all at the hospital. Apparently, a so-called
fan recognized Tom, snapped pictures on her cell phone,
and sent them into the gossip site.

Kara plays with the edges of her cell phone. "Drew
doesn't have to know about this."

"I don't care."

"But Tom has been texting me, asking what you want
to do."

"Why is he asking you?" I set the tablet on the bed
before I give in to the temptation to contact him myself.

"I told him your phone is off for the day." She taps
something into her phone. "Anything he wants to say is
going through me." Kara looks at me. "Whatever happens
with the band, you and I are family. Even if Drew does
something stupid to get himself killed or thrown in jail."

"You think he would?"

"He knows better." She shoves her phone back into her
pocket.

"The guys are always teasing Drew that he'll never find
anyone as good as you."

"He won't. Drew hates everyone. Except the people he
loves. He's pretty black or white."

"They never tease Miles about not doing better than
Meg."

Kara plops on the couch. "Miles doesn't take the bait.

Drew is easy to rile up. Sure you noticed. But Miles would be just as lost without her. More even."

"You know, I hated you when we were kids."

"Really?"

"Drew was my only friend in San Francisco. And my ally against our parents. It felt like you stole him."

"Sorry about that. Can't say I regret it."

I push the tablet aside to sit next to her.

Her phone buzzes. She groans as she checks it. "Tom sounds really upset. But there's no way I'm letting him talk to you right now."

"He didn't do anything wrong. He can't help not loving me."

Sympathy fills her eyes. "Um. How do you want to spin the story?"

"I don't care. Tom can decide."

Kara taps her phone. "If he decides, it will be something about threesomes and bondage. And your name will get connected sooner or later."

"Probably sooner being the guitarist's innocent baby sister. It's a lot more scandalous with that detail."

"True." She looks at me. "Are you sure? I can fuck with him. Tell him to make the story about your secret love affair with Pete, how you two are hiding it from Tom because he is a much better lay."

"No thank you." I lie back on the bed and stare at the stucco ceiling. "Tell him not to spin it. To make it the truth. That I handed him my heart and he stared at it like it was a hand grenade."

Kara plops next to me. "Oh honey, I'm sorry." She taps a reply and tosses her phone aside. "Are you okay?"

I say nothing.

She's quiet for a minute. Eventually, she gets up and

looks over my camera. "What have you been thinking about up here?"

"Only what I'm doing with my life."

"So no big deal?" She smiles.

"Yeah."

Her voice is calm, friendly. "What are your options?"

"Hazel, the band's photographer, offered me a job as her assistant on another tour."

"Or?"

"Or I can stay in LA and try to set up my own studio. Or a million other things."

Kara's text tone interrupts my train of thought. She stares at the phone with temptation in her eyes. It only takes a few moments for her to break.

"Oh." She presses her fingers into her phone. "Tom wants to take you somewhere tomorrow."

"Where?"

"He won't say. Only that it's important. And some bull-shit about how you're both adults, and he should be having this conversation with you." Her voice drops to a mutter. "He's lucky he's not having this conversation with my boot."

A flutter of hope builds in my stomach. He wants to see me. That might mean he's figured things out.

"I can tell him to go fuck himself," Kara offers.

"No. I want to see him."

She purses her lips in distaste. "If you're sure."

"Tell him he has to get through Drew first."

She smiles. "That's quite the obstacle."

"He deserves to work for it."

Chapter Thirty-Six

Kara refuses to return my phone. For my own good, supposedly. She arranges everything with Tom. He's set to arrive at eleven a.m.

I sleep in fits. Come morning, I'm too nervous to do much more than brush my teeth, shower, and dress. Of course, I manage to pick out a particularly low cut top and short skirt combination, so I'm not that out of it.

Drew makes coffee and breakfast. Scrambled eggs with vegetables. They have a taste. Mostly hot sauce, but it's something. The coffee too. I can smell it. It's nutty, robust, bitter. I fix it with sugar and almond milk until it's sweet.

Kara distracts me with another round of *Crash Team Racing* while Drew sulks in his room. Or sharpens his blade. Or prepares some plan to kill Tom and get away with it. There's no telling what my brother is doing.

I give up on the game at a quarter to eleven. The minutes pass slowly. My skin is flushed, slick with sweat. It's summer in Los Angeles. Warm. But not warm enough to justify this.

The doorbell rings.

That must be him.

I remind myself to breathe. In. Out. Easy. No big deal.

Drew descends the stairs with a serious look on his face. He motions for us to stay then answers the door.

Sure enough, Tom is standing there. He looks normal in jeans and a t-shirt, his sunglasses pulling down the v of his v-neck.

He doesn't wait for Drew's response. "Do whatever you have to do. Hit me. Declare you're never speaking to me again. Hand me the paperwork your lawyer drew up about quitting the band. I don't care. I'm not here for you. I'm here for Willow."

"I'm not going to hit you." Drew's voice is calm, unreadable.

Tom stares back, tapping his fingers against his thigh impatiently.

Drew presses his hand against the doorframe, blocking my view of Tom. "Doesn't mean I'm going to let you make my sister cry again."

"Last thing I want is to hurt her."

I can't see Tom but his voice is sweet, earnest.

"Intentions aren't always good enough," Drew says.

"If we're gonna have this conversation, let's do it privately," Tom says.

Drew looks back to me as if to ask my permission. When I nod, he steps outside and closes the door behind him.

Kara plays with her cell phone with a not quite calm expression. "I haven't been this nervous in forever. Are you okay?"

I nod.

She unlocks her cell phone and navigates to the browser. "I probably shouldn't show you this, but—"

She's interrupted by the door opening. Drew steps back inside.

He looks at me. "Do what you want to do, Wil."

Kara hides her phone and makes eye contact with Drew. "You shouldn't phrase that like she has to earn your permission."

"No, it's fine," I say. I asked Drew to be my first line of defense. He's only doing as I ask. "I'll see you guys later."

"You need anything?" Drew asks.

I shake my head.

He hugs me on my way out the door.

And then I'm outside, and the door is shut, and Tom is staring at me with the most intense expression.

He smells good. Every impulse in my body tells me to wrap my arms around him. Somehow, I resist.

"How is your mom?" I ask.

"Great. Pete's treating her like a queen. You okay?"

I shake my head. "Whatever you're going to say, can we get it over with? I'm not in the mood for anticipation."

He reaches out to touch me but stops himself. "I want to show you something first. It's important. It will only take twenty minutes to get there."

His expression is earnest enough that I believe him. Okay. I've come this far. I can survive another twenty minutes.

Tom pulls his car keys from his pocket and offers them to me. "You have a license?"

"Yeah, but it's been a while."

"You want to drive her? She's a lot of fun."

"I guess so." I take the keys, slide into the driver's seat, and turn the car on.

"Got you something." Tom reaches into the glove box and pulls out a pair of women's sunglasses. He hands them to me. "You'll need them if you decide to stay in Los Angeles. It's bright as hell here."

"Thank you." They're nice shades. Designer. A black frame with a slight cat eye. Grey lenses. I slide them on and check my reflection. Not bad. I almost pull off rock star girlfriend. But then I shouldn't get ahead of myself.

TOM DIRECTS ME SOUTH ON A STREET THAT RUNS PARALLEL to the ocean. By the time he tells me to leave the main drag, I have the hang of driving.

He points to a parking space in front of a small white and grey apartment complex. We're a few blocks from the beach, close enough to hear the waves and smell the salt. There's beautiful soft light everywhere. And the ocean seems to go for miles.

"It's through here." Tom leads me to a door marked *Three*. He takes back the keys and uses one of them to unlock the door.

Okay. We're going into a strange apartment. It's not his. He lives in Hollywood. What the hell is he trying to show me?

It's a beautiful place. Light streams through the wide-open windows. There's a small kitchen along the wall. A bed, a couch, a dresser, a changing screen in the back.

And there's photography equipment. A tripod. A lighting kit. Gold and silver bouncers. Stands. There must be a few thousand dollars worth of accessories here.

"What is this?" I ask.

"It's your photo studio."

"I can't afford this."

"The lease is paid for the next twelve months. If you

don't want it, ignore it. But it's yours." He takes the key off the ring and hands it to me.

It's sharp edges press against my palm. I meet his gaze. "I don't even know if I want to run my own studio."

"Yes, you do. You get this look of excitement in your eyes whenever you talk about it. Whenever you look at your photos. You can think whatever you want about me, kid. But I'm not going to watch you run away from your ambition." He stares back at me. "You deserve the world. This is the least I can do."

"I can't take your money."

"Then consider it a payment."

"For what?"

"I need your help with something."

Sounds implausible. I take a deep breath. "What?"

He pulls his cell phone from his pocket. "You told me to spin the story as the truth."

I nod.

"That's what I did." He taps the screen a few times and hands the phone to me.

It's the same gossip site but the headline is totally different.

Tom Steele Confirms Identity of the Mystery Girl and He's Madly in Love.

What?

Madly in love.

With me.

My heartbeat picks up until it's the only thing I can hear.

"Keep going, gets better," he says.

I do.

There's a picture. A selfie Tom took. From his gorgeous green eyes to the jut of his hipbone. Only.

No.

There's fresh ink on his hipbone. A single word.

Willow.

My hands are so sweaty I nearly drop the phone.

"Miles did it first, but he got his on his chest. Figured this was the best way to one up him."

I stare back at Tom. "You... You didn't."

He nods, unbuttons his jeans, and pulls them down low enough to reveal the ink. There it is, in curving black letters. My name. On his body. Forever.

"Tom." I set the phone on the windowsill before I break the damn thing. "I..."

"I love you, Willow. Took me a while to figure out what that meant, two people loving each other, but I'm sure." He slides his arms around my waist. "Now I need your help making sure the whole world knows it."

"How?"

He points to the camera poking out of my purse.

"And you're paying me for this service with a year of studio rent?" I ask.

"Unless you demand two years." He pulls me closer.

"No, one year is plenty." My laugh is nervous. He loves me. I tug at his jeans. "Show me again."

He does.

I trace the letters with my fingertip.

Tom runs his hand through my hair and looks me in the eyes. "I hope you're okay with the whole world thinking you're my girlfriend."

"As long as the whole world knows you're my boyfriend."

He nods and presses his lips into mine. The world shifts into focus. Everything is easy. Light. Perfect.

Then he pulls back and he brings his mouth to my ear.

"I love you," he whispers.

And somehow the world gets better.

I whisper back. "I love you too."

He teases. "How can I be sure you're not saying that because you want to get into my pants?"

"You can ask me again after I'm done with you."

He takes my hand and leads me to the bed. "I can arrange that." Tom does away with his t-shirt as he pulls me into the bed.

His lips go to mine. It's like all the kisses before it but it's better in every way. Feelings pour between us. Love. Affection. Tenderness.

I've got no patience. I need our bodies joining. I need this love pouring between us with nothing in the way. No clothes. No deceit. No holding back our feelings.

I pull off my tank top and do away with my bra. Tom responds with the same eagerness. Kissing my lips, my neck, my chest.

He pulls my underwear to my knees and runs his fingertips over me. It's too much. I'm already sensitive. And I need him. All of him.

I push his jeans and boxers off his hips. Then they're at his feet and my hand is tracing the lines of that tattoo again and again.

That's a lot to live up to. But I'm game to try.

I spread my knees. "Please."

He groans as he slides into me. I'm home. Every time we've been together has been amazing, but it's never been like this.

We move together, arching and groaning and thrusting together. Our lips lock and we kiss hard and deep. In no time at all, an orgasm races up inside me. I hold him close, groaning his name again and again as I come.

It's beautiful, watching pleasure spread over his face. Better now that he's mine. After a few more thrusts, he's coming, moaning against my skin as he fills me.

Tom stays on top of me, inside me. God, it feels right, our bodies together.

I stare up into his eyes. This is everything. "I still love you."

He smiles. "You just came. I'm not sure your word is trustworthy."

"Guess you'll have to try again later."

"I have plans to make you come again later."

"Tomorrow?"

"You're definitely coming tomorrow."

"The next day?"

"Every day for the rest of our lives."

A smile spreads across my lips. "I love you so much."

He runs his fingertips over my jaw line. "I love you too."

Epilogue

The most respected photo editor in the country is shaking my hand. There are words coming out of her mouth, something about loving my portraits, about wanting to hire me to shoot a feature for her magazine. A feature spotlighting an A-list, Oscar winning actress. Something edgy, with personality, like all these lovely photos on the wall.

I nod *yes* and point her to my agent. Do I really have an agent? It's hard to believe that this is my life.

A familiar voice grabs my attention.

"Willow, sweetheart, these photos are amazing." Hazel takes my hand and pulls me away from the editor. She scans the walls of the gallery and settles on the first of my dozen pictures—a moody portrait of Tom. "I was worried you'd given up photography to follow him around the country when you turned me down."

"No way in hell I'd give this up."

Hazel smiles. "I'm almost glad you aren't my assistant."

"Almost?" I ask. "What's wrong with my replacement?"

"His ego is bigger than your boyfriend's and he's not

351

even half as attractive." Hazel nods to Tom in the corner, directing a star struck gallery attendee to one of my portraits with a proud look on his face. "Enjoy this night. It's the only time you'll be more in demand than he is."

"Thank God. I'm not sure how the guys do this celebrity thing. It's exhausting."

Hazel kisses me on the cheek. "I'm proud of you honey. Your parents here?"

I shake my head. "No. We're not close. But——" I point to Ophelia, in the corner next to Tom. "Tom's mother is here. She's sweet and badass. You'd like her."

Oh. They're looking at the portrait of Ophelia, the one I took, in her words, to immortalize her one good tit. It gave me an idea—to offer discounted and free boudoir shoots to cancer patients, to help them feel at home in their bodies again.

The demand has kept me busy. Really busy. But it's more than worth the time crunch for the joy that spreads over people's faces as they look at their finished pictures.

Hazel laughs. "You've always been a daydreamer. I'm glad you haven't changed. Good luck with everything."

She nods goodbye. There's someone else ready to talk to me. A fan. I have a fan. It's totally bizarre. I have a dozen portraits in the most prestigious gallery in all of Los Angeles. A showing of my work. For the next six months. The owner is charging outrageous sums for my work.

It's dizzying.

I make it through another five introductions. Then ten. I'm about ready to drop when I feel arms around my waist. My body floods with warmth as Tom pulls me closer.

"You hanging in there, kid?" Tom presses his lips against my neck.

"Mmmm. I'd rather be doing this somewhere else."

"You sure?"

"Positive."

I scan the packed room. It's been a solid three hours of schmoozing. It's overwhelming, everyone here to support me, to see my work.

My studio business started slowly—a few clients here, a few clients there, but now I'm booked Monday to Thursday and every other Saturday. I mostly shoot boudoir but I make time to squeeze in editorials, head-shots, even engagement photos. At first, Tom helped with the practical bits, but now I have the hang of it.

I'm a real, honest to goodness business owner.

A real working artist.

His hands go to my hips. "I have something to show you."

"What is it?"

"A surprise."

"Can I have a hint?"

"No."

"What if I have a surprise for you?" I do. I can't believe I've managed to keep it a secret the last few days.

"Oh, you're after a quid pro quo, are you?" He pulls me out of the gallery, onto the quiet Beverly Hills street. "Maybe if you go first..."

My cheeks flush. I know he'll love it, but I'm still nervous. "Has to be at home."

He leads me to the neighborhood around the corner. His red sports car is parked in front of some several-million-dollar mansion. It's a nice place. Too nice, as Hazel would say.

Tom pulls the passenger's door open. "Then my surprise first. You'll have to wait."

"You're a tease."

He slides into the driver's seat and turns the car on. "You keep talking like that, and I'll get ideas, kid."

———

Tom doesn't drive towards his place in Hollywood. He goes west.

The top is down. The cold air sends goosebumps up and down my arms. But it's worth it for the view of the sky. The stars come into focus the further we get from the center of the city. By the time we're in Venice Beach, the sky is filled with them.

"Where are we going?" I ask. "Your place is in the other direction."

"Is it?"

I turn towards Tom to take in every ounce of affection in his expression. "You're up to something, Mr. Steele."

"Not yet." He winks. "But soon."

Okay. It's a surprise. Something tells me it's an amazing surprise.

After five minutes driving city streets, we pull into an eclectic neighborhood. Into the driveway of a house on the beach.

It's actually on the beach. The backyard is sand.

My heartbeat picks up. We're staying in a house on the beach? There are a lot of ways this can go, and they're all amazing.

Tom turns the car off. He holds up his key ring, showing off one key in particular. It's shiny. New.

This place is gorgeous on the outside—very modern, all sharp corners and glass. Big white window shades provide plenty of privacy. If privacy is what we want. If not, well... it has quite the potential for showing off.

It's just as beautiful and modern inside. The den has all sorts of options for seating or screwing. A couch. A rug. An armchair. Wait. That's Tom's armchair, the one that is usually in his bedroom.

Huh.

He's smiling wide. Proud. Excited.

"That's your chair." I scan the room again. It's flashy and classic at once. There's only one possibility. "This is your new place? But... when did you move? I saw you two days ago." The gallery opening has kept me busy.

"It's our new place." He pulls another key ring from his pocket and hands it to me.

"What about Pete?"

"He has a mansion to himself. Don't think he's complaining."

My fingers curl around the key. "Our new place?"

He nods. "You like it?"

"It's perfect."

"Good. I bought it." He slides his arms around my waist. "It's ours, even if my name is on the deed. It won't matter soon... It will..." He runs his fingers through his hair. "It's only a ten minute walk to your studio."

He's nervous about something. It's hard to focus on that when I'm in such an amazing house. Our house. That he bought. For us.

The words bounce around my head. "We're living together."

He smiles. "Yeah, we are."

"And in the mornings, I'll wake up to the smell of coffee and you in the kitchen all sweaty from the gym."

"You sleep that late?"

"I'm a business owner. I can sleep as late as I want!"

"There's an office upstairs." He presses his lips against my neck. "It's yours."

I have my own office. I take his hand and pull him towards the stairs. "Let's see."

"Mmm, bossy today."

Tom leads me into the office. Everything is set up—a

thick, white sit to stand desk, an ergonomic chair, a very expensive desktop computer. The one I've been eying for ages.

There are framed prints on the wall. My work. A smattering of different styles but all in black and white.

He squeezes me then leads me through a tour of the place. The master bedroom is especially gorgeous. It's decked with a king bed, string lights, and a disco ball. There's a walk in closet and a master bathroom with a tub that fits two.

Tom leans in to whisper. "There's a particularly spacious shower in the bathroom downstairs."

"Whatever would we use that for?"

"Getting clean." He runs his fingers over my neck. "In fact, I'm thinking it's about time for that."

I look up into his eyes. "I have to show you something first."

He stares back at me. "You want to show me something before seeing me naked? Must be pretty good."

"It's better." I take a deep breath as I reach for the light switch. I want him to see this in as much detail as possible.

Okay. Here goes nothing. I pull my dress up my thighs and hips.

"Hate to break it to you, kid, but I've seen this before." He smiles. "Not that I'm complaining."

"No, I..." I push my panties to my knees and point to my hipbone. To my fresh ink. *Tom* in curvy letters, the same script as his tattoo.

His eyes go wide. "You... you..." He drops to his knees and runs his fingertips over my skin. "Willow." He looks up at me with all this wonder and affection in his eyes. "When did you get this?"

"Remember when I went shopping with Kara and Meg a few days ago?"

He nods.

"I went with them. But not shopping."

"You..." He swallows hard. "You're that sure you'll never leave?"

"More."

"How the fuck did I get so lucky?" He slides his hand to my stomach, holding my dress above his head as he traces the lines of the tattoo with his tongue. "As much as I love that dress, I need it gone."

I love it too. It's the same dress I wore the first night we were together.

But I'm just as desperate to get rid of it. After one swift movement, it's a pile on the floor. My bra joins it quickly.

"You're fucking perfect." He presses his lips against my stomach.

Then lower.

Lower.

Almost.

I tug at his hair.

Tom plants soft kisses up my thigh, starting at my knee and working his way up until he's almost there. Then he switches to my other leg and starts at my knee again.

He does it again.

My sex throbs with protest. I need him in every way it's possible to need a person.

Again.

And again.

Then his tongue is against me and everything else melts away. I dig my hands into his hair as he licks me. Up and down and left and right, almost where he needs to be.

When he finally presses his tongue against my clit, my knees buckle. I stumble.

Tom rises to his feet in time to catch me. He throws me into the bed, spreading my knees and planting his face between my thighs. No more teasing. His tongue plunges inside of me.

Pleasure spreads through my core. I pant. I scream. I tug at the clean white comforter.

He works his way back to my clit, teasing with light strokes. Then harder. Harder. I'm close. Every inch of me feels so good, so utterly his.

Harder.

There.

I squeeze his shoulder. With the next flick of his tongue, I come. My sex spasms, pleasure spilling all the way to my fingers and toes.

I relax into the bed, reveling in after shocks as Tom kisses his way up my stomach, chest, neck, chin. He presses his lips to mine. I'm not shy about kissing him back, tasting myself.

His body sinks into mine. His chest. His legs. His crotch.

He's hard.

God yes.

I pull back to stare into his eyes. Okay. There's no beating around the bush here. I have to come out with it. My cheeks flush. "I have an idea."

He brushes my hair behind my ears. "If you were wearing clothes I'd ask what you have up your sleeve, kid."

"There's a tripod in my office. And my camera is in my purse. The memory card has room for thirty minutes of video."

His eyes go wide.

"I was thinking we could record ourselves... If you want to."

"Fuck yeah. You sure?"

I nod. "Have you ever done it before?"

"No."

"Really?"

"Yeah." He pushes up and pulls me to my feet. "Never trusted anyone with sexy pictures, much less video."

My lips curl into a smile.

"You're a genius. Have I mentioned that?" He plants a kiss on my lips.

"Not recently."

Nerves threaten to swallow me whole as I collect the necessary equipment. Makes it difficult to attach my camera to the tripod.

But the excitement on Tom's face is more than enough to convince me to continue. I get behind the camera, adjusting it so the angle gives us plenty of room to play.

God, I'm going to film me and Tom having sex.

It's going to be immortalized. On my memory card. Forever.

The thought sends a thrill down my spine. As soon as I hit the record button this is happening.

There.

It's happening.

I explain the angle of the shot to him. We have most of the bed and all the space in front of it. This won't be fancy —one angle, straight on—but it will be us, ours.

Tom slides his hand over my side. "When did you get this adventurous?"

"When I met you."

He pulls my body into his. "You sure about this, kid?"

"Don't you want something you can take with you on tour? Something of me."

His eyes go wide. He nods.

Then his eyes are closed and his lips are on mine. I kiss him long and hard, taking my time exploring his mouth. Like it's the first time.

I pull his shirt over his head and show the muscles of

his torso the same appreciation. Every part of him is hard and strong. My fingers dig into his skin. Shoulders, back, chest, stomach. He's yummy.

In fact.

I want him to feel as good as I do. I suck on his earlobe until he's panting and clawing at my skin. Then I move to his other ear and do the same.

"Willow," he groans.

My fingers find the zipper of his jeans. I push them aside and trace the letters of his tattoo. My name on his body forever. And his on mine forever.

It's perfect.

I kiss my way down his stomach and chest as I lower myself to my knees. Ah, the view of my name is much better here. *Willow.* The lines are months old now, but they're still clean and defined. I work his jeans and boxers down his hips as I trace the letters with my tongue.

Tom's eyes are wide with desire. It does something to me. Makes me want him even more.

"Fuck, I'm going to watch this so many times." He slides his hand into my hair. "You're amazing."

I run my fingers over his tattoo. "*We're* amazing."

I wrap my hand around his cock and tease him the way he teases me. I brush my lips against his tip. Again and again, until I'm desperate to have him in my mouth.

Even then, I take my time sliding my tongue around his tip and playing with the metal balls of his piercing. God do I love the way it makes him groan.

He brings his other hand to the back of my head, nudging me forward.

I've teased him enough.

I take him as deep as I can.

I'm doing this on film.

Holy shit.

The thrill of the exhibition spurs me on. I let Tom guide me with his hands and his groans, taking him deep or shallow, sucking harder or softer. It's still amazing, watching the pleasure spread over his face.

His eyes roll back into his head. His lips part. His thighs quiver. One hand goes to my shoulder and squeezes.

I keep my pace. Until he's groaning.

His fingers knot in my hair. "I want to come inside you. Get on the bed on your stomach."

God yes.

I release him and shift to my feet. Tom presses his hands against my back, kissing me so hard and so deep that I forget how to breathe.

When he breaks the kiss, he helps me onto the bed, positioning me to give the camera a perfect view of us from the side.

God, I want to watch this.

Want him to watch this.

He shifts behind me, his hands on my hips.

His cock nudges against my sex. No teasing this time. With one swift thrust, he enters me. It's hard. Deep. I grab at the sheets, spreading wider, giving myself to him.

Tom and I... we're having sex on our bed... in our house.

On camera.

Everything about this is forever.

Pleasure wells up inside me with every thrust. I arch my back to meet him, desperate to come with him this time.

I'm not going to make it.

"Tom," I breathe. "Touch me. I want to come with you. Please."

He groans. "Fuck yes."

His hand slides around my hip and between my thighs. Then his fingers are on my clit, and I lose track of everything except the pleasure spilling through my body.

My sex clenches. Almost. The way he's shaking—he's almost there too. I let my eyelids flutter closed. I soak in everything about him—the skin on skin, the soft brush of his fingers, the sharpness of his teeth scraping against my shoulder, and his hard cock driving into me again and again.

Tom, God, Tom.

My sex clenches, pulling him closer. He's there. Pulsing inside me. Filling me. It pushes me over the edge.

Tension spills out from my core as I come. It takes me a full minute to catch my breath.

Tom untangles our bodies. He lies next to me, presses his lips to mine, runs his fingers through my hair.

"We christened the new bed," he says.

I nod. "We can get the balcony next.

"Then the couch."

"And the armchair."

"We've already fucked on that chair a dozen times," he says. "But I'm not complaining."

I kiss him deeply.

When he pulls back, he stares into my eyes. "You hungry?"

"A little."

"There's leftover pasta in the fridge. I'll meet you on the balcony."

"What do you mean leftover? You don't cook."

He laughs. "I tried." He pushes off the bed and motions to the closet. "Should be a new robe in there for you."

This day is already amazing. Now, on top of everything else, I have a present. I take my time pouring through the closet. All the clothes I usually keep at Drew's place are here. Most of the space is occupied by Tom's clothes. How can one person own this many different pairs of canvas sneakers? He has a rainbow of them.

The robe is a beautiful silk fabric in a lovely shade of pink. I pull it around my shoulders and cinch it tightly.

Tom is already waiting on the balcony. Our balcony. It's decked with a patio table and two chairs and it looks out on the ocean. God, the ocean is only a few hundred feet away. I can hear the waves. I can taste the salt in the air.

It's beautiful.

And cold. The wind rolls in from the beach. I cinch my robe tighter but that only helps so much.

Tom slides his arm around me and points to the plates of pasta pomodoro on the table. "You eat lunch or dinner?"

"Sort of." I take a seat and dig into the pasta. The basil is scorched and the pasta is undercooked, but so what? Tom made it. As far as I'm concerned, it's perfect. "Setting up for the gallery kept me busy."

I practically inhale my plate. Tom takes two bites of his then passes it to me. Okay, it would be rude to reject the food he cooked me. I eat until the plate is clean.

Tom smiles as he wipes stray bits of sauce off my cheeks. There's something different about his expression. An uncharacteristic shyness.

He slides the table out of the way, leans back into his chair. "You know, you're the best thing that ever happened to me, kid."

"You're the best thing that ever happened to me," I say.

He stares into my eyes. "It used to be that when I thought about the future, it was mom, and Pete, and Sinful Serenade. How we'd hit higher on the Billboard charts or how our next video would be bigger. All this stuff about taking on the world." He lowers his voice. "But I didn't think about what I wanted at the end of the day, when I was home, by myself in my head. I didn't want anything until I met you."

He lowers himself onto the tile.

Onto one knee.

Holy shit.

He looks up at me. "You make me happy. In a way nothing ever has."

My heart thuds against my chest.

Tom slides his hand into his pocket. He pulls out a ring box. "You're what I want."

He opens the box to reveal a three-stone ring. It's huge, classic and flashy at once.

It's so Tom.

He looks up at me. "Willow Denton, will you marry me?"

Warmth floods my body. "Yes. Of course."

He slides the ring onto my finger.

Tom rises to his feet. He wraps me in a hug and whispers in my ear. "I love you."

"I love you too."

I press my lips to his and, once again, the world gets a little bit better.

Want More Sinful Serenade?

Sign up for <u>the Crystal Kaswell mailing list</u> to get exclusive alternate POV scenes from *Sing Your Heart Out, Strum Your Heart Out, Rock Your Heart Out,* and *Play Your Heart Out.* You'll also get exclusive teasers and news on new releases and sales.

Turn the page for a teaser from <u>*Play Your Heart Out,*</u> featuring Pete and his heroine, Jess.

Sinful Serenade
<u>*Sing Your Heart Out*</u> - Miles
<u>*Strum Your Heart Out*</u> - Drew
<u>*Rock Your Heart Out*</u> - Tom
<u>*Play Your Heart Out*</u> - Pete
<u>*Sinful Ever After*</u> – series sequel
<u>*Just a Taste*</u> - Miles's POV

Teaser from Play Your Heart Out

Get *Play Your Heart Out* Now

"*Oh. Ohhhhh. Ohhhhhhh.*"

The entire bar echoes with the sounds coming from the single-stall bathroom in the corner.

"Jess, that one is yours." Rick points to the shaking bathroom door and hands me his set of manager's keys. "You're off after that."

Great. I'm off after I tell the people fucking in the bathroom to break it up.

"*Ohhh. Yes. YES. GOD, PETE. OHHH.*"

"Now, Jess." Rick's voice is dripping with irritation. His gaze is fixed on the cleavage of the copper-haired woman leaning over the bar.

What does he have to be irritated about? He's getting laid tonight. Sure, he's not going to get the woman screaming as loud as this Pete guy is, but he's not going home alone.

I press my eyelids together. Only two more weeks

working here. My loan will go through. I'll quit this hell-hole and officially enroll at USC Law.

Life will be under control.

My lips curl into a customer service smile. Rick is my boss. I have to be polite. "Of course, sir."

I take a deep breath and turn towards the bathroom.

It's late enough that the bar is down to a dozen customers. Half of them are lost in drunken misery. The other half are staring at me, licking their lips in anticipation of the drama about to unfold.

Attention from concerned strangers, my favorite. I steel my nerves. This is nothing compared to standing in front of a jury. If I want to be a trial lawyer, I need to learn to project strength and confidence.

"Oh, God, Pete you feel so good. MMM."

A sigh escapes my lips as I tap a knock on the door. Must be nice to be that uninhibited.

Is it even possible to enjoy sex that much? It's not like the guy is at an ear piercing volume. I can barely make out his grunts.

Okay, that's enough of listening to the strangers having sex. I knock again. "Excuse me. You can't—" I'm a grown adult, I can say the word—"engage in sexual activities here. Please get dressed and leave."

This does nothing to quiet them.

I knock again.

"MMM. PETE DON'T STOP." The woman squeals.

Rick is watching me with that same stern *do my bidding* expression. Dammit. Our bouncer only works weekends. I'm the last cocktail waitress on the floor. Either I take care of this or I escalate to calling the police.

Deep breath.

I pound on the fucking door. "I have the key. I'm opening the door in five seconds." My hands are so sweaty

I can barely grip the thing. "Five. Four." I slide the key into the lock. "Three. Two." I turn it. My fingers curl around the door handle. God help me. "One."

I open the door.

A tall, broad-shouldered man has a thin brunette pinned against the wall. Her red dress is at her waist. His jeans are at his feet. Even in the dim light of the bathroom, the hard muscles of his ass and legs are clear as day.

He's still pumping into her. She's still screaming. No more words. It's a collection of incomprehensible sounds. She claws at the wall, shaking and panting with orgasmic bliss.

The guy, Pete I guess, waits until she's finished. Then he stops pounding and he turns to me.

My cheeks flush as our eyes connect. He's handsome.

And familiar. Really familiar.

He's not a regular. Certainly not from Long Island.

I don't know anyone in LA. Why do I recognize him?

I shove my hands into the pockets of my apron. I'm here to accomplish something and it's not checking out the manwhore with an exhibitionist streak. "Excuse me, but you can't do that here. Please take a minute to get dressed and leave or I'll have to call the police."

"Can you make it two minutes?" he asks with a deep, even voice.

He's ballsy. I'll give him that much.

My gaze is drawn to the tattoo curving around his hip and thigh.

Get a grip, Jess. Six months is a long dry streak but you don't need to stoop to being some player's sloppy seconds.

"Uh..." I can negotiate too. "Two minutes if you keep it down."

"Thanks." He turns back to the woman. One hand

plants on the wall in front of her. The other stays over her mouth, muffling her groans.

He has the decency to wait until I close the door to resume fucking her.

Pete.

I know him.

But how?

I do a mental run through of every dark-haired man I know as I add up my tips. Time to close out with Rick. And to plead for an extra weekend shift.

He's sitting with the copper-haired woman, his arm around her waist.

Great. I'm interrupting his flirtation. That will put him in a good mood.

Someone bumps into me. Hard. It's her—the woman from the bathroom.

She scowls at me. "Thanks a lot."

I bite my tongue. Telling her to go to hell is above my pay grade. Better to step out of the way and let her storm off. Besides, she looks embarrassed. I'm not going to rub salt in the wound.

I try to step aside. Her eyes narrow. She goes out of her way to bump into me again.

Shit. My balance falters. I land right on my ass, my glasses sliding off my face.

I can't make out any of the details of her expression. But I can hear her frustrated sigh, her loud stomping steps, the cracking of plastic.

Dammit. I know that sound. There's no chance my frames are still in one piece.

Her footsteps get quieter as she storms out of the bar.

Where the hell did my glasses go? I'm about to swallow my pride and launch into a full on hands and knees search when I hear his voice. The man from the bathroom. Pete.

"You okay?" He kneels next to me and offers his hand.

I stare back at him. Does he really think I'm going to take that hand? God knows where he was touching the girl in the red dress. "Where has that been?"

"Just washed and scrubbed."

Not clean enough.

He's close. I can make out his expression. Concern. About me or something else?

"Your friend ran off." I push myself to my feet. "You should hurry if you want to catch her."

He looks up at me. "You were wearing glasses."

I rub my eyes. It does nothing to help my vision or my comprehension of the situation. His voice is even, his posture is confident. Three minutes ago, he was screwing that girl in the bathroom. Now, he's worried about my glasses.

I can't help but laugh. "You noticed what I was wearing while you were pounding the screaming brunette."

"Stopped pounding when you opened the door," he teases.

"I guess you did."

He reaches for something on the floor then pushes himself to his feet. "These *are* yours?"

He holds up my glasses. I squint to make out the damage. They're broken at the bridge. Damn.

"You have tape?" he asks.

I nod. "Yeah. It's through here." I lead him to the back room. After two months taking every shift I can get, I know the bar well enough to navigate sans corrected vision.

Supplies are in the Manager's Office. Booth against the wall is the only place to sit. I point everything out to him and slide into the bench seat.

A few moments later, he slides into the booth next to

me with a roll of tape. My heart beats faster. A flutter builds below my stomach.

This beautiful image pops into my head—the two of us in the bathroom, him pressing me against the wall, one hand tugging at my long blond hair, the other sliding under my skirt.

I want to be lost in pleasure the way that woman was.

Is it even possible for sex to feel that good?

"Here." His deep voice pulls me out of my thoughts. He holds up my now taped together glasses.

"You're good with your hands."

He chuckles. "True."

"I didn't mean it like that."

His laugh gets deep. "Years of playing the bass guitar does good things for your dexterity."

The bass guitar.

No. He can't be Pete Steele, the bassist of the alternative rock band, Sinful Serenade. They're Madison's favorite band. Her wall is covered in pictures of them and especially pictures of the enigmatic bassist.

"These will hold for tonight." His deep brown eyes meet mine. "I'll buy you new glasses tomorrow."

"You're going to buy me glasses?"

"My fault these are broken."

"What if I never want to see you again?"

"Then you wouldn't have let me help you."

I bite my lip. I can't afford new glasses and I can't work with these for long. But seeing him again is dangerous. His proximity has my body buzzing. Will I really be able to resist him?

Last thing I need is some player breaking my heart. Even if he is rock star bassist Pete Steele.

"What if I have a policy of rejecting players who get into fights?" I ask.

"You getting at something?"

"Have you ever heard of asking?"

He nods. That's it, a nod.

I wipe my hands on my apron. "Are you going to ask?"

"If it will make you feel better about how badly you want to say yes."

Damn, he's cocky. I usually hate that kind of thing, but on him, it's sexy. I swallow hard. "It will."

"Will you allow me to buy you glasses?"

"Yes."

His fingertips skim my temples as he slides the frames back onto my face.

Now that I can see, there isn't a doubt in my mind. "You're Pete Steele."

"Unfortunately." His eyes meet mine. "And you are?"

"Jess."

"Nice to meet you." He shakes my hand. "Where's your phone?"

My heart is beating too fast. I need to tell him to get lost, to pull back so I won't get hurt.

My body won't allow it. My hands and arms move of their own volition. Before I know it, my phone is in his palm.

He taps his number into my cell then sends himself a text. "Jess what?"

"Jess James. Technically Jessica," I say. "People called me Jessie James all throughout elementary school."

"Sweet, innocent blond on the outside. Outlaw on the inside. I see it." His lips curl into a smile.

I melt. It's the most beautiful smile in the history of the world.

He texts me an address. "Meet me at one."

I wait for my judgment to kick in, but all I can feel is the flutter of desire in my stomach. "Okay."

His eyes meet mine. "You gonna be alright, Jess? You look a little flushed."

"I'm not used to breaking up sex in the bathroom." I play with my skirt. "That girl was screaming loud enough to wake the dead."

His smile turns cocky. "I've heard louder."

"Really?"

"Yeah." He pushes himself out of his seat. "I'll see you tomorrow."

"See you then."

I rub my eyes, pinch myself to see if I'll wake up from this daydream.

But I'm not daydreaming.

That's Pete Steele.

He knows my name.

And he's buying me glasses tomorrow.

What happened to my normal life?

Get *Play Your Heart Out* Now

Author's Note

Thank you so much for reading *Rock Your Heart Out*. I hope you loved Tom and Willow's story as much as I did, and I hope you love Sinful Serenade as much as I do.

If you enjoyed the story, please help other readers find it by leaving an honest review on Amazon or Goodreads.

Want news about new releases and sales before anyone else? How about exclusive sneak peeks and bonus scenes? Sign up for the Crystal Kaswell mailing list.

If you love to review and want to get books before anyone else, join the Crystal Kaswell ARC team.

Want to talk books? I love hearing from my readers. Contact me through Facebook, Twitter, or email.

You can find more of my books here.

Acknowledgments

My first thanks goes to my husband, who not only tolerates but loves all my weird quirks (even my rants about grammar). The second goes to my father for always encouraging me to follow my dreams and especially for taking me to the book store when I was supposed to be grounded.

Tonya, you are the best developmental editor out there. Thank you for always pushing me to take the draft to the next level. To my critique partner and fellow rock star addict, Athena Wright, thank you so much for the notes (but thank you even more for listening to my terrible song title puns and telling me they are comedy gold). And, of course, thank you to Giselle at Xpresso book tours and to all the bloggers who are helping to promote this book. And to all my beta readers and my ARC team, a million thank!

As always, my biggest thanks goes to my readers. Thank you for taking a chance on Sinful Serenade. I hope you'll be back for *Play Your Heart Out*.

Printed in Great Britain
by Amazon

27915389R00216